More Praise for
CAT CRIMES

"Scary, funny, clever and traditional, each story has its own special flavor. . . . This is a grand collection, indeed."

Mostly Murder

"Original stories guaranteed to give you paws."
The Kirkus Reviews

"Admirable for the ease with which skilled writers were able to thread a plot around the furry ones."
Chicago Sun-Times

CAT
CRIMES

edited by
Martin H. Greenberg
and Ed Gorman

IVY BOOKS • NEW YORK

Ivy Books
Published by Ballantine Books
Copyright © 1991 by Martin H. Greenberg and Ed Gorman

Library of Congress Catalog Card Number: 90-56050

ISBN 0-8041-0979-6

This edition published by arrangement with Donald I. Fine, Inc.

Manufactured in the United States of America

First Ballantine Books Edition: June 1992

Contents

Author Notes

Peter Lovesey has written many good novels and short stories, most in a prose style far too literate and graceful for the bloodthirsty tastes of our time. For me, *Rough Cider* is his best novel thus far, a fetching and haunting look at World War II that I come back to again and again.

Bill Pronzini's Nameless Detective series is one of my generation's major bodies of work. Good as he was to begin with, Pronzini has continued to grow, both as stylist and social commentator, so much so that the Nameless books are revered as much for their wisdom as their stories. He's a real writer in all respects.

Joan E. Hess' novels are deceptively light. True, they're funny, fast and almost relentlessly good-natured, but they also say a great deal about small-town life in this part of the century. Joan has a good eye and a good ear for the sound of sorrow in laughter, and so if you read her carefully you'll find that her purpose is just as serious as her dandy prose.

Jon L. Breen is one of the best mystery critics of the past three decades, maybe the best since Anthony Boucher. Unlikely as it sounds, he's also a very good novelist and short-story writer, thereby putting to rest the notion that critics can't do anything but carp. Breen is his own man, working in a quiet voice all his own.

Dorothy B. Hughes is one of my favorite writers. I've spent years stealing effects from her books, and hope to go on stealing even more. *The So Blue Marble* is still one of the most disturbing mysteries ever written, and *In a Lonely Place* a more perfect Jim Thompson novel than Thompson ever wrote. The length of her career has blessed us all.

Barbara Paul has a wry soft Virginia voice filled with laughter and wisdom, the same wry soft voice you find in her novels. *First Gravedigger*, one of her early books, remains for me one of the best serio-comic novels I've ever read, the first half bitchy and droll as George Baxt, the second half sad and hopeless as James M. Cain. Her later books are even better.

William J. Reynolds is a former advertising man (he got out before the mutation was complete) who writes very good private-eye novels in the Nebraska series. His style is sly and wry, which makes him very readable, and he knows how to parody certain conventions without reducing his books to silliness. You should give him a try real soon.

Christopher Fahy is a middle-aged Irishman who may be the most self-effacing guy around. Tell him a book of his is good and he'll give you fifteen reasons why you're wrong. *Eternal Bliss* is his best book to date, a very dark and in some ways superior variation on *The Collector.* Hopefully a publisher will soon get behind him and help the rest of America learn just how good he is.

Bill Crider writes both mysteries and westerns and does them in an easygoing manner that sometimes conceals his more serious intentions. He has a strong talent for structure and pace, and perhaps an even stronger talent for the wry observation that reveals character. He is developing a real following.

David H. Everson has written several novels, one of the best of which is *Recount*, a fine funny book about politics in

Springfield, Illinois. He works his own side of the street and nobody's doing anything quite like him. He's a comer.

To date, **Douglas Borton** has written horror novels, though his forthcoming *White Rose* will show readers that he's equally good at writing straight suspense novels as well. Spend a little time and try to find his earlier novel *Kane*. It's a frightening, hallucinatory experience about a small dusty California town beseiged by a strange and unsettling stranger.

Les Roberts has spent a good deal of his life in various aspects of show business, which perhaps explains why his excellent private-eye novels are so world-weary. In addition to being a fine storyteller, Roberts is also a good writer, one of those people worth reading slowly, so you can enjoy his deceptively simple style. He gets better with each book and will someday have the major following he deserves.

John Lutz is one of the field's best writers. From his recent best-seller *SWF Seeks Same* (shortly to be filmed as a major motion picture) to his wonderful tales of Alo Nudger (*Buyer Beware* being my favorite private-eye novel of the seventies), Lutz has demonstrated that he can do it all, including win an Edgar for his short story "Ride the Lightning," one of the most powerful pieces in all of crime fiction.

J.A. Jance came from nowhere, a series of Avon paperback originals making her a major voice in mystery fiction of this decade. She's very good with place description, especially, which is why her version of Seattle is as indelibly etched as Chandler's Los Angeles and John D. Hammett's San Francisco. This is her first short story, and a good one.

Gene DeWeese is one of those real pros whose praises are too seldom sung. Author of several "Star Trek" bestsellers, and a man who has written in a variety of other fields including gothic suspense and juveniles, DeWeese is the writer of a very unappreciated novel called *Jeremy Case*, one of the best treatments ever of a man who can heal others through telepathic means.

Barbara D'Amato is a key player in the Chicago mystery scene, a bright, energetic and tirelessly decent woman whose first novel *Hardball* got the kind of rave reviews that most authors are smart enough to envy. A major career awaits her. Her already sizable readership will be happy to know she's just completed her second novel and will soon start number three.

Barbara Collins is the only confirmed cat-hater in the book. Just doesn't like the little devils. But Barbara more than makes up for this by writing one of the book's cleverest stories about our little friends. While this is officially Barbara's first published story, she has done considerable writing for the ''Mike Mist'' stories in the *Ms. Tree* comic books written by her husband Max Allan Collins, Jr., plus she's well into her first novel. This story would have made a dandy episode of the old half-hour ''Alfred Hitchcock Presents,'' being perverse in just the way Hitchcock seemed to love.

—Ed Gorman

Introduction

I didn't always like cats. I suppose this had something to do with my own self-image. Cats were for men destined to be poets while dogs were more for, you know, regular guys. I wanted—how I wanted—to be a regular guy.

This went on well into my thirties when, one drab spring morning, I awoke knowing neither my name nor my present whereabouts, and found next to me a woman who spoke a language other than English. Years later, this would all be funny in a grisly sort of way but that morning it was not funny at all. My life was completely out of control. I was an alcoholic.

That afternoon, without a word to anybody—the nice thing about being divorced and a bad father is that your time is completely your own—I went up on the gorgeous rolling Iowa River where for two weeks I stayed in a cabin and attempted to detoxify myself. I put several fists through several walls, I cried enough tears to prove I was no regular guy at all, and I made a pact with myself to never take another drink of alcohol.

Seventeen years later, I've managed to keep this pledge and I've done it, I think, with the help of two cats in particular.

When I got back from the Iowa River, I called my nine-year-old son Joe and told him where I'd been and why I'd been there and how afraid I was of the days ahead. He said it sounded as if I needed some steady companionship, that both he and his mother worried about me and how I spent so much time alone.

The next afternoon, windows open to soft spring, me

banging away at the free-lance ad copy I wrote for a living in those glum days, somebody knocked at my door and when I opened it there stood Joe with a tiny kitten followed by his mother bearing a litter box and litter.

They set everything up and then let the kitty loose to prowl. I couldn't find it in myself to tell them that I didn't much care for kitties.

Weeks went by and Ayesha (so named for H. Rider Haggard's eternal goddess) became my best friend. Those long nights when I wanted a drink, she sat in my lap and watched TV. Those long days when I wrote stories for minor literary magazines, she lay next to my typewriter and slept. She even went for rides with me in the country, liking to sit up on the dashboard and gaze on the dairy cows and beautiful horses not far from where we lived.

But she didn't grow at all and this began to trouble me. One day I took her to a veterinarian. He called me a few days later to say that Ayesha had leukemia and would be dead soon. And so it was. She began to vomit and lose weight. She went for days without being able to hold anything down. And finally when I realized that I was keeping her alive for my sake instead of hers, I brought her to him, very much like delivering a prisoner for execution, and he took her with professional solemnity and I never saw her again, though her picture still hangs in my office.

I've never gotten over the loss of Ayesha or later Doc or little Eloise. They were friends and companions and soulmates. Right now, as I'm writing this, a cat named Tess is sprawled on my monitor watching me. To the right of my machine sits beautiful Tasha and bounding over to the food bowl at the moment is Crystal, who genuinely believes that my wife Carol is her mother.

And speaking of my wife, at the time we met, she didn't like cats at all. But one day, not long after we were married, she came home from her teaching job with a small kitten in her arms and said, "Here's a new one," a classically striped kitty that some schoolboys had been throwing rocks at. A month later, Carol brought home a second homeless cat. She had apparently changed her mind about felines.

Many of the writers in this volume have likewise said that at one time they disliked cats, too. At least one writer (a misguided woman to be sure) says she *still* dislikes cats. She wasn't impressed when I told her that in ancient Egypt cats were considered gods, and that when the cat died Egyptian families went into formal mourning, the father even shaving his head to symbolize how they had been shorn of their beloved.

You'll find stories of all kinds in this book—cute, funny, sad, even (in one case) violent. And you'll find unabashed love, too, because cat lovers are just as passionate in their affections as dog lovers (plus we have the satisfaction of knowing that our animals are smarter).

So why not put your cat in your lap, lean back in your favorite recliner, and start reading? Just remember to keep scratching kitty's head all the time because otherwise she might tend to get a little grumpy. I think you know what I mean.

—Ed Gorman

Ginger's Waterloo

·

Peter Lovesey

This story was drafted by my son, Phil, who commutes by train to London, and I'd like to record my thanks to him.—P.L.

And this is how bad things can happen.

I stood on the new station, in the new suit for the new job, with no idea whose ground I was invading. The regular commuters were streaming along the platform for the 8.16 to Waterloo.

A glance at the flipping metal digital clock told me I had eight minutes before the train pulled in. Bad news. I would have preferred to get straight on to a waiting one without having to negotiate this minefield.

Grey clouds hung indolently over Shipley. Rain was threatening. Only threatening. A pity, this. Even a light drizzle would have forced a hasty rearrangement under Shipley's station canopy. The two uncovered ends of the platform would then have been given up except by the few willing to unfurl their tightly rolled umbrellas.

But the rain held off. Since Joyce and I had moved to 19, Winter Gardens three weeks previously, the sun had not once broken through. The weather here was as implacable as the inhabitants. Still, I tried telling myself, this was October, a time of the year when it was unfair to judge the potential of any town. Joyce, an unfailing optimist, was sure our small square of rear garden would be a sun-trap in summers to come.

I'd ventured along the platform to the less populated end and found a space. Enough room here to swing a cat, I thought. Yes, that insensitive phrase truly came into my head that Monday morning just minutes before I met Colin.

This end was where the singles hung out. Or loners, if you like; anyway, the people who preferred their own company to anyone else's. Executive briefcases, broadsheet newspapers and definitely no eye contact. Naked without a *Times* of my own, I positioned myself the requisite eighteen inches from the platform edge, pretending to be completely absorbed in the billboard opposite, an advert for cigarettes.

At the edge of my field of vision I noticed another minute flip down on the station clock. Five more to go. The man on my left saw my eyes move. He flinched and closed his paper a little in case I sneaked a glimpse of the headlines. Probably he was relishing the arrival of whoever it was who usually stood where I had taken up position. The space had asked to be filled—a sure sign it already had an owner. I expected hot breath on the back of my neck any second.

I actually felt homesick for Barton Vales Station. The tree-lined car park, Joe punching tickets and apologizing to every passenger for late-running trains. The sound of birds, not buses. But that was gone now. I couldn't even imagine it existing any longer. Surely Barton Vales had ceased to be, out of respect, the minute I left?

I'd exchanged that rustic idyll for a City job with the biggest insurance company in Europe. In no time at all, I'd promised Joyce, we'd reap the benefits.

Four minutes. I read the health warning on the cigarette ad. Didn't smoke myself.

Then Colin came into my life.

"I shouldn't stand there if I were you."

Ignore. Ignore. Read the health warning again.

"You're in the wrong place, mate."

Jesus, he's definitely talking to me, I thought. And this

was worse than I'd imagined. I'm no snob, but the accent wasn't the sort you expected on the 8.16 to London.

"I can always spot a new face."

His face, and a gust of garlic breath, invaded me from my right. I stared ahead like a guardsman. No paper to hide behind. I cursed myself for walking past the newsstand.

"I mean you, mate."

A note of aggression in the voice. Because I'm a coward, I responded by sliding my eyes a fraction his way.

Fatal.

Eye contact. He was in.

"This is a gap, see?"

I didn't need telling.

The others around me relaxed and started to read the share prices again. They weren't being spoken to. I was.

"The carriages all stop at certain places, right?" The stocky, scruffy figure pointed a denimed arm at the sign 6 which hung directly above my head. "There won't be no door here when it comes. You'll be stood facing the gap between the carriages."

I nodded and tried to appear grateful for the information.

He stabbed a finger at several people around me and said, embarrassingly in the circumstances, "These clever buggers here, see, they've got it sorted. They're stood ready by the doors, ain't they? You won't get a look in, mate."

I remained as deadpan as I could, allowing how acutely uncomfortable I felt. Just go away now, please.

"Straight up," he said. "I tell no lies. They've got it down to inches here, mate. Worst station on the line. Cut-throat. You're new to the game, I can see—a butterboy."

Brilliant. New job, my first day on the 8.16, and I'd found the loudmouth.

"Don't take offence, squire. I like your style."

Perhaps it was the compliment that did it. Or just relief that he wasn't about to turn nasty.

Stupidly, I felt compelled to respond. "It's coming, I think."

"Bang on time, for once."

"Unusual, is it?"

"Unheard of, these days. Better expect a hold-up at Clapham Junction."

A joke. I rewarded it with a grin.

The 8.16 cruised in, brakes squealing, and the melee started. Doors opened and released a few sleepy-eyed shop assistants and schoolteachers to a day's work in Shipley, while the London-bound lot plunged in and planted cold-trousered rears on still-warm seats.

"This way, mate," my newfound friend bawled in my right ear, grabbing my sleeve. "Always space in a smoker."

Now, I have never smoked in my life—nor do I intend to. I had until that day avoided smoking compartments in restaurants and trains. I travel on the lower decks of buses, avoiding any contact with the noxious weed. But that day, that Monday, because I was too weak to antagonize the loudmouth, I clambered in with him.

Tobacco stung my nostrils. We sat opposite each other, squeezed on the ends of seats of three.

"Good to get some cloth under your bum, eh? Never failed to find a seat in a smoker before it pulls out. Standing-room only in the other carriages. By the way," he continued, offering a muscular hand, "mine's Colin. What's yours?"

My cynical old Dad once told me that friends are like fish. Kept too long, they begin to smell. Three weeks after our first encounter, Colin stank.

That may sound mean, but I hadn't sought him out in the first place. We had, by now, become regulars. I deeply regretted my initial wish to blend into Shipley's status quo. I was discovering it had unforeseen consequences. I just couldn't fend Colin off. Every morning I endured him for the twenty-seven minutes from Shipley to Waterloo. I'd arrive at the terminus with my paper unread and tightly curled, my hands black from the newsprint, my face aching from the polite smile as he talked at me.

You see, there was no escape from his conversation. He enjoyed a chat, he told me. There wasn't much chatting in his work as a contract-plumber on the new Nomura building in the City. He must have been the only tradesman on the train. I've nothing against plumbers, but Colin was redefining my limits of tolerance. My new suit reeked of stale tobacco. The smoke clung to my hair. My eyeballs, soft from sleep, stung from the exhaled poison from Colin's roll-ups.

As the days passed, my frustration increased. Frankly it was becoming intolerable. Colin's outspokenness was acutely embarrassing. At the beginning, I'd been willing to put up with it just to avoid a scene, even tried to persuade myself that it was amusing. By now it was confirmed as uncouth and insupportable. My fellow-travellers, well-bred to the core, said nothing, but rolled their eyes at each other and rustled their papers during particularly unpleasant harangues.

So what held me back? What prevented me from avoiding him? Why didn't I step smartly into a different carriage—a non-smoker—to enjoy some privacy and my paper?

Cowardice. I didn't dare provoke him. My dread of an ugly outburst grew daily in me like a cancer, stronger than the rage I felt at the daily imposition.

"Take women, for instance. Take my wife. Are you listening, Davey?"

How I loathed his distortion of my name. Why didn't I correct him? I suppose it was better he called me that, than David, which I reserved for friends who were, frankly, more my type. Oh God, not again! He was about to come out with it once more.

"I said take my wife, and I wish you would." Followed by the quick look around to see who was smiling. "No, wouldn't wish that on Adolf Hitler. I mean, I don't know about your missus, Davey boy, and believe me I don't want to pry, but, like, it's different once they get that ring on their finger. Your sex bomb turns into a couch potato, know what I mean?"

I just nodded, aware that every woman in the carriage expected me to put a stop to his boorish talk. As I didn't, they could only assume I was another bigot. If only the voice weren't so loud, so coarse.

"Take Louise, right? She's got her life to lead, the same as you or me. She's out all day and comes back knackered. We're both knackered, right? Now, I'm no chauvinist."

You could have fooled me, I thought—and so, no doubt, thought everyone else in the carriage.

"No, very liberated I am. I do my share. I don't mind washing up. And I'll open a tin for the cat. It was my cat in the first place. I just think, as a bloke, I'm entitled to some sort of dinner on the table. Nothing fancy, just meat and two veg, maybe. I mean, marriage is supposed to be a partnership, am I right?"

Here it came again, as familiar now as Vauxhall Bridge flying by. The wife-and-cat diatribe. Colin felt left out. Couldn't stand the wife all woosey over the cat.

"Don't get me wrong, Davey. I've nothing against cats. I grew up with cats. And Ginger, well, she's affectionate. It's her nature. She's looking for attention, like they do. She wants fussing up, but there are limits. I get home, like, and all I see is Louise and Ginger all over each other. Okay, so Louise hasn't seen her all day, but I need my dinner. The cat gets fed. I see to that. And I'm bloody starving."

A silence. Time for my lines. Wearily, like an actor in a long run, I said, "Why not make yourself a sandwich?"

"Ain't the food for a hungry fella, is it, Davey, eh? Ain't the food to send vigour coursing through these veins, is it? No, not a pesky sandwich."

A pause. I hadn't been listening. Missed my cue. Fortunately the script was unchanging.

"I always enjoy a takeaway myself," I said too late and too flatly, watching the silver rails collide and cross in rhythmical patterns beneath me.

"Ah, now you *are* talking, Davey. Don't mind a bit of foreign myself. Louise, God bless her, just laps up that Chinky grub. Ever tried that chicken chop-suey thing? Hey, it's no wonder they're all walking round like this . . . I say, Davey, like this, eh?"

Dreading this, I looked up to see his fingers at the outer corners of his eyes, pulling the skin sideways. A goofy mouth, bottom lip pulled under top teeth, completed the hideous parody.

"Fu Manchu, ain't I? Numburrhh flifty-two wi plawn balls and flied ri. Ginger likes a bite of the old sweet and sour, you know. They're canny creatures, females, whatever bloody species they are. Listen to this. I reckon Ginger has twigged that if she plays with Louise for half an hour when she comes in, then there's no meal for me. So it's off down the takeaway. I bring back the sweet and sour, and Ginger gets her portion, see?"

"I see."

But I didn't want to see. I sincerely hoped the mental images of Colin's crass domestic life, his apathetic wife and his manipulative cat, would be erased from my mind, replaced by something more uplifting.

The airbrakes swished and hissed under our feet, the points clattering repeatedly, a sombre drumming into Waterloo, and work. Very likely I was the only passenger arriving there with a sense of release. Each day I longed to leave that train, to step into anonymity, knowing that our captive audience was dispersing. The appalling Colin would disappear, too, bound for his plumbing contract.

And now I have to explain something, and it's not easy, so bear with me.

Between the train and the ticket-barrier, I talked to Colin each morning. I felt the pressure to respond to the diatribe he'd given me all the way from Shipley. I'd said very little in the train. Now, with no one else eavesdropping, I could humour the man. I didn't want to part on bad terms. I've already admitted to being a coward. I'm also a humbug. So I pretended to share his opinions.

"I couldn't agree with you more, old man," I'd find myself saying as I eyed the approach of the ticket collector's gate.

"Yeah?" he'd say.

"Women. And cats. They need training. They don't like it, but it's got to be done."

"Just what I said, Davey. You and me, we think alike. Not like these wimps, eh?"

"Absolutely not, Colin."

"Your meal always on the table, then?"

"Every day, Colin—or else." An absolute lie, but strangely exhilarating to plant a fictional seed of my own chauvinistic home life in his head.

"You got it well sussed, Davey." He put a comradely hand on my shoulder. "So what would you do, then, about Louise and Ginger?"

"Well, Colin," I said, raising my voice to compete with the Tannoy. "It's a matter of priorities. Who wears the trousers?" We had reached the gate. That morning I paused to finish the conversation. "Just talk to Louise. Tell her you expect certain standards. She has to know you're boss. You'll be fine after that."

"Talk to her? You reckon?"

"They love it, Colin, they love it."

"Yeah?"

"See you, then."

He looked grateful, if doubtful. "Yeah, Davey. Tomorrow, eh?"

And I left him and stepped out briskly to the sanctuary of the Underground, where nobody talked. There was just the drone of the trains that whisked my away from the station, and my shame.

In those few weeks I had made a good start with my insurance giant. I rose to the challenges my new post offered. Moving from small claims to the juicier stuff proved stimulating. I had my own office, too—a distinct improvement on the ghastly impersonality of the open-plan system I had endured before. The others in my group proved a lively lot and were quick to invite me to join them for pub-lunches in shoulder-to-shoulder London bars, where the outrages of previous claims (mostly apocryphal, I'm sure) were cheerfully discussed.

My Group Head, Mr Law, was less approachable, a bit of a stickler for procedures (we speculated over lunch one day that he was probably into bondage in his sex life), but scrupulously fair. He dispensed advice without ever knocking my small-claims background. He even referred to it as a useful training-ground that had developed my attention to detail, a definite asset in my present post.

"You see, Walters," he told me in confidence, "we all have to start somewhere. I've studied every one of your reports. You don't miss anything. The others here . . . well, there's a tendency to rush things. Successful broking, Walters, begins with a sharp eye. You seem to have it. Indeed, I have a feeling you could go far."

Naturally, this conversation sent my confidence soaring, with its hint that I was ahead of the others in the group. I cast myself as the young hopeful, sure of promotion. That four years in the sticks sorting small claims was bearing fruit. So I had nothing to fear, one evening when I had volunteered to work late, when Mr Law called me into his office.

"Ah, Walters. Still enjoying the work here?"

"Tremendously, Mr Law."

"Good, good. Sit down, please. Just an informal chat. I see from the records you reside in Shipley, yes?"

"Yes, sir," I replied, a trifle uncertain what bearing this might have on my promotion prospects.

"Never been to Shipley myself," he continued, his back to me as he stared at the lighted cityscape eighteen floors below.

Feeling the need to contribute something, I volunteered, "It suits me, Mr Law. Suits me fine. At this stage in my career. Good amenities. Convenient for London." I was slipping smoothly into the staccato-style speech Mr Law himself used, the businesslike delivery that fitted me for the role of Deputy Group Head.

He continued to survey the trail of antlike humanity on its way home. "My sister moved there not long ago. She's an artist. Abstract stuff. I don't understand it at all. It sells, I'm told. I haven't seen much of her lately. Don't care much for the man she married. We're not a marrying family."

He turned from the window quite suddenly and looked at me. "Walters, I need help."

Christ. Now I was out of my depth. I had a hideous feeling it was going to be personal. Was he, perhaps, infatuated with one of the secretaries? I could see myself as a go-between pandering to Mr Law's perverted tastes.

What relief, then, as he continued, without mention of whips and handcuffs, "I'm down your way at sissie's next week. Tuesday. Duty visit. Her first exhibition. The preview. Sure to run late. The last train leaves at eleven-oh-five—too early for me. Have to use their sofa-bed. Inevitably I shall travel up by train on Wednesday. You're a good timekeeper, Walters. Always in by nine-thirty. Tell me, which train do you catch from Shipley?"

"The eight-sixteen," I told him.

"In that case I'll look out for you on Shipley Station on Wednesday morning."

"Splendid."

"Shall we say ten past, just to be sure?"

"Fine, Mr Law," I said, without a thought of Colin.

But I was sharply reminded the next time I saw him, on the Monday.

"Cha, mate."

"Hello, Colin."

"Didn't do no good, what you told me last week," he announced, attaching the verbal tow-rope that would drag me once again up the cat-and-wife alley.

"Really?" I responded without interest.

"Louise has taken it bad. I gave her a rollicking like you said, and she walked out."

"Left you?" I said, more concerned. I didn't want to be responsible for a broken marriage.

"Not for keeps. She's not that daft. Just pushed off, God knows where. She did the same Friday, Saturday and Sunday. She's got a pal, I reckon."

"Maybe." I tried to sound casual, as he had. From his tone, it hadn't dawned on him yet that the pal might be a boyfriend.

Then he added, "Doesn't come home until after I've gone to bed."

"What do you do?"

"Sit around all evening with Ginger for company."

The train was approaching. I had something more urgent on my mind than Colin's domestic crisis. Wednesday was too close.

"You, er, working all this week, Colin?"

"Sure thing, mate."

"Wednesday?"

"Same as ever."

We were seated in the smoker as usual. I wondered frantically how I might disentangle myself from the routine for one day. In a perfect world, I would just ignore Colin on Wednesday and travel up with Mr Law. But our arrangement was too entrenched for that. Colin regarded me as a soulmate. I'd got in too deep, particularly in our conversations between train and ticket barrier at Waterloo.

What if the two met? I shuddered at the prospect of Mr Law being subjected to Colin's inane monologue all the way to London. In my mind's eye I could see my Group Head grimly enduring the barrage, and later adding a note to my personal file: *Showed early promise, but betrayed a lack of discrimination in the company he keeps. Might be better employed, after all, in some limited capacity. Small claims, perhaps?*

The nightmare was interrupted.

"Louise and I, we go back years. Then wallop. Ginger's on the scene. Don't ask me how. She sort of adopted us both. Mind you, I didn't object at first. It was good company for Louise. Me, too. Let's be honest. But now Louise ignores me, it's hurtful, Davey, and I'm getting flaming mad with her. I blame the cat. I shouldn't, but I do."

"Well, yes."

"She could be jealous of Ginger. Is it possible? Do you think she's jealous of Ginger?"

I caught eyes observing me, peering over the tops of the *Times* like snipers in the trenches at the Somme. "I wouldn't know."

Then, unexpectedly, came an impassioned plea, made all the more ludicrous by the presence of the other passengers: "I couldn't bear to lose Louise. I want her back. I want my Louise back, Davey. That's all." He was on the verge of tears.

I looked at the thick-set plumber and mentally commanded him to snap out of this. Pitiful though he was, my major concern was my own predicament. For God's sake, he was just someone I met in the train each morning.

"Help me, Davey. You have an answer, don't you?"

Oh, this was great entertainment for the others. A highlight in the saga, like the murder of a well-known soap-opera character to push up the ratings at Christmas.

Vauxhall came up. We were just a few minutes from Waterloo. I had to settle this today. It couldn't be allowed to run on, not into Wednesday.

"I'll need to think," I told him. "Take it easy while I consider the matter."

Believe me, my brain worked overtime.

Colin watched me, mercifully silent until we reached the terminus.

On the platform, away from the eavesdroppers, I gave him the advice he'd begged for. I tried to sound calm. "From all you've told me, it's obvious that Ginger is a problem. She came between you and Louise, and now you want to get back on the old footing with your wife and you can't. It won't work. The solution to me, an outsider, is this. Get rid of Ginger."

His eyes widened. "But how, Davey, how?"

For once we were walking quite slowly along the platform, and anyone who travelled with us must have got far ahead, out of earshot.

Speaking as if to a child, I said, "Any way you choose.

In a sack, isn't that the way it's done? Tie the top and drop it in a river. No more Ginger."

"But what about Louise? She's not going to like this."

"She's out every evening, isn't she?"

"Well, yes, but . . ."

"How will she know? Cats run away, Colin."

"True, but it seems kind of—"

I lost my patience with him. "Do what you bloody want. You asked for advice and I gave it to you."

I heard him say, "I'll think about it, Davey," as I marched on and gave up my ticket.

Colin wasn't on the train next morning and my hopes were raised for Wednesday. I got to the station early, really early. I had a dozen possible strategies in mind and just one purpose: to keep Colin and Mr Law apart. I bought a copy of the *Financial Times*, to impress my boss, and stood by the station entrance. Mr Law, being tall, would be easy to spot.

"What you doing here, Davey?"

God, no! Colin had caught me on the blind side.

"Er, Colin, I, er . . ." But I didn't have to fumble long for an excuse.

He was keen to tell me something. "Done it, mate. Like you said. Monday night. Louise and me, it's all made up, at least for now, anyway."

"Ah."

"Look," he went on, "don't take offence, Davey, but I'm going to sit by myself this morning, okay?"

"Fine," I said, trying to sound just a little despondent as the tidal wave of relief crashed over me.

"Ah, there you are, Walters."

The worst possible outcome. Mr Law, bang on 8.10, and just ten seconds too early for me. Colin was lingering.

"You're not offended, are you, Davey? Listen, why don't you come round for a drink tonight? I'll be fine by then. You can meet Louise. You know, put some names to faces, mate?"

My toes curled. I was caught between two conversations.

"Is it always so crowded?" from Law.

"Just for an hour, eh?" from Colin.

"Eight-sixteen on schedule, I hope?" Law.

"Forty-seven, Cramer Way. The green door. About seven." Colin.

"Yes, Colin. I'll do my best."

"Champion!" And Colin was away.

My toes uncurled.

"A friend?" enquired Law.

"I wouldn't put it so strongly as that, Mr Law. Actually he's a local plumber. The fellow gave me some advice about installing central heating. Seems to think I want to get to know him better, which I don't."

"Ah, I know the sort."

The 8.16 arrived dead on time. It hadn't let me down. Moreover, Mr Law and I stepped into a non-smoking carriage and found two empty seats. I glowed with satisfaction.

I was so relieved at how the day had turned out that I decided that evening to take up Colin's invitation. I needed a drink. And Colin's decision to travel alone had given me the break I needed. I was willing to show some gratitude. We would drink to our futures.

I might even get to like travelling in Colin's company now that the cat-and-wife saga had come to an end. We'd have something different to talk about. Football, perhaps. Or television. But I would avoid any more marriage counselling.

Forty-seven, Cramer Way was fronted by the green door Colin had mentioned. A council-built house with a carport and a white van standing there. I pushed the doorbell.

"Davey—come in, mate." Colin reached out and grasped my arm. He was towel-drying his hair. "Just had a shower. The brick-dust gets everywhere. Come through to the kitchen."

The kitchen was a tip. I stood, conspicuous in my coat, surveying unwashed pans and piles of aluminum takeaway trays. And he'd brought me in here from choice.

A beer was offered. "You don't mind drinking from the

can? I don't have a glass handy. Give us your coat, Davey. Louise'll be through that door any minute.''

I took a sip of beer, grateful that it came from a sealed container. My eyes travelled around the cramped room and spotted a grease-spattered photograph standing on the fridge. Colin's wedding. The couple stood on what I recognized as Shipley Library's steps, confetti scattered over an ill-fitting suit and summer dress and jacket. She looked attractive, face vibrant with the occasion. Colin's remark about the couch potato came back to me. I felt uncomfortable knowing so much about Louise before I met her.

"The wedding snap," said Colin, opening a can. "Don't times bleeding change, eh?"

I passed no comment.

"Hey up," he said. "Here she comes now, bang on cue."

I turned to face the front door, first placing my can on the kitchen table. It didn't seem right to be drinking when the lady of the house arrived.

But nothing happened. The door didn't open. I looked towards Colin and saw that he was watching the back door. That, also, remained closed—apart from one small section. The bottom left-hand panel. The cat-flap.

It opened.

"Louise, my little beauty!" Colin cried as he swept the creature into his arms, a small, white cat. "Look, we've got a visitor. Remember I told you about Davey, the man on the train?"

I froze.

"Davey told me what to do with Ginger."

Louise purred approvingly in Colin's arms.

Stroking her head, Colin said to me, "Honestly, Davey, I could cheerfully have killed you as well the other night. Do you know how difficult it is tying a live woman into a sack?"

Bedeviled: A "Nameless Detective" Story

·

Bill Pronzini

"**Y**oung Man," Mrs. Abbott said to me, "do you believe in ghosts?"

The "young man" surprised me almost as much as the question. But then, when you're eighty, fifty-eight looks pretty damn young. "Ghosts?"

"Crossovers. Visitors from the Other Side."

"Well, let's say I'm skeptical."

"I've always been skeptical myself. But I just can't help wondering if it might be Carl who is deviling me."

"Carl?"

"My late husband. Carl's ghost, you see."

Beside me on the sofa, Addie Crenshaw sighed and rolled her eyes in my direction. Then she smiled tolerantly across at Mrs. Abbott in her Boston rocker. "Nonsense," she said. "Carl has been gone ten years, Margaret. Why would his ghost come back *now*?"

"Well, it could be he's angry with me."

"Angry?"

"I'm not sure I did all I could for him when he was ill. He may blame me for his death; he always did have a tendency to hold a grudge. And surely the dead know when the living's time is near. Suppose he has crossed over to give me a sample of what our reunion on the Other Side will be like?"

There was a small silence.

Mrs. Crenshaw, who was Margaret Abbott's neighbor,

friend, watchdog, and benefactor, and who was also my client, shifted her long, lean body and said patiently, "Margaret, ghosts can't ring the telephone in the middle of the night. Or break windows. Or dig up rose bushes."

"Perhaps if they're motivated enough . . ."

"Not under any circumstances. They can't put poison in cat food, either. You know they can't do *that*."

"Poor Harold," Mrs. Abbott said. "Carl wasn't fond of cats, you know. In fact, he used to throw rocks at them."

"It wasn't Carl. You and I both know perfectly well who is responsible."

"We do?"

"Of course we do. The Petersons."

"Who, dear?"

"The Petersons. Those real estate people."

"Oh, I don't think so. Why would they poison Harold?"

"Because they're vermin. They're greedy swine."

"Addie, don't be silly. People can't be vermin *or* swine."

"Can't they?" Mrs. Crenshaw said. "Can't they just?"

I put my cup and saucer down on the coffee table, just hard enough to rattle one against the other, and cleared my throat. The three of us had been sitting here for ten minutes, in the old-fashioned living room of Margaret Abbott's Parkside home, drinking coffee and dancing around the issue that had brought us together. All the dancing was making me uncomfortable; it was time for me to take a firm grip on the proceedings.

"Ladies," I said, "suppose we concern ourselves with facts, not speculation. That'll make my job a whole lot easier."

"I've already told you the facts," Mrs. Crenshaw said. "Margaret and I both have."

"Let's go over them again anyway. I want to make sure I have everything clear in my mind. This late-night harassment started two weeks ago, is that right? On a Saturday night?"

"Saturday morning, actually," Mrs. Abbott said. "It was just three A.M. when the phone rang. I know because I looked at my bedside clock." She was tiny and frail and she couldn't get around very well without a walker, and Mrs. Crenshaw had warned me that she was inclined to be "a little dotty," but there was nothing wrong with her memory. "I thought someone must have died. That is usually why the telephone rings at such an hour."

"But no one was on the line."

"Well, someone was breathing."

"But whoever it was didn't say anything."

"No. I said hello several times and he hung up."

"The other three calls came at the same hour?"

"Approximately, yes. Four mornings in a row."

"And he didn't say a word until the last one."

"Two words. I heard them clearly."

" 'Drop dead.' "

"It sounds silly but it wasn't. It was very disturbing."

"I'm sure it was. Can you remember anything distinctive about the voice?"

"Well, it was a man's voice. I'm certain of that."

"But you didn't recognize it."

"No. It was muffled, as if it were coming from . . . well, from the Other Side."

Mrs. Crenshaw started to say something, but I got words out first. "Then the calls stopped and two days later somebody broke the back porch window. Late at night again."

"With a rock," Mrs. Abbott said, nodding. "Charley came and fixed it."

"Charley. That would be your nephew, Charley Doyle."

"Yes. Fixing windows is his business. He's a glazier."

"And after that, someone spray-painted the back and side walls of the house."

"Filthy words," Mrs. Abbott said, "dozens of them. It was a terrible mess. Addie and Leonard . . . Leonard is Addie's brother, you know."

"Yes, ma'am."

"They cleaned it up. It took them an entire day. Then my rose bushes . . . oh, I cried when I saw what had been done to them. I loved my roses. Pink floribundas and dark red and

21

orange teas." She wagged her white head sadly. "He didn't like roses any more than he did cats."

"Who didn't?"

"Carl. My late husband. And he sometimes had a foul mouth. He knew *all* those words that were painted on the house."

"Margaret," Mrs. Crenshaw said firmly, "it wasn't Carl. There is no such thing as a ghost, there simply *isn't.*"

"Well, all right. But I do wonder, Addie. I really do."

"About the poison incident," I said. "That was the most recent thing, two nights ago?"

"Poor Harold almost died," Mrs. Abbott said. "If Addie and Leonard hadn't rushed him to the vet, he would have."

"Arsenic," Mrs. Crenshaw said. "That's what the vet said it was. Arsenic in Harold's food bowl."

"Which is kept inside or outside the house?"

"Oh, inside," Mrs. Abbott said. "On the back porch. Harold isn't allowed outside. Not the way people drive their cars nowadays."

"So whoever put the poison in the cat's bowl had to get inside the house to do it."

"Breaking and entering," Mrs. Crenshaw said. "That was the final straw."

"Were there any signs of forced entry?"

"Leonard and I couldn't find any."

Mrs. Abbott said abruptly, "Oh, there he is now. He must have heard us talking about him."

I looked where she was looking, behind me. There was nobody there. "Leonard?"

"No, Harold. Harold, dear, come and meet the nice gentleman Addie brought to help us."

The cat that came sauntering around the sofa was a rotund and middle-aged orange tabby, with a great swaying paunch that brushed the carpet as he moved. He plunked himself down five feet from where I was, paying no attention to any of us, and began to lick his shoulder. For a cat that had been sick as a dog two days ago, he looked pretty fit.

"Mrs. Abbott," I said, "who has a key to this house?"

She blinked at me behind her glasses. "Key?"

"Besides you and Mrs. Crenshaw, I mean."

"Why, Charley has one, of course."

"Any other member of your family?"

"Charley is my only living relative."

"Is there anyone else who . . . *uff*!"

An orange blur came flying through the air and a pair of meaty forepaws almost destroyed what was left of my manly pride. The pain made me writhe a little but the movement didn't dislodge Harold; he had all four claws anchored to various portions of my lap. I thought an evil thought that had to do with retribution, but it died in shame when he commenced a noisy purring. Like a fool I put forth a tentative hand and petted him. He tolerated that for all of five seconds; then he bit me on the soft webbing between my thumb and forefinger. Then he jumped down and streaked wildly out of the room.

"He likes you," Mrs. Abbott said.

I looked at her.

"Oh, he does," she said. "It's just his way with strangers. When Harold nips you it's a sign of affection."

I looked down at my hand. The sign of affection was bleeding.

It was one of those cases, all right. I'd sensed it as soon as Addie Crenshaw walked into my office that morning, and I'd known it for sure two minutes after she started talking. City bureaucracy, real estate squabbles, nocturnal prowlings, poisoned cats, a half-dotty old lady—off-the-wall stuff, with seriocomic overtones. The police weren't keen on investigating the more recent developments and I didn't blame them. Neither was I. So I said no.

But Addie Crenshaw was not someone who listened to no when she wanted to hear yes. She pleaded, she cajoled, she gave me the kind of sad, anxious, worried, reproving looks matronly women in their fifties cultivate to an art form—the kind calculated to make you feel heartless and ashamed of yourself and to melt your resistance faster than fire melts wax. I hung in there for a while, fighting to preserve my better judgment . . . until she started to cry. Then I went all soft-hearted and soft-headed and gave in.

P. T. Barnum would have loved me. Yes he would.

According to Mrs. Crenshaw, Margaret Abbott's woes had begun three months ago, when Allan and Doris Peterson and the city of San Francisco contrived to steal Mrs. Abbott's house and property. The word *steal* was hers, not mine. It seemed the Petersons, who owned a real estate firm in the Outer Richmond district, had bought the Abbott property at a city-held auction where it was being sold for nonpayment of property taxes dating back to the death of Mrs. Abbott's husband in 1981. She wouldn't vacate the premises, so they'd sought to have her legally evicted. Sheriff's deputies refused to carry out the eviction notice, however, after a Sheriff's Department administrator went out to talk to her and came to the conclusion that she was the innocent victim of circumstances and cold-hearted bureaucracy.

Margaret Abbott's husband had always handled the couple's finances; she was an old-fashioned sheltered housewife who knew nothing at all about such matters as property taxes. She hadn't heeded notices of delinquency mailed to her by the city tax collector because she didn't understand what they were. When the tax collector received no response from her, he ordered her property put up for auction without first making an effort to contact her personally. House and property were subsequently sold to the Petersons for $186,000, less than half of what they were worth on the current real estate market. Mrs. Abbott hadn't even been told that an auction was being held.

Armed with this information, the Sheriff's Department administrator went to the mayor and to the local newspapers on her behalf. The mayor got the Board of Supervisors to approve city funds to reimburse the Petersons, so as to allow Mrs. Abbott to keep her home. But the Petersons refused to accept the reimbursement; they wanted the property and the fat killing they'd make when they sold it. They hired an attorney, which prompted Mrs. Crenshaw to step in and enlist the help of lawyers from Legal Aid for the Elderly. A stay of the eviction order was obtained and the matter was put before a Superior Court judge, who ruled in favor of Margaret Abbott. She was not only entitled to her property, he decided, but to a tax waiver from the city because she lived on a fixed income. The Petersons might have tried to take the case to a higher court, except for the fact that negative media attention was harming their business. So, Mrs. Crenshaw said, "They crawled back into the woodwork. But not for long, if you ask me."

It was Addie Crenshaw's contention that the Petersons had commenced the nocturnal "reign of terror" against Mrs. Abbott out of "just plain vindictive meanness. And maybe because they think that if they drive Margaret crazy or straight into he grave, they can get their greedy claws on her property after all." How could they hope to do that? I'd asked. She didn't know, she said, but if there was a way, "Those two slimeballs have found it out."

That explanation didn't make much sense to me. But based on what I'd been told so far, I couldn't think of a better one. Margaret Abbott lived on a quiet street in a quiet residential neighborhood; she seldom left the house anymore, got on fine with her neighbors and her nephew, hadn't an enemy in the world nor any money or valuables other than her house and property that anybody could be after. If not the Petersons, then who would want to bedevil a harmless old woman? And why?

Well, I could probably rule out Harold the psychotic cat and the ghost of Mrs. Abbott's late husband. If old Carl's shade really was lurking around here somewhere, Addie Crenshaw would just have to get herself another soft-headed detective. I don't do ghosts. I definitely do not do ghosts.

Mrs. Crenshaw and I left Margaret Abbott in her Boston rocker and went to have a look around the premises, starting with the rear porch.

A close-up examination of the back door revealed no marks on the locking plate or any other indication of forced entry.

But the lock itself was of the push-button variety: anybody with half an ounce of ingenuity could pop it open in ten seconds flat. The cat's three bowls—water, dried food, wet food—were over next to the washer and dryer, ten feet from the door. Easy enough for someone to slip in here late at night and dose one of the bowls with arsenic.

Outside, then, into the rear yard. It was a cold autumn day, clear and windy—the kind of day that makes you think of football games and the good smell of burning leaves and how much you looked forward to All Hallows Eve when you were a kid. The wind had laid a coating of dead leaves over a small patch of lawn and flower beds that were otherwise neatly tended; Mrs. Crenshaw had told me her brother, Leonard, took care of Mrs. Abbott's yard work. The yard itself was enclosed by fences, no gate in any of them and with neighboring houses on two sides; but beyond the back fence, which was low and easily climbable, was a kids' playground. I walked across the lawn, around on the north side of the house, and found another trespasser's delight: a brick path that was open all the way to the street.

I went down the path a ways, looking at the side wall of the house. Mrs. Crenshaw and her brother had done a good job of eradicating the words that had been spray-painted there, except for the shadow of a *bullsh* that was half hidden behind a hedge.

In the adjacent yard on that side, a man in a sweatshirt had been raking leaves fallen from a pair of white birches. He'd stopped when he saw Mrs. Crenshaw and me, and now he came over to the fence. He was about fifty, thin, balding, long-jawed. He nodded to me, said to Mrs. Crenshaw, "How's Margaret holding up, Addie?"

"Fair, the poor thing. Now she thinks it might be ghosts."

"Ghosts?"

"Her late husband come back to torment her."

"Uh-oh. Sounds like she's ready for the loony bin."

"Not yet she isn't. Not if this man"—she patted my arm—"and I have anything to say about it. He's a detective and he is going to put a stop to what's been going on."

26

"Detective?"

"Private investigator. I hired him."

"What can a private eye do that the police can't?"

"I told you, Ev. Put a stop to what's been going on."

Mrs. Crenshaw introduced us. The thin guy's name was Everett Mihalik.

He asked me, "So how you gonna do it? You got some plan in mind?"

People always want to know how a detective works. They think there is some special methodology that sets private cops apart from public cops and even farther apart from those in other public-service professions. Another byproduct of the mystique created by Hammett and Chandler and nurtured—and badly distorted—by films and TV.

I told Mihalik the truth. "No, I don't have a plan. Just hard work and perseverance and I hope a little luck." And of course it disappointed him, as I'd known it would.

"Well, you ask me," he said, "it's kids. Street punks."

"What reason would they have?"

"They need a reason nowadays?"

"Any particular kids you have in mind?"

"Nah. But this neighborhood's not like it used to be. Full of minorities now, kids looking for trouble. They hang out at Ocean Beach and the zoo."

"Uh-huh." I asked Mrs. Crenshaw, "There been any other cases of malicious mischief around here recently?"

"Not that I heard about."

"So Margaret's the first," Mihalik said. "They start with one person, then they move on to somebody else. Me, for instance. Or you, Addie." He shook his head. "I'm telling you, it's those goddamn punks hang out at Ocean Beach and the zoo."

Maybe, I thought. But I didn't believe it. The things that had been done to Margaret Abbott didn't follow the patterns of simple malicious mischief, didn't feel random to me. They felt calculated to a specific purpose. Find that purpose and I'd find the person or persons responsible.

* * *

27

Addie Crenshaw lived half a block to the west, just off Ulloa. This was a former blue-collar Caucasian neighborhood, built in the thirties on what had once been a windswept stretch of sand dunes. The parcels were small, the houses of mixed architectural styles and detached from one another, unlike the ugly shoulder-to-shoulder row houses farther inland. Built cheap and bought cheap fifty years ago, but now worth small fortunes thanks to San Francisco's overinflated real estate market and a steady influx of Asian families, both American- and foreign-born, with money to spend and a desire for a piece of the city. Original owners like Margaret Abbott, and people who had lived here for decades like Addie Crenshaw, were now the exceptions rather than the norm.

The Crenshaw house was of stucco and similar in type and size, if not in color, to the one owned by Mrs. Abbott. It was painted a garish brown with orange-yellow trim, which made me think of a gigantic and artfully sculpted grilled-cheese sandwich. The garage door was up and a slope-shouldered man in a Giants baseball cap was doing something at a workbench inside. Mrs. Crenshaw ushered me in that way.

The slope-shouldered man was Leonard Crenshaw. A few years older than his sister and on the dour side, he had evidently lived here for a number of years, though the house belonged to Mrs. Crenshaw; Leonard had moved in after her husband died, she'd told me, to help out with chores and to keep her company. If he had a job or profession, she hadn't confided what it was.

"Don't mind telling you," he said to me, "I think Addie made a mistake hiring you."

"Why is that, Mr. Crenshaw?"

"Always sticking her nose in other people's business. Been like that her whole life. Nosy and bossy."

"Better than putting my head in the sand like an ostrich," Mrs. Crenshaw said. She didn't seem upset or annoyed by her brother's comments. I had the impression this was an old sibling disagreement, one that went back a lot of years through a lot of different incidents.

28

"Can't just live her life and let others live theirs," Leonard said. "It's Charley Doyle should be taking care of his aunt and her problems, spending *his* money on a fancy detective."

Fancy detective, I thought. Leonard, if you only knew.

"Charley Doyle can barely take care of himself," Mrs. Crenshaw said. "He has two brain cells and one of those works only about half the time. All he cares about is gambling and liquor and cheap women."

"A heavy gambler, is he?" I asked.

"Oh, I don't think so. He's too lazy and too stupid. Besides, he plays poker with Ev Mihalik and Ev is so tight he squeaks."

Leonard said, "You know what's going to happen to you, Addie, talking about people behind their backs that way? You'll spend eternity hanging by your tongue, that's what."

"Oh, put a sock in it, Leonard."

"Telling tales about people, hiring detectives. Next thing you know, *our* phone'll start ringing in the middle of the night, somebody'll bust one of *our* windows."

"Nonsense."

"Is it? Stir things up, you're bound to make 'em worse. For everybody. You mark my words."

Mrs. Crenshaw and I went upstairs and she provided me with work and home addresses for Charley Doyle and the address of the real estate agency owned by the Petersons. "Don't mind Leonard," she said then. "He's not as much of a curmudgeon as he pretends to be. This crazy business with Margaret has him almost as upset as it has me."

"I try not to be judgmental, Mrs. Crenshaw."

"So do I," she said. "Now you go give those Petersons hell, you hear? A taste of their own medicine, the dirty swine."

The impressive-sounding Peterson Realty Company, Inc. was in fact a storefront hole-in-the-wall on Balboa near Forty-sixth, within hailing distance of the Great Highway and Ocean Beach.

Coming to this part of the city always gave me pangs of nostalgia. It was where Playland-at-the-Beach used to be, and Playland—a ten-acre amusement park in the grand old style—had been where I'd spent a good portion of my youth. Funhouses, shooting galleries, games of chance, the Big Dipper roller coaster swooping down out of the misty dark, laughing girls with wind-color in their cheeks and sparkle in their eyes . . . and all of it wrapped in thick ocean fogs that added an element of mystery to the general excitement. All gone now; closed nearly twenty years ago and then allowed to sit abandoned for several more before it was torn down; nothing left of it except bright ghost-images in the memories of graybeards like me. Condo and rental apartment buildings occupied the space these days: Beachfront Luxury Living, Spectacular Views. Yeah, sure. Luxuriously cold gray weather and spectacular weekend views of Ocean Beach and its parking areas jammed with rowdy teenagers and beer-guzzling adult children.

It made me sad, thinking about it. Getting old. Sure sign of it when you started lamenting the dead past, glorifying it as if it were some kind of flawless Valhalla when you knew damned well it hadn't been. Maybe so, maybe so—but nobody could convince me Beachfront Luxury Living condos were better than Playland and the Big Dipper, or that some of the dead past wasn't a hell of a lot better than most of the half-dead present.

There were two desks inside the Peterson Realty Company offices, each of them occupied. The man was dark, forty, dressed to the nines, with a smiley demeanor and earnest eyes that locked onto yours and hung on as if they couldn't bear to let go. The woman was a few years younger, ash-blonde, just as smiley but not quite as determinedly earnest or slick. Allan and Doris Peterson. Nice attractive couple, all right. Just the kind you'd expect to find in the front row at a city-held tax auction.

They were friendly and effusive until I told them who I was and that I was investigating the harassment of Margaret Abbott. No more smiles then; unveiling of the true colors.

Allan Peterson said, with more than a little nastiness, "That Crenshaw woman hired you, I suppose. Damn her, she's out to get us."

"I don't think so, Mr. Peterson. All she wants is to get to the bottom of the trouble."

"Well, my God," Doris Peterson said, "why come to us about that? *We* don't have anything to do with it. What earthly good would it do us to harass the old woman? We've already lost her property, thanks to that bleeding-heart judge."

"I'm not here to accuse you of anything," I said. "I just want to ask you a few questions."

"We don't have anything to say to you. We don't know anything, we don't want to know anything."

"And furthermore, you don't give a damn. Right?"

"You said that, I didn't. Anyway, why should we?"

Peterson said, "If you or that Crenshaw woman try to imply that we're involved, or even that we're in any way exploiters of the chronologically gifted, we'll sue. I mean that—we'll sue."

"Exploiters of the *what*?" I said.

"You heard me. The chronologically gifted."

Christ, I thought. Old people hadn't been old people—or elderly people—for some time, but I hadn't realized that they were no longer even senior citizens. Now they were "the chronologically gifted"—the most asinine example of new-speak I had yet encountered. The ungifted ad agency types who coined such euphemisms ought to be excessed, transitioned, offered voluntary severance, or provided with immediate career-change opportunities. Or better yet, subjected to permanent chronological interruption.

So much for the Petersons. A waste of time coming here; all it had accomplished was to confirm Addie Crenshaw's low opinion of them. I would be happy if it turned out they had something to do with the nocturnal prowling, but hell, where was their motive? Assholes, yes; childishly vindictive bedevilers, no. And unfortunately there is no law against being an asshole in today's society. If there was, five percent of the population would be in jail and another ten percent would be on the cusp.

Charley Doyle's place of employment was a glass-service outfit in Daly City. But it was already shut down for the weekend when I got there; glaziers, like plumbers and other union tradesmen, work four- or four-and-a-half-day weeks. So I drove back into San Francisco via Mission Street, to the run-down apartment building in Visitacion Valley where Doyle resided. He wasn't there either. The second neighbor I talked to said he hung out in a tavern called Fat Leland's, on Geneva Avenue, and that was where I finally ran him down.

He was sitting in a booth with half a dozen bottles of beer and a hefty, big-chested blonde who reminded me of a woman my partner, Eberhardt, mistakenly came close to marrying a few years ago. They were all over each other, rubbing and groping and swapping beer-and-cigarette-flavored saliva. They didn't like it when I sat down across from them; and Doyle liked it even less when I told him who I was and why I was there.

"I don't know nothing about it," he said. He was a big guy with a beer belly and dim little eyes. Two brain cells, Addie Crenshaw had said. Right. "What you want to bother me for?"

"I thought you might have an idea of who's behind the trouble."

"Not me. Old Lady Crenshaw thinks it's them real estate people that tried to steal my aunt's house. Why don't you go talk to them?"

"I already did. They deny any involvement."

"Lying bastards," he said.

"Maybe. You been out to see your aunt lately?"

"Not since I fixed her busted window. Why?"

"Well, you're her only relative. She could use some moral support."

"She's got the Crenshaws to take care of her. She don't need me hanging around."

"No, I guess she doesn't at that. Tell me, do you stand to inherit her entire estate?"

"Huh?"

"Do you get her house and property when she dies?"

His dim little eyes got brighter. "Yeah, that's right. So what? You think it's *me* doing that stuff to her?"

"I'm just asking questions, Mr. Doyle."

"Yeah, well, I don't like your questions. You can't pin it on me. Last Saturday night, when them rose bushes of hers was dug up, I was in Reno with a couple of buddies. And last Wednesday, when that damn cat got poisoned, me and Mildred here was together the whole night at her place." He nudged the blonde with a dirty elbow. "Wasn't we, kid?"

Mildred giggled, belched, said, "Whoops, excuse me," and giggled again. Then she frowned and said, "What'd you ask me, honey?"

"Wednesday night," Doyle said. "We was together all night, wasn't we? At your place?"

"Sure," Mildred said, "all night." Another giggle. "You're a real man, Charley, that's what *you* are."

I left the two of them pawing and drooling on each other— one of those perfect matches you hear about but seldom encounter in the flesh. Cupid triumphant. Four brain cells joined against the world.

Even though it was too late in the day to get much background checking done, I drove down to my office on O'Farrell and put in a couple of calls to start the wheels turning. Credit information and possible arrest records on the Petersons and Charley Doyle, for openers. I had nothing else to go on, and you never know what a routine check might turn up.

At five-thirty I quit the office and drove home to Pacific Heights. Poker game tonight at Eberhardt's; beer and pizza and smelly pipe smoke and lousy jokes and somebody always wanting to "liven things up" by playing a silly wild-card game. I was looking forward to it. My lady friend, Kerry

Wade, says all-male poker games are "bonding rituals with their roots in ancient pagan society." I love her anyway.

While I was changing clothes I wondered if maybe, after the game, I ought to run an all-night stakeout on Margaret Abbott's home. It had been two days since the last incident; if the pattern held, another was due any time. But I talked myself out of it. I hate stakeouts, particularly all-night stakeouts. And with two easy ways to get onto her property, front and back, I could cover only one of the possibilities at a time from my car. Of course I could run the stakeout from *inside* her house, but that wouldn't do much good if the perp stayed *outside*. Besides, I was not quite ready to spend one or more nights on Mrs. Abbott's couch, and I doubted that she was ready for it either.

So I went to the poker game with a clear conscience, and won eleven dollars and forty cents, most of it on a straight flush to Eberhardt's kings full, and drove back home at midnight and had a pretty good night's sleep. Until the telephone bell jarred me awake at seven-fifteen on Saturday morning. Addie Crenshaw was on the other end.

"He broke into Margaret's house again last night," she said.

"Damn!" I sat up and shook the sleep cobwebs out of my head. "What'd he do this time?"

"Walked right into her bedroom, bold as brass."

"He didn't harm her?"

"No. Just scared her."

"So she's all right?"

"Better than most women her age would be."

"Did she get a good look at him?"

"No. Wouldn't have even if all the lights had been on."

"Why not?"

"He was wearing a sheet."

"He was . . . what?"

"A sheet," Mrs. Crenshaw said grimly, "wearing a white sheet and making noises like a ghost."

When I got to the Abbott house forty-five minutes later I found a reception committee of three on the front porch:

Addie and Leonard Crenshaw and Everett Mihalik, talking animatedly among themselves. Leonard was saying as I came up the walk, ". . . should have called the police instead. They're the ones who should be investigating this."

"What can *they* do?" his sister said. "There aren't any signs of breaking and entering this time either. Nothing damaged, nothing stolen. Just Margaret's word that a man in a sheet was there in the first place. They'd probably say she imagined the whole thing."

"Well, maybe she did," Mihalik said. "I mean, all that nonsense about her dead husband coming back to haunt her . . ."

"Ev, she didn't say it was a ghost she saw. She said it was a man dressed up in a sheet pretending to be a ghost. There's a big difference."

"She still could've imagined it."

Mrs. Crenshaw appealed to me. "It happened, I'm sure it did. She may be a bit dotty, but she's not senile."

I nodded. "Is she up to talking about it?"

"I told her you were coming. She's waiting."

"Guess you don't need me," Mihalik said. A gust of icy wind swept over the porch and he rubbed one reddened hand with the other, winced, and said, "Brr, it's cold out here. Come on, Leonard, I've got a pot of fresh coffee made."

"No thanks," Leonard said, "I got work to do." He gave me a brief disapproving look and then said pointedly to his sister, "Just remember, Addie—chickens always come home to roost."

Mrs. Crenshaw and I went into the house. Margaret Abbott was sitting in her Boston rocker, a shawl over her lap and Harold, the orange tabby, sprawled out asleep on the shawl. She looked tired, and the rouge she'd applied to her cheeks were like bloody splotches on too-white parchment. Still, she seemed to be in good spirits. And she showed no reluctance at discussing her latest ordeal.

"It's really rather amusing," she said, "now that I look

back on it. A grown man wearing a sheet and moaning and groaning like Casper with a tummy ache.''

''You're sure it was a man?''

''Oh yes. Definitely a man.''

''You didn't recognize his voice?''

''Well, he didn't speak. Just moaned and groaned.''

''Did you say anything to him?''

''I believe I asked what he thought he was doing in my bedroom. Yes, and I said that he had better not have hurt Harold.''

''Harold?''

''It was Harold crying that woke me, you see.''

''Not the man entering your bedroom?''

''No. Harold crying. Yowling, actually, as if he'd been hurt. Usually he sleeps on the bed with me, and I think he must have heard the man come into the house and gone to investigate. You know how cats are.''

''Yes, ma'am.''

''The intruder must have stepped on him or kicked him,'' Mrs. Abbott said, ''to make him yowl like that. Poor Harold, he's been through so much. Haven't you, dear?'' She stroked the cat, who started to purr lustily.

''Then what happened?'' I asked. ''After you woke up.''

''Well, I saw a flickery sort of light in the hallway. At first I couldn't imagine what it was.''

''Flashlight,'' Mrs. Crenshaw said.

''Yes. It came closer, right into the doorway. Then it switched off and the intruder walked right up to the foot of my bed and began moaning and groaning and jumping around.'' She smiled wanly. ''Really, it *was* rather funny.''

''How long did he keep up his act?''

''Not long. Just until I spoke to him.''

''Then he ran out?''

''Still moaning and groaning, yes. I suppose he wanted me to think he was the ghost of my late husband. As if I wouldn't know a man from a spirit. Or Carl, in or out of a sheet.''

I sat quiet for a little time, thinking, remembering some

things. I was pretty sure then that I knew the *why* behind this whole screwy business. I was also pretty sure I knew the *who*. One more question, of Mrs. Crenshaw this time, and I would go find out for sure.

Everett Mihalik was doing some repair work on his front stoop: down on one knee, using a trowel and a tray of wet cement. But as soon as he saw me approaching he put the trowel down and got to his feet.

"How'd it go with Margaret?" he asked.

"Just fine. Mind answering a couple of questions, Mr. Mihalik?"

"Sure, if I can."

"When I got here this morning, you were on Mrs. Abbott's porch. Had you been inside the house?"

"No. Wasn't any need for me to go in."

"When was the last time you were inside her house?"

". . . I don't remember exactly. A while."

"More than a few days?"

"A lot longer than that. Why?"

"Do you own a cat?"

"A cat?" Now he was frowning. "What does a cat have to do with anything?"

"Quite a bit. You don't own one, do you?"

"No."

"Then how did you get that bite on your hand?"

"My—?" He looked at his left hand, at the iodine-daubed bite mark just above the thumb. I'd noticed it earlier, when he'd winced while rubbing his hands together, but the significance of it hadn't registered until I'd talked with Mrs. Abbott.

"Fresh bite," I said. "Can't be more than a few hours old." I held out my own bitten hand for him to see. "Fresher than mine, and it's only about twenty hours old. Similar marks, too. Looks like they were done by the same cat— Mrs. Abbott's cat, Harold."

Mihalik licked his lips and said nothing.

"Harold is an indoor cat, never allowed outside. And he

likes to nip strangers when they aren't expecting it. Somebody comes into his house in the middle of the night, he'd
not only go to investigate, he'd be even more inclined to take
himself a little nip—especially if the intruder happened to
try to pat him to keep him quiet. Mrs. Abbott was woken up
last night by Harold yowling; she thought it was because the
intruder stepped on him or kicked him, but that wasn't it at
all. It was the intruder swatting him after being bitten that
made him yell.''

''You can't prove it was Harold bit me,'' Mihalik said. ''It
was another cat, a neighborhood stray . . .''

''Harold,'' I said, ''and the police lab people *can* prove
it. Test the bites on my hand and yours, test Harold's teeth
and saliva . . . they can prove it, all right.''

He shook his head, but not as if her were denying my
words. As if he were trying to deny the fact that he was
caught. ''You think I'm the one been doing all that stuff to
Margaret?''

''I know you are. Dressing up in that sheet last night,
pretending to be a ghost, was a stupid idea in more ways than
one. Only one person besides Addie Crenshaw and me knew
of Mrs. Abbott's fancy about her dead husband's ghost. You,
Mihalik. Mrs. Crenshaw mentioned it when we talked to
you yesterday afternoon. She didn't mention it to anybody
else, not even her brother; she told me so just a few minutes ago.''

Another headshake. ''What reason would *I* have for has-
sling an old lady like Margaret?''

''The obvious one—money. A cut of the proceeds from
the sale of her property after she was dead or declared incompetent.''

''That don't make sense. I'm not a relative of hers . . .''

''No, but Charley Doyle is. And you and Charley are buddies; Mrs. Crenshaw told me you play poker together regularly. Charley's not very bright and just as greedy as you are.
Your brainchild, wasn't it, Mihalik? Inspired by that auction
fiasco. Hey, Charley, why wait until your aunt dies of natural
causes; that might take years. Give her a heart attack or drive

her into an institution, get control of her property right away. Then sell it to the Petersons or some other real estate speculator for a nice quick profit. And you earn your cut by doing all the dirty work while Charley sets up alibis to keep himself in the clear."

Mihalik stood tensed now, as if he were thinking about jumping me or maybe just trying to run. But he didn't do either one. After a few seconds he went all loose and saggy, as though somebody had cut his strings; took a stumbling step backward and sank down on the stairs and put his head in his hands.

"I never done anything wrong before in my life," he said. "Never. But the bills been piling up, it's so goddamn hard to live these days, and they been talking about laying people off where I work and I was afraid I'd lose *my* house . . . ah, God, I don't know. I don't know." He lifted his head and gave me a moist, beseeching look. "I never meant that Margaret should die. You got to believe that. Just force her out of there so Charley could take over the house, that's all. I like her, I never meant to *hurt* her."

Three brain cells to Charley Doyle's two. Half-wits and knaves, fools and assholes—more of each than ever before, proliferating like weeds in what had once been a pristine garden. It's a hell of a world we live in, I thought. A hell of a mess we're making of the garden.

I went to see Mrs. Abbott again later that day, after Everett Mihalik and Charley Doyle had been arrested and I'd finished making my statement at the Hall of Justice. Addie and Leonard Crenshaw were both there. All three were still a little shaken at the betrayal of a neighbor and a relative, but relief was the dominant emotion. Even Leonard was less dour than usual.

A celebration was called for, Mrs. Crenshaw said, and so we had one: coffee and apple strudel. Harold joined in too. Mrs. Abbott had some "special kitty treats" for him and she insisted that I give him one; he was, after all, something of a hero in his own right. So I got down on one knee and gave him one.

In gratitude and affection, he bit me. Different hand, same place.

A Weekend at Lookout Lodge

·

Joan E. Hess

"It's very nice to have you staying with us again, Mr. Curry," said Fallinger, the day manager. Beads of sweat popped up on his forehead like a light frost, and despite his polished demeanor and obsequious voice, he looked as if he were confronting a heavily armed mugger. What he was actually confronting was a short man in a plaid jacket and polyester pants. A man who'd been in pretty good shape until ten years ago, when he'd begun to lift beers instead of barbells. A man who assumed no one could see his blotchy pink scalp under the dozen hairs combed over it like oily black wires. A man whose fondness for overindulgence was written in his bloodshot eyes and red nose. A man who spoke too loudly, grinned too broadly, and now was breathing too heavily from the minor exertion of climbing the few steps from the sidewalk to the veranda.

Ed Curry mopped his neck with a handkerchief as he gazed at the large lobby. It looked exactly as it had two years ago—and all the tedious years before that, from the droopy potted plants to the excesses of rustic wood, amateurish landscapes, and worn leather upholstery. A trio of little old ladies reigned from a cozy seating arrangement near the elevators. No one could go into the restaurant, out to the veranda, or even to the restrooms without being scrutinized. Ed wondered if they were the same biddies, or facsimilies replaced with a minimum of fuss whenever one died.

41

Fallinger was still hovering uncertainly, clearly debating what, if anything, would be tactful.

In a rare spurt of generosity, Ed said, "Yeah, it's been two years since I was here, but it looks the same. It won't feel the same, that's for sure."

"Poor Mrs. Curry," Fallinger intoned in an appropriately gloomy voice. "We shall all miss her. She had been coming here since she was a child, first with her parents and then with you. I know how dearly she loved Lookout Lodge. Perhaps it was fitting that she should . . . well, that she should . . ."

"Die here?" Ed suggested. When he'd been selling life insurance, he used all the acceptable euphemisms, but they made him wince inwardly. Pass away. Meet one's Maker. Seek one's reward. Malarkey, dead was dead and Caroline Fitzweller Curry was deader than a doornail (he liked that one) and tucked away next to her parents in a mossy corner of the cemetery.

"Ah, yes," Fallinger said unhappily.

"I thought about suing you guys, but when I recovered from my grief, I realized it was just a senseless accident that no one could have prevented. She lost her footing, that's all. I kinda think Princess got loose somehow, and Caroline might have been trying to coax her away from the edge of the cliff."

Fallinger blanched, although the reference to a law suit was the more likely culprit. "A senseless accident and a terrible tragedy. How is Princess? She must miss poor Mrs. Curry. The two were so devoted."

"Princess is fine," Ed said. For all he knew, she was, and he worried more about tire pressure than he did about the damn cat.

"I'm so happy to hear that. I understand your new wife is traveling with you, and I look forward to meeting her. May I dare to hope that Princess is with you, too, so that I may give her my regards and perhaps a dab of caviar to welcome her back?"

"Sorry, Princess is at the vet's having her claws manicured," Ed said with a shrug. "My wife's outside, admiring the view, and she adores caviar. We met here, you know. In fact, I was out in the parking lot helping her with a dead battery when poor Caroline went for her last, fateful stroll."

Despite his years of experience, Fallinger could not prevent his smile from slipping. His chin rose until he was looking down his nose, and his voice took on a faintly nasal twang of disapproval. "Oh, I didn't realize you had married the former Miss Lisbonnet. She was the singer in our lounge, wasn't she? My predecessor had hired her, but I felt her style was a bit too . . . too much for our clientele. They seem to prefer someone more, shall we say, restrained."

"Yeah, Madeline could really belt 'em out," Ed said, grinning. The same grin and a slap on the back had sold a lot of insurance policies, but not enough to keep him in Porsches and voluptuous young women. That had required Caroline's family money and the proceeds of a few modest insurance policies, all with accidental-death riders to double the payoff.

He poked Fallinger's chest. "We're in your best room, right? The former Miss Lisbonnet said she remembers how she was treated when she worked here, and now she wants to see if she's treated any better. You will see to that, won't you? Flowers and champagne in the room would be nice, and one of those baskets of fruit. Chocolates on the pillow, all that sorta thing. Nothing's too good for my Madeline." He dropped his key ring on the desk. "Our stuff's out in the car. It's a silver Porsche."

"Of course, sir. The Sycamore Room on the fourth floor." Fallinger gestured to a bellboy. "Fetch Mr. and Mrs. Curry's luggage, and be quick about it."

Ed went back outside and stood on the veranda, savoring the redolent autumn air. The mountains were covered in a ruffly quilt of oranges, yellows, and flashy reds. The grounds leading down to the lake were discreetly perfect. The grass was smoother than some carpets he'd seen, and even the chrysanthemums were aligned like little bearded soldiers. As he turned away, he caught a glimpse of something white flit

43

behind the flowers, but when he looked back, he saw nothing.

"Eddie, honey, what's wrong?" his wife said, clattering up the steps on spiked heels. Although the temperature was moderate, she wore her full-length mink, having muttered something about showing that priggy manager a thing or two about class.

He forced himself to smile at her. "Naw, it must have been a bird or something."

"What must have been a bird?"

At times her lack of perception irritated him, and he often wondered if she simply preferred to allow him to do the thinking in order not to risk mussing her elaborate hairdo. "I thought I saw a bird in the flowerbed," he explained patiently.

Madeline blinked. "And?"

"And nothing, okay?" He took her arm and escorted her into the lobby. As they sailed past Fallinger, Ed winked at him. The manager responded with a stiff nod.

When they reached the room, Ed made sure the little niceties were in place. The bellboy arrived shortly with the luggage, and Ed felt benevolent enough to tip him a whole dollar.

"Come out on the balcony," Madeline called. "It's really pretty."

Ed had to agree. Lookout Lodge was perched on the top of a mountain so its guests could, well, look out, which was the major pastime between meals, the afternoon croquet games, and tea. The mountains appeared to be cushiony, but there were a few sheer cliffs and steep, rocky inclines that could prove dangerous to clumsy strollers. Caroline hadn't been clumsy.

"That's the path," he said, pointing at a broad swath of gravel that led away from the lodge.

"That leads to the vista?"

"No, muttonhead, to the outhouses," he answered. Her lower lip shot out so promptly that he regretted his remark, and he began to caress her shoulder and nibble at her neck.

44

As usual, she relented, and, not long after that, whispered an invitation that delighted him.

Ed increased his attentions as they inched their way to the french doors. As they reached the threshold, he opened his eyes briefly, and once again saw something white move between the trees at the edge of the lawn.

"What the hell?" he said, releasing her. He returned to the rail and stared at the woods, his heart beginning to thud like a lopsided wheel. All he'd seen was a flash of white. But if it was a piece of paper, how could it have moved so quickly and disappeared? There was no wind, not even a breeze. A bird? The only white birds he could think of were ducks, swans, and sea gulls. The ocean was a hundred miles away. There were no ducks or swans on the lake at the foot of the lawn, and it was absurd to think either could dart like that.

"Eddie! Eddie!"

He realized Madeline was hanging on his arm, shaking it so hard it was liable to pop out of the socket. "Ease up, honey," he said. "I saw another damn bird."

"I don't understand what this thing about birds is," she said. Her blue eyes welled with tears, and the pout was definitely back in place. "You told me this was going to be our honeymoon, Eddie. You promised me that you'd be extra-special nice and we could be together without the telephone ringing and football games on television and appointments with the lawyers and poker games and trips to the race tracks. You promised, Eddie."

He squinted at the spot where the white thing had been, but he had enough sense to say, "I know I did, darling, and I meant every word of it."

"Then what's this thing about birds? You never told me you had a thing about birds. Did you bring binoculars and a dumb little book so we can wander around in the woods and look for robins?"

He squeezed the rail until he calmed down. "No, we're not going to look for robins or anything else we can't see from right here. I just wonder what I saw, that's all."

"I thought you said you saw a bird," Madeline said, rather pleased with her relentless logic.

"It must have been," he said, then made a risqué suggestion in her ear. Minutes later they were inside the room, the champagne cork was on the floor, and the white flash was forgotten.

After dinner, they strolled around the veranda until that became boring. Madeline wanted to dance, but Ed appeased her with a promise to dance the following night, and they started for the elevator.

"Aren't you Mr. Fitzweller?" said a thin voice. It belonged to one of the three old ladies, all of whom were regarding Ed as if he'd been convicted of child molestation.

Ed shook his head. He punched the elevator button, but before he and Madeline could escape, a second lady said, "Of course he's not, Doris. Caroline was a Fitzweller by birth. This gentleman was her husband."

Madeline marched over to them. "Well, he's my husband now, and his name is Curry, not Fitzweller."

"Isn't she charming?" said the third. Her faded eyes assessed Madeline rapidly but shrewdly. "Please forgive me if I'm being presumptuous, but haven't I seen you on television, Mrs. Curry?"

By the time Ed gave up on the damn elevator, Madeline was sitting on the sofa between two of them, modestly admitting she'd been in show business for five years but had never appeared on television. "I was in a movie once," she was saying as Ed came over. "Well, it was a small part, mostly standing in a crowd, but one of the cameramen said I did really good."

"Fascinating," breathed the first. "And Mr. Curry, how nice to have you back at Lookout Lodge. When I saw you checking in, I was quite surprised. I told Lydia that you must have recovered from your tragic loss. Are you planning to place a memorial wreath at the vista?"

"You bet your ass," he said, then took his wife's elbow, pulled her up, and propelled her to the elevator. "Why are you telling them your life story?" he whispered harshly.

Madeline's chin trembled, but she didn't respond, and they ascended to their floor in silence. Ed figured she'd sulk all night if he didn't do something, so he called room service for another bottle of champagne. She was back out on the balcony, he realized. He didn't know why this made him feel uneasy, but it did and he paced in the room until the order arrived.

"Champagne for my bride," he called.

"Bring it out here. The moon's fantastic. It makes the lake look like it's covered with silver dust or something, and the trees look all soft."

He filled two glasses and joined her, determined to make the right noises to lure her to the king-sized bed. "Real pretty," he said expansively. "Here, have a little bubbly, doll. I'm sorry I snapped at you in the lobby. Those old ladies were giving you a compliment, and it's not your fault you look like a glamorous actress."

"Do you really think so, Eddie? You're not just saying that?"

He was making progress. He nuzzled her neck, but before he could assure her that he really did think so (even if he really didn't, but what the hell), an eerie noise drifted from the flat black shadows of the woods at the edge of the lawn. It began as an almost inaudible growl. It grew louder, swooped from low to high, at first lilting and smooth, then raggedly brittle. When it finally faded, it seemed to leave colored lines, both glaring and pastel, indelibly etched in the darkness.

The champagne glass slipped from Madeline's hand and splintered on the floor. "What was that?" she gasped, clinging to him.

Ed had to fight for a breath as his heart lurched. "I don't know. It sounded like a banshee."

"Do you think somebody just got murdered? You know, stabbed or thrown off a cliff?"

"You've been watching too many mystery shows on television," he snapped. "I don't know what the hell that was, but we're paying good money for romantic moonlit nights,

47

and I'm not going to have some clown playing tricks in the woods." He went into the room and called the desk. "You better get a security guard out in front," he said, wiping his damp forehead with his sleeve and trying not to allow the horrible noise to echo in his head. "There's somebody out there making spooky noises. It's gonna keep us all up till you catch the jerk."

"Spooky noises, sir? Exactly what kind of spooky noises?"

"Get off it, buster. You must be having complaints from everybody on this side of the lodge."

"No, sir. Yours is the only one thus far."

"You'll get more. Trust me." Ed said. He banged down the receiver and told Madeline to come inside and close the doors. She wanted to leave them open. He slammed them closed and switched on the television. By the time they went to bed, they were reduced to glowers, snorts, and, on Madeline's part, tears of self-pity.

When Ed woke up the next morning, she was gone. He made sure the doors to the balcony were still secured, then took his sweet time showering and shaving and trying not to think about the banshee below the balcony.

"Yoo-hoo," she said as she came into the room, dressed in tight shorts and gossamer blouse. "Are you gonna be a sleepyhead the whole honeymoon?" When he merely looked at her, she walked past him, flung open the french doors, and said, "Come on, Eddie, don't be grouchy. It's so warm and sunny this morning. I had breakfast out on the veranda with those nice old ladies."

He decided he was being stupid and went out to the balcony. "Did you have a cozy chat about your career?"

"It may have been mentioned," she said. She tossed her chin, daring him to continue, but he shrugged and leaned over the balcony to study the edge of the woods. "Don't lean so far, Eddie. You're gonna fall on your head. Actually, Miss Eleanor thought she remembered me in that crowd scene. Miss Doris and Miss Lydia—they're sisters, you know—

hadn't seen the movie, but they agreed that I have charismatic cheekbones.''

He squinted at the row of chrysanthemums. Nothing.

Madeline tapped him on the shoulder. "Are you listening, honey? Anyway, Miss Doris and Miss Lydia were staying here when I sang in the lounge, or at least the three nights I did before I was canned. And they knew Caroline from when she was a little girl. Her mother used to play bridge with them.''

Out of the corner of his eye, Ed caught a flash of white. He jerked his head around, but it was only a white-coated waiter gliding across the lawn, a tray balanced on his fingertips.

"If you're gonna ignore me—"

"No, I heard it all.'' He straightened up and gave her his twenty-four-carat grin. "So they played bridge with Caroline's mother. So what?''

"So they did, that's all. They asked me some funny questions about Caroline's cat, Eddie. I didn't even know she had a cat, but they went on and on about some Persian cat named Princess and how Caroline used to feed it imported sardines and caviar at tea time.'' She blinked several times, and a faint line appeared between her eyebrows. "They acted like we still had it with us at home.''

He ran his tongue around his lips for a minute. "Yeah, Caroline had this fancy pedigreed cat named Princess. She was all the time fawning over it. It wore a rhinestone collar, although for what she shelled out for it, it should have been real ice. The damn thing slept on a satin pillow beside the bed, and if Caroline so much as stepped out of the penthouse, you can bet she was carrying the cat and cooing at it in French. Made me wanna puke sometimes.''

"So where's the cat now?''

"What's with the third degree? I haven't even had coffee.'' Ed went back inside and called room service. After he'd ordered an elaborate breakfast, he called the desk and asked to speak to Fallinger. "What did you do about that noise last night?'' he demanded. He listened to the response, then hung up and flopped down on the sofa with a scowl.

"Did they find something?" Madeline asked from the doorway.

"Hell, no! It seems ours was the only complaint. Fallinger said the night manager sent out a guard with a flashlight, but he didn't find anything out of the ordinary. The night manager concluded that it was an owl.''

"Maybe it was," she said as she snuggled down beside him and began to toy with his limp hand. "What happened to Caroline's cat?''

"It was kind of a fluke, like Caroline's accident," he said, resigned to getting it over with. Madeline was a few slices short of a loaf, but she was stubborn. "You remember the police investigation and all that? Well, once they decided it was an accident, I was told I could leave. I didn't want to stick around on account of the painful memories, you know.''

She stroked his hand as if it were a small, scaly pet. "Poor Eddie. I remember how awful it was for you. Those policemen were real nasty. It's a good thing you were helping me in the parking lot, so I could tell them you were with me the whole time. I might still be out there crying if you hadn't gone to your car in that lot on the other side of the lodge to get jumper cables.''

"That's right, Madeline—I was with you. But anyway, I packed all the stuff, threw it in the car, and started back to the city, trying not to dwell on Caroline's accident. Princess had this posh travel box, with a door and a couple of screened windows. I guess I didn't hook the door so good, because just as I reached the highway, the cat leapt over my shoulder and went on out the car window. Lemme tell you, I about had a heart attack.''

Madeline touched her lips. "Was it killed?''

"It was out of sight before I hit the brakes," he said, striving to sound overcome with remorse. "The woods are real thick along in there, with bushes and trees and dead branches and stuff. I got out of the car, and wasted a good half hour calling its name, but that was the last I ever saw of Princess.''

''Oh, that's so sad. First you lose Caroline, and then her beloved pet. You must have wanted to cry.''

He lowered his face and blinked mistily. It really had been touching, his farewell to Princess. He'd waited until there was no traffic, parked at the side of the road, grabbed the cat by its collar, and slung it as hard and far as he could at the undergrowth. He felt much more cheerful when he heard a muted cry of pain. He hadn't known what broke, but he'd hoped it was its bejewelled neck.

A waiter arrived with a cart, and Madeline watched her husband eat breakfast, solicitously refilling his coffee cup and dabbing his chin with a linen napkin when he finished. They spent the day strolling around the grounds, lunching on the veranda, and snickering at the incompetent croquet players. Each time they went through the lobby, Madeline waved coyly at the three old women, who responded with sweet smiles for her and cool ones for him.

''I want to change for tea,'' Madeline announced after she'd dropped nearly a hundred dollars in the gift shop on T-shirts, ashtrays, painted dishes, and enough postcards to bring the postal system to a stop.

Ed carried the sacks to the elevator, loaded her up, and told her he'd meet her on the veranda. He hadn't seen any more furtive flashes of white, and the view, although unexciting, was a pleasant change from noisy, polluted streets, litter-strewn pavements, harsh concrete walls, and the bums who seemed to reside in every doorway these days.

Winking at the old ladies, Ed lazily circled the lobby and then headed for the door, but as he went past the desk, Fallinger hurried out of his office to intercept him.

''Mr. Curry! Your wife just called the desk, and she sounds hysterical,'' he said urgently. ''Please accompany me to your room.''

As they stepped off the elevator, they could hear Madeline's sobs, and they found her huddled on the carpet just inside the door. Her face was streaked with ribbons of mas-

51

cara, and her fingernails cut into Ed's arm as she clutched him. "Oh, Eddie," she moaned, "it's terrible. You got to do something."

"What's wrong, honey?" he said.

Fallinger stepped around them. "Mrs. Curry said she found a distasteful item on the bed," he murmured as he went across the room. "Oh, dear, it is indeed distasteful. I'll call housekeeping immediately."

Ed pried Madeline off his arm and joined the manager, who was rubbing his hands fretfully. On the bed was a green dress, and on its skirt was a small, bloodied lump. Ed bent down to study it. "It's some kind of little animal," he said. "There's not much left of it, but it looks like maybe a mouse"—Madeline squealed—"or a baby rabbit. I said to put chocolates on the pillows, not dead animals on the bed."

"I can assure you that no one on the staff is responsible for this," Fallinger said coldly. He used the telephone, and shortly thereafter a maid arrived with a small bag. While Madeline moaned and hiccuped from the balcony, the lump was removed. After a round of apologies and promises that the dress would be sent immediately to the dry cleaners in the village, the manager and the maid left.

"Is there any blood?" demanded Madeline, declining his repeated requests to come back into the room.

"No," Ed said, "but if it bothers you, I'll tell those jerks to change the bedspread. Hell, we can get a different room if you want."

"No, I already got everything unpacked. I don't understand how that awful thing got there." She came to the doorway, then hesitated. "It's real weird, Eddie. I decided to wear my green silk, so I put it on the bed and went into the bathroom to do my makeup. When I came out, there it was."

"Did you open the french doors?"

"Yeah, just to let in some fresh air. I was gonna close them when I left. I don't care any more about tea. I'm going to take a long, steamy bath."

Once she was in the bathroom, Ed made sure the doors were latched, and he tested them again before they went downstairs for dinner. Afterwards, they drank steadily and danced until midnight. They were both giggling and weaving as they crossed the lobby, and it took Ed several attempts before he connected with the elevator button.

As far as he could tell through unfocused eyes, the room had not been disturbed. Madeline avoided looking at the bed as she dropped her purse on the sofa and continued to the french doors. "Come kiss me in the moonlight," she purred, then opened the doors and slipped out to the balcony before he could protest.

Ed took off his jacket and tie, dropped them on a chair, and began to unbutton his shirt with uncooperative fingers. It was just a balcony, he told himself in the hearty voice he used to spread a trio of aces or collect a significant sum at the track. Ed Curry wasn't scared of some damn duck in the flowerbed.

He was splashing whiskey into a glass when he heard Madeline clap her hands together. "Oh, you are a sweetie," she said. "You're the most thoughtful husband in the whole wide world, Eddie!"

"I am?" he said as he drained the glass and refilled it. "Why don't you come in here and prove it?"

"But it's so pretty in the moonlight. Come on out here and see how it sparkles."

He took a swallow of whiskey, set down the glass, and forced himself to go to the doorway. Madeline's back was to him, and he couldn't see what she was holding.

"What is it?" he asked.

She looked at him over her shoulder, her eyes smoldering and her mouth curled into a sensual invitation. "Come here and get your reward, lover boy."

Wishing he had the glass in his hand, Ed made it the short distance to the rail and let his arm brush hers. "I'm sure I deserve a reward for something, but you'll have to tell me what it is."

She draped a glittering band over her wrist. "For giving me this present, silly. Did you leave it out here on the table to surprise me?"

Bewildered, he gawked at the object. "I—I didn't leave anything out here," he managed to say, his throat paralyzed.

"Aren't you the sweetest thing!" she said. "Promise me you'll wait right here. I'm going to slip into that black lace teddy you like so much, and when I get back, I'm going to show you exactly how sweet I think you are." Wiggling her fingers at him, she went into the room.

He rubbed his eyes, still struggling to understand what had happened. His blood seemed to spurt through his body, alternately hot and cold, making his head throb. His skin felt clammy, and he began to shiver.

The first cry came from the woods, an exact replica of the sound they'd heard the night before. The second seemed to come from the lake, the third from the inky veranda below the balcony. Ed spun back and forth, frantically trying to locate the source. Now they came from all sides. Louder, closer, angrier. Invisible slashes of color stung him like needles. The cloud of noxious noise was suffocating him. He struggled to breathe, to force his feet to move, even to sink to the floor and cover his ears.

"Eddie?" Madeline called from inside the room. "What's going on out there?"

He turned around. Just above the door two yellow eyes glittered at him. The devil's eyes, he thought wildly. A white tail swished like a blade. Gasping, Ed stumbled backward until he felt the rail cut into his back. "Get away from me," he croaked.

The two yellow eyes flew at him. Claws ripped into his face and neck, and his mouth was muffled by a fierce, hot body. He tried to scream as he scrabbled to pull the thing off of him, but he gagged on matted, filthy hair, and then on blood. His blood. The banshee was inside his head, deafening him. Pain exploded in snakes of lightning.

By the time Madeline rushed through the french doors, the balcony was empty, and the only sound was the distant call of a whippoorwill. She looked over the rail and began to scream.

* * *

"You poor, poor child," Miss Doris said, handing Madeline a cup of tea. "And on your honeymoon, too." Miss Lydia and Miss Eleanor nodded soberly.

Madeline sighed. "The doctor said Eddie must have had a heart attack, and that's why he passed out and fell off the balcony. I knew before I married Eddie that he had a heart problem. That's one of the reasons I insisted we come here, so he could relax. But, as you know, he was acting real jumpy from the minute we got here. All he wanted to talk about was birds. He never used to talk about birds. I didn't know he even noticed them, much less wanted to talk about them."

"And you both had been drinking," Miss Lydia inserted.

"Yeah," Madeline said sadly. "Champagne in the moonlight. It was supposed to be romantic."

Miss Doris clucked her tongue, and was pressuring Madeline to have another cucumber sandwich when the elevator doors slid open. A bellboy wheeled a laden cart toward the desk.

Madeline put down the tea and stood up. "There's our luggage. You were all real nice to me, and I appreciate it. This hasn't been the best time in my life, but I'll always remember how kind you were." She held out her wrist, and moistly added, "And I'll have this diamond bracelet to remember Eddie by. He was so generous."

The three ladies watched Madeline as she went across the lobby, smiled bravely at the manager, and continued out to the veranda for a final look at the undulating, autumn-hued slopes of the Catskill Mountains.

"What a stupid girl," Miss Lydia pronounced to her companions. "My eyes may be failing, but I know rhinestones when I see them."

Her companions nodded once more, then the three settled back to see who would be next to check in for a restful weekend at Lookout Lodge.

Tea and 'Biscuit

•

Jon L. Breen

Do have a cup of tea, and I'll tell you a story.

My nephew Jerry Brogan sometimes accuses me of trying to escape reality. That is, of course, absurd. No one my age would think such a thing possible. Reality will always come after you, whether in the form of the unavoidable processes of aging or the more dramatic form of finding a dead body on the grounds of your own home, as I did some years ago when jockey Hector Gates was murdered there. I solved that one, with some help from Jerry, and yet when he has become involved in other puzzles of a criminal nature, he has never called on me, despite my deep knowledge of detection from a lifetime of reading about it. Am I trying to evade reality or is Jerry trying to shield me from it?

I should introduce myself before I go on. My name is Olivia Barchester, widow these many years of the late Colonel Glyndon Barchester, who campaigned Vengeful and other fine thoroughbreds on California tracks. I myself raced Vicar's Roses, among others, after my husband's death.

Odd to say I raced them. I never saw any of my own horses in person, since I never went to the track after the Colonel died, but they ran in my colors. So if a trainer or a jockey's agent can say, "I hooked the favorite at the head of the stretch and beat him by a nose at the wire," I suppose I can say I raced Vicar's Roses.

While I won't admit to evading reality, I do take the prerogative of one who is fairly advanced in years and comfortably off (say old and rich if you must) and control my environment to the greatest extent possible. I don't consider myself a recluse, but I see little need to leave my home and my books. After my husband's death, I decided to follow racing to the extent possible on television. That decision came after Go for Wand's tragic death in the Belmont stretch the day of the 1990 Breeder's Cup. Now I videotape the races on my VCR and watch them at my leisure the evening of the day they are run, relying on Jerry to let me know if anything tragic occurred that I can shield myself from seeing. Self-indulgent, I'll admit, but I can enjoy a race so much more when I know all the runners and their jockeys will reach home safely.

Now I must introduce you to my black cat Seabiscuit, a handsome fellow from a rather distinguished litter who has been my companion for the past fifteen years. All of Seabiscuit's siblings were named for notable one-word racehorses—Stymie, Citation, Equipoise, Swaps, Nashua, Regret. They were born on the backstretch to a stable pet from the barn of an English trainer who insisted, contrary to American superstition, black cats were *good* luck.

There are many cats in racetrack stable areas, though most of them are strays, semi-wild. They are seldom pets for racehorses. Goats are more often cast in that role, for their calming effect on the highstrung thoroughbred.

Thus it is hardly surprising that, while most of Seabiscuit's litter found homes with persons connected to racing, only one followed in his mother's footsteps as a stable mascot. That brings me, you'll be relieved, to the subject of my story.

On a coolish fall evening, toward the end of the annual Surfside Meadows meeting where my nephew Jerry works as track announcer, I was visited by an old acquaintance, trainer Walter Cribbage. I brought him into my library, where Seabiscuit was lying by the fire and I had been engrossed in a vintage Agatha Christie novel from my extensive collection. I offered Walter a choice of beverage. I was sipping tea, but he opted for a straight bourbon, an indication of his troubled state of mind.

Walter is of my generation, thus nearing eighty, but he still has a trim figure and an erect, almost military carriage, and he still is up early mornings seeing to his string of horses. On this particular evening, we began by exchanging good-natured banter in the old way, but it seemed a bit forced on his part. He was clearly worried about something, and I was relieved when he got to the point of his visit.

"Olivia, Exterminator died this morning."

Remembering the post-World War I gelding, I said, "I should think he died years ago."

"Not the horse. The cat. He lived in my stable all these years. He came from the same litter as Seabiscuit. Remember?"

"Oh, of course. I am sorry to hear it. Still, fifteen is a good age for a cat, and one cannot hope—"

"That litter is notably long-lived, Olivia. Citation and Stymie are both still around. And he didn't die of old age, Olivia. He was murdered. Poisoned."

"Oh, dear. But why? Some superstitious backstretch worker, I suppose."

"He survived fifteen years without superstition getting the better of him. I think I know why he was killed. I have a horse in my barn named Band Wagon."

"Walter, as I think you know very well, that was one of the last horses I bred. Odd to say I bred him—I wasn't there in the shed after all—but I did plan the mating of his parents, Red Band and Hay Ride."

"I thought you'd be concerned about his welfare."

"Most certainly. You're doing very well with him, I understand. Jerry tells me he may be favored for the Surfside Handicap. But I'm sorry he doesn't belong to my friends the Burnsides any more."

Walter made a face. "As one who has to deal with the current owners, Mr. and Mrs. Preston Fremont and son, I sometimes share your sorrow. Still, if the Burnsides still had him, I wouldn't have got the chance to train him, would I? I got him just over a year ago. He was a bad actor and had never run up to his potential. Since I've had him, he's gotten better and better, and I don't take a smidgen of the credit. He fell in love with Exterminator. As long as that black cat was around the barn, he was as calm and as kind as can be. He started training well and racing better. That black cat made him a stakes horse. Now he's gone into a tailspin, not eating well, acting up. In the state he's in now, I don't think he'd win a ten-thousand-dollar claimer, let alone the Surfside Handicap.''

Very sad, of course, for my last good horse to fall on bad days, but how could I help? After considerable hemming and hawing, Walter finally got to the point.

"Olivia, I have a big favor to ask of you. I want to borrow Seabiscuit.''

"Borrow Seabiscuit? You must be joking.''

Hearing his name twice in quick succession, Seabiscuit woke from his slumber and strolled over to sit by my chair, happily oblivious to the significance of our conversation.

"He and Exterminator are virtually identical,'' Walter continued. "Maybe having him around the barn would bring Band Wagon back into form.''

I shook my head. "Walter, I'd like to help you, but I can't believe you'd ask me that. To begin with, cats, even much younger ones than Seabiscuit, don't always adjust well to new surroundings. He has grown accustomed to this house and these grounds, a quiet and predictable environment.'' I reached down to scratch Seabiscuit's ear, and he appreciatively rubbed his head against my palm. "Put him in the middle of the furor of the backstretch at his age, and who knows how he would react? Second, cats as much as horses have very distinct personalities. There is no reason to think Seabiscuit could establish that same special bond with Band Wagon simply because he and Exterminator are closely related. And finally, Walter, you are asking Seabiscuit to fill in where his brother has already been poisoned. You think I would consider putting him in that situation?''

Walter looked crestfallen. "You're quite right, of course.

59

I never should have asked. But I don't know what else to do.''

It was at that moment that Jerry phoned to assure me that the day's racing at Surfside, as well as ESPN's coverage of a midwestern stake, had passed without a hitch and was safe for me to watch. Not sharing my nephew's tendency to keep a mystery to himself, I invited him to join Walter and me for a discussion of the problem. He seemed to treat it as a command appearance, though of course it was nothing of the kind. He turned up at my door within minutes.

When he had settled his considerable bulk into an easy chair and accepted a cup of tea and a scone, Jerry listened closely to Walter's story and said rather archly, "It reminds me of the curious incident of Barnbuster's goat."

Walter seemed to brighten slightly. "Barnbuster had no goat."

"That was the curious incident."

"Really," I said, "while nothing delights me more than Sherlockian allusions, I haven't any idea what you two are talking about."

"Don't you remember a horse called Barnbuster a few years ago? He only lived up to his name when his pet goat Mary Poppins wasn't around. The owner-trainer was down on his luck and forced to sell the horse. He got a good price based on the horse's record, but he cleverly withheld Mary P. Barnbuster proved unmanageable for his new owner, and the original owner was able to buy him back for considerably less than he'd been paid for him. Reunited with his nanny, Barnbuster resumed his winning ways."

Walter chuckled at what was obviously a familiar story, then turned grim again. "Doesn't apply to my situation."

"Not exactly, no, but I wouldn't rule out the former owners. Could they be looking for a way to get Band Wagon back cheap? Or maybe seeking revenge against the new owners?"

I was scandalized. "Jerry, what a suggestion! You've known Matthew and Helen Burnside all your life."

"A lot of people probably knew Jack the Ripper all *his* life, too."

"Do be serious! He's just talking this way to irritate me, Walter."

"All right, all right. I don't really suspect the Burnsides, okay?"

"Besides, they've been living on Maui for over a year," I had to add.

"Then let's see what else we can figure out," Jerry said, truly applying himself to the problem for the first time. "How do you know Exterminator was poisoned?"

"The vet recognized the symptoms," Walter said, "and it wasn't the first time someone had tried to kill him. A week or two before, I discovered someone had put a rubber band around the poor cat's stomach. It was eating into his flesh, and there was nothing he could have done about it. It surely would have killed him eventually, and very painfully. I got it off him, and saved his life."

"What a terrible thing to do to an innocent animal," I said, more thankful than ever I had declined to loan Seabiscuit. He cooperated reluctantly as I protectively gathered him into my lap.

"Any new stable employees?" Jerry asked.

"They've all worked for me for years."

"Any of them unusually superstitious?"

"Perhaps, but not about black cats."

Annoyingly, Jerry resumed his anecdotal posture. "It's not always just black cats. I once knew a hotwalker who was heavily into numerology. To him, *any* cat was bad luck in a barn. You take a horse's four legs and add them to a cat's nine lives, and what do you have? Thirteen."

Walter seemed as impatient with Jerry's digression as I was. "Everybody who works for me loved the cat," he insisted.

"Do the owners of Band Wagon visit the backstretch often?"

Walter nodded. "What a bunch. If I didn't like their horse so much, I'd dump them in a minute. Old Preston Fremont is a mean bastard with a short temper and no real regard for horses. He'd run them into the ground if I'd let him. He's smart enough not to even try to do that to Band Wagon, though, and he certainly wouldn't have harmed the cat no matter how angry he was. He loves the money Band Wagon makes him too much.

"Then there's Millicent Fremont, his wife. Kids herself she can dress like a woman half her age, and every time she comes to the stable she seems to resent those filthy things you have to have around a barn—you know, dirt, dung, people. Imagines herself a horse-lover, though. Makes a big deal of feeding her horse carrots. I wonder how'd she react if one of them bit her polished nails!

"And the son is the prize of the lot. Young Delbert. Twenty-five and never did an honest day's work. Doesn't know one end of the horse from another but always has big plans for the stable. A terrible snob with all his other sterling qualities. It was his bright idea Band Wagon should prove his worth by racing in Europe next spring. Even had his old man half convinced it was a good plan. I told them it was impossible, and Preston understood, but the kid practically threw a tantrum."

"What relationship did the three owners have to the late Exterminator?" Jerry asked.

"Relationship with the cat? None at all, really. Preston understood why we had to keep him around, but I don't remember he ever came near him. Millicent would make a big fuss over him until he got pawprints over one of her thousand-dollar dresses one morning. Since then, she's kept her distance. Delbert's gone on record as hating all domestic animals, and I guess that includes horses as well as cats, though money-makers like Band Wagon he manages to take some interest in."

"Are any of *them* superstitious?"

"Just the opposite, if anything. You have to understand, Jerry, the role of Exterminator in that barn was not a matter of superstition. It was just the relationship he had with Band Wagon. They were pals. Mr. and Mrs. Fremont accepted that, but the son always figured it *was* superstition, and the idea drove him nuts."

"How frequently do you see the owners, Walter?"

"More than I want to. I sometimes think they're there every day, but it probably just seems that way."

Jerry nodded. "I think I know who killed the cat," he said, with the offhand casualness appropriate to a brilliant amateur. I'm sure he puts that on for my benefit. "Not that it will do you much good. Killing a domestic animal isn't nearly as serious a criminal offense as it ought to be, and knowing who did it won't help your problem with Band Wagon . . ."

Jerry shook his head solemnly and stared into the fire, letting his dramatic pause lengthen intolerably.

I cleared my throat. "Jerry, if you'll permit me, whodunits form a large part of my recreation. I still might like to know who the killer was."

"So would I," Walter said.

"Sure," Jerry said obligingly. "It has to be the son."

Walter wagged his head. "How on earth did you figure that out?"

"Go back a minute, Walter. You didn't say racing Band Wagon in Europe would be just a bad idea because he didn't like to run on grass or something. You said it would be impossible. Why impossible?"

Before Walter could answer, I belatedly caught on to Jerry's line of reasoning. "The quarantine! A domestic cat would probably have to be quarantined for months before he would be permitted in a European country. It wouldn't be possible for Band Wagon to travel with his pal. And without Exterminator's companionship, Band Wagon would have been useless on the track. So the idea really was impossible from your point of view, Walter."

Jerry nodded. "But young Delbert thought Exterminator's role was just superstitious nonsense. He thought if he killed the cat, and if Band Wagon then carried on his winning ways as before, his scenario of campaigning the horse over European tracks could be realized."

"I ought to have known!" Walter Cribbage exclaimed. "The last time Delbert visited the stable area he had a scratch on his face."

"Probably he got that on his first attempt, when he put the rubber band on Exterminator," Jerry said. He reached down to stroke Seabiscuit, who had fled my lap when the thrill of detection made me too animated.

So among the four of us we seemed to have solved the whodunit. But what good did that do Walter Cribbage, you ask, in his effort to restore Band Wagon to form? Jerry was able to offer him a small ray of hope. One of Regret's off-spring, thus a nephew of Exterminator, was a backstretch resident at Santa Anita and might conceivably be available as a new companion for Band Wagon. If bloodlines meant anything at all, Jerry argued, why not give him a try?

I remained dubious about the probable success of a surrogate, but when I heard the cat's name, I felt it was a good omen. It was Vengeful, after my late husband's best runner.

Band Wagon did win the Surfside Handicap, but Delbert Fremont wasn't around to see it. Died of an infected cat scratch, poor lad.

Well, I wouldn't have told you the story if it didn't have a happy ending.

Horatio Ruminates

·

Dorothy B. Hughes

Some people don't like cats. Some cats don't like people. We try to like all people. We do try. At least, some of us do. But, after all, how can we like people who don't like us? There's something in the atmosphere that measures like to like. And off-putting to off-putting.

Some people hate cats. I mean they say it out loud. With special emphasis. *"I hate cats!"* Alexander called Xan is one of those. He comes to visit his Aunt—she is Milady—and says right out, "I hate cats." It is little wonder that I don't like him. Yet I try. Every time he comes, I try. To no avail. I no sooner rub against his ankles than he explodes, "I *hate* cats!" And follows this by his usual threatening, "Scat, Cat!"

Most people don't know that cats understand people talk. We are born with that knowledge. It doesn't matter whether it's Micronesian or Asiatic or English or Whatever, we understand it. A cat can't make words. Our voice box is different from the human kind. But we understand spoken words.

Aunt Christobel—Milady—loves cats. I have long noticed that female people like cats better than male people do. Not that there aren't exceptions. But on the whole it's that way. Males seem to think that dogs are male and cats are female. They thus identify with dogs. Strange ideas some human people get. I could take on any dog I've ever met and send him yelping. Like that poodle up the street. I can inform you that he no longer ventures onto our property when I am reposing on the front stoop.

Milady has always loved cats, I've heard her say so many times. When I was so little that I could curl in the palm of her hand, I became her Kitty Kat. When I grew to man's estate, I was addressed by my official name, Horatio Ebony Corkindale. Xan knows my given name. Milady has told him so often enough. Yet he never calls me anything but That Damn Cat.

Another thing. Every time he comes to visit her, he takes my special place on the living room sofa. And when I rub against his shoulder or arm to let him know he is in my place, he yells at his aunt, "That damn cat. Why do you keep that damn cat around?" and yells at me, "Scat, Cat!"

When she was not in the room, he used to pick me up and throw me onto the floor. I put an end to that by using a claw here and a claw there, and by adding a certain spitting ejaculation followed by a loud strangle sound of m'yowers. This would always bring Milady in to confront the cat hater. Her mildest warning would be, "If you touch that cat again, you can pack up and leave. Now. Not tomorrow. Now."

His riposte invariably was, "You're a witch! That's what you are. You wouldn't have that damn black cat, if you weren't."

She would sigh patiently and explain to him again, and again and again, each time he makes this ridiculous accusation, "A black cat is not a witch's familiar. It is a black dog."

She might as well be addressing that yappy poodle.

"Then why keep that damn cat around? All she does is sleep, eat her fool head off, scrounge the best pillow . . ."

She could have said, "Which is exactly what you do. And you don't even belong to this household."

But she would not lower herself to his level. She would explain as always, "Horatio is not a female cat. He is a male. A macho male." She had learned about macho from TV.

Xan is decidedly not macho. He is a whine-baby. Actually no baby, he is near thirty years old. His full name is Montrevor Alexander Corkindale. He is the son of Milady's eldest brother. She is Christobel Aylwin Corkindale. She never married. I daresay her brother's achievements in producing progeny discouraged her. Before she retired, she was a professor of mathematics at our University. You can see she is no timorous little woman.

But Xan defeats her. Not only is he a whiner, he is far worse. A taker. Milady is a giver. Generous to persons and to cats. Probably even to dogs, like that yappy poodle up the street. Xan takes all, gives nothing. When he comes to visit Milady, always uninvited, he takes over the best guest room. And its adjoining guest bath, with all the fancy soaps and colognes and face creams and special shampoo she keeps there for her lady visitors. Xan uses all of them. That's why he smells.

When he is present at dinner, he helps himself first, taking the most succulent bits of meat and the finest of the vegetables and fruits. Far worse, after he has served himself these and sees other garden items which he likes better, he puts back again from his plate into the serving dish his initial choosing and takes the others. It makes you wonder if he is actually a Corkindale changeling.

In the living room after dinner, I have seen him empty the crystal candy jar where Milady keeps Belgian chocolates for her invited guests. Empty the entire jar, piece by piece! I have never understood how anyone can have a taste for chocolate. Some dogs like it but cats have finer tastes than that.

Xan is just the kind of human person who would stuff himself with chocolate. Fortunately for our well-ordered household, his branch of the Corkindale family lives somewhere back east, Ohio or Pennsylvania or Kentucky. So he can't come to visit very often and normally can't stay long.

He has not married. Of course not. He wouldn't share with anyone, certainly not a wife. A wife is a female. And he condescends to females, even to his Aunt Christobel. Anyway he couldn't support a wife. He's never been in work long. Once a bossman has a chance to observe him, he is booted out. From what I overhear, even his own father won't have him around the office. Mr. Corkindale is an architectural consultant. When Xan does temporarily arrange for a job—or the family arranges for him—not only does he slump the work, he also informs his superiors just how they should conduct their businesses. He knows more than anybody about anything. His opinion. Obviously no one else concurs. Imagine the governor of a state—and big-city businesses have a much larger organization than most governors—having some hireling clerk tell him how to conduct his affairs.

Presumably Xan came out to his Aunt Christobel's this time as he had some job interviews in our town. Whether she or some other family member arranged these, I haven't yet overheard. However, he certainly isn't stirring himself to meet those interviewers. He stays in bed until near noon. Unwashed, uncombed, and in his crumpled pajamas, he then comes downstairs for breakfast. He has to see to it himself, the coffee is left for him in the thermos on the breakfast table, and some bread on a plate by the toaster. Milady no longer leaves her jar of good English marmalade for him to mess up and leave half empty. Instead she spoons out some grape-smelling American jam into a saucer and that is that. If he wants a real breakfast he has to be at the table, clean and shaven, by eight in the morning.

By noon, Mrs. Odo, our Daily, has vacuumed the downstairs, cleaned Milady's room and bath upstairs, and is arranging Milady's lunch tray, usually a chicken sandwich on brown bread, a green salad with vinaigrette dressing, and hot Jackson's tea. Mrs. Odo does not do a tray for Xan. "He will be out for lunch," Milady tells her every day. Mrs. Odo catches on.

Of course Xan leaves his breakfast mess on the table for either Milady or Mrs. Odo to redd up. He goes back upstairs, takes his shower, drops the towels on the bathroom floor. He gets dressed, then preens in front of the mirror—he loves to look at himself—until he is satisfied with his style and image of the day. (Men say women spend hours before the mirror. They should witness Xan.) He then dashes off to some luncheon date. For which someone else is paying, you can bet. A female, no doubt. A man wouldn't put up with his antics.

When he first arrived on this visit, he asked Aunt Christobel if he might borrow her car. She thought it was for something connected with the job interview and loaned him the key. But after he kept it all day, and then took it again at night, not returning until past midnight, she took back the key. She's a busy woman and uses her car.

He evidently found someone to rent a car for him. His mother, no doubt. From what I've heard Milady tell her friends, his mother has spoiled him from the day he was born. He was the first son in the family, a late arrival, after four daughters, one every twoyear.

If he doesn't have a dinner invitation, he comes back for dinner at our house. He doesn't let Milady know in advance, one way or the other. But she always has a bountiful dinner. Mrs. Odo's niece, Ethel, comes in the afternoon to prepare and serve, whether Milady is alone or having friends in to dine.

After dinner Xan rushes off again, either to a party—to which he probably invited himself—or to join with friends the likes of himself. From what I overhear he has plenty of ne'er-do-wells like himself in the after-college set, perhaps a half dozen of them went to the same Ivy League schools (Xan went to several on his flunk circuit), and perhaps they too are mother-spoiled.

Or Xan is off to chivvy some female, according to Milady. She explains to her friends, "A girl without a date will go out with anything who shaves his face." You can bet he selects only the ones with plenty of money to spend, and happy to take on an escort with whom to spend it. What time he returns, and in what condition, Milady does not stay awake to find out.

I knew things were intolerable. But I didn't know that Milady was at her wits' end until I heard her say so to her best friend, Letty, on the telephone one morning near to three weeks after Xan moved in.

"He simply won't leave," she was saying. "I'm at my wits' end. Every time I ask him when—and I make no bones about it, Letty—he informs me that he can't leave yet, not until he concludes his business appointments. Of course, it's not true. I know it and he knows it and he knows I know it. But he delivers that line just as if it's factual. He's good at that sort of delivery, he's been using it enough years." She concluded her heart-pouring with hard fact. "He's shiftless. That's the only word for it. Perhaps it's an infection, from the womb. No one in our family is that kind." She didn't say, perhaps he inherited it from his mother's family. But I knew she was thinking it, the mother who spoiled him and continues to spoil him.

This long divulgence was of course interrupted over and over again by Letty's exclamations; but I have no way of knowing what she said. I could invent, but why? Anyone who knows Milady's friend Letty could fill in the breaks as well as I. Letty does not suffer fools gladly.

But when Milady finished with that phone call and sat down on the couch quietly for a brief moment, rubbing her forehead with her Irish linen handkerchief, I became aware of how very troubled she was. I heard her deep sigh, watched her pull herself together and prepare to leave for an alumnae meeting in town. I realized she wasn't as young as she had been when I first came to her house. And it was then that I realized I must do something about this situation.

It came to me like a twitch of a tail. Getting rid of Xan depended on Cats. But how?

I would start by sniffing his room. If it is the way he usually leaves it, this should lead to an idea. As I had expected and hoped, he had not bothered to close his bedroom door. I started my prowl-about in his bathroom. It was the usual. Soggy towels on the floor, wet washcloths flung down on the shower tiles. I sprang up to the tiled washbasin ledge. Same as usual. Every one of the bottles left uncapped, puddles about most of them where he had slopped the liquid. Of course all tubes were uncapped, from toothpaste to tinted shaving cream. When I sprang off the ledge I almost lost my footing. I landed on his discarded underpants which he'd left on the floor after evidently using them to mop up some spill or other.

I retreated to the bedroom which was as bad or a worse mess. The carpet was littered with his discards from yesterday or the day before or longer. Whatever he took off he left there, slacks, shirts, socks, more underpants, even the bathrobe which he must have worn some time this morning.

While I was making a cursory examination of the pieces, Mrs. Odo came to the doorway. She was accustomed to talking out loud to herself and to me. "Look at that!" she said to both of us. "Just look at this room! He's a slob. That's what he is. I don't care if he is her blood nephew." She toed his pajamas and underpants half under the bed where she didn't have to see them. She didn't touch them. "Miz Corkindale says I'm not to do his room or his laundry. Horatio, that's what she says to me." Mrs. Odo was carrying her laundry basket, one of those plastic ones with latticed sides. She had succumbed to that modern mode a year or so ago. She didn't want to change from her heavy straw-plaited one, the kind her grandmother and her mother and she had used for generations. Milady convinced her to give the plastic one just a try. Once Mrs. Odo found out it wasn't half so heavy as the other, she accepted it. Neither she nor Milady are as youthful as once they'd been. Nevertheless Mrs. Odo still resented the plastic substitute. She kicked it often.

Through the latticing I could see she'd already gathered Milady's towels and other laundry. She now carried the basket over to the bathroom to pick up the soggy sogs he had left there. She repeated her complaint, "She says I'm not to do his room or his laundry. That's what she says to me." Obviously she wasn't happy about it. Her life was to make everything clean and shipshape. She didn't feel right, leaving a responsibility untouched. "So I do like she says." She went "Ugh" when she picked up the washcloths from the shower floor. "I been working for Miz Corkindale now for some thirty years, I guess. And I've always done like she says. That's how we get along so well." There were more ughs and grunts as she gathered up the rest of the debris. Leaving the clothes, just like "Miz Corkindale says."

It was while she was making her way through the mess that the idea flashed into my head, just like one of those electric light bulbs in cartoons. I stayed right there while Mrs. Odo finished her monologue and made her way to the door. In a quiet corner but in plain sight.

She completed her outburst and stumped away with her basket to the laundry room downstairs. She wouldn't shut me in. But if I left the room it would be just like her to close the door, close the mess from our sight.

I needed to prowl about. I surveyed every nook and cranny of that room while the idea began to take on a substance which was credible.

My next move was to visit my friend, Mignonette, more familiarly known to persons and felines as Mimi. In these days, the romance of the French nickname seems to have been forgotten. Or never known by today's cultural illiterates. No longer is Mimi known as the exquisite light of love. Today—believe it or not!—Mimi is a pet name for a *grand-mother*. Don't ask me why. Too often human people are beyond understanding.

At any rate, my friend Mignonette known as Mimi is no grandmère. Nor is she a courtesan although she well could have been. She is a blue-eyed white cat, exquisitely fluffed and groomed by her Lady, Milady's friend Fran. Their house is over on the next block and up the hill, about three blocks in all. Just a pleasant prowl.

Not too many months ago Mimi birthed six Jellicle kittens. As Mr. Thomas Eliot has pointed out, Jellicle cats are black and white. The three boys of Mimi's litter were black with moonlit eyes. The three girls were white with Mimi's crystal blue eyes. Many human persons and also some cats believe I was sire to the Jellicles. This could not be. I was spayed, or "fixed" in the vulgar, when I was but a kitten. Hence, I cannot reproduce.

The Jellicles, according to Mr. Eliot, are "rather small," and are "merry and bright." Exactly like Mimi's kits. I had seen the Jellicles shortly after they emerged. I followed Milady when she walked over to see the sight. Mimi's Lady had named them. The black males she called The Stuffs. Ruff Stuff was all black but for the tip of his tail and the peak of his left ear. Gruff Stuff had a white collar and one white leg; Tuff Stuff, two white stockings and a white moustache.

The females were all Ee's. Muff had one black ear and one black sock. Fluff was all white but for some black polka dots on her tail. Nuff—her Lady called her EeNuff—was last of the litter. She was all white except for two black zebra stripes, one on each side of her coat.

All of the Jellicles are still at home with their mother. The Lady is not going to put them out for adoption until they are older. All are spoken for by friends of the Lady, this was quite a spectacular litter, you can imagine.

Today was a perfect day for visiting Mimi. Milady was attending her sorority luncheon at noon. It would be near to five o'clock before she returned, there was always a meeting after lunch. Then she was going out for the evening as this was the night of an annual charity supper and ball. She would be away by eight of the evening, being called for by friends, and it would be near midnight before she returned. Xan as usual would be off by six or seven o'clock to dine with whatever friends he'd favored for the evening. I never could understand how it was that he could be tolerated for so many days and nights. There must have been some secret talent he had which those of us at Milady's failed to see. Maybe he was like the Court Fool, not exactly acceptable but amusing. For the most part he probably battened on those females who would endure anything male rather than be unescorted.

The house would thus be free of human folk from early eight to near midnight. Mrs. Odo would leave promptly at six which was her time-honored custom. And as there would be no dinner, Ethel would not be here tonight.

I found Mimi on her cushion in the back garden, blinking as was her wont while resting for the night. She was a night wanderer. Which explains the black-and-white Jellicles.

It was easy enough to map out my plan. "I need your Jellicle kittens," I told her. And then elucidated. She was beautiful but also intelligent. Don't let anyone tell you that beauty and stupidity go together. Far from it. Most of the beautiful cats or people I have studied are as bright (intellectually, that is) as they are beautiful.

And once I had made clear to Mimi my need of the Jellicles, she was as excited as I about some of the ideas I had evolved. In fact, she was eager to impart the ideas to her Jellicle brood, rehearse them if need be, and she assured me that she would be outside my private entrance no later than nine o'clock tonight. With her little ones. My private door is in the downstairs hallway. I did suggest to Mimi that she leave a bit early in order to taunt the poodle, who is not permitted to roam as are we cats. A city ruling.

I went back to my own domicile to await the hour. It was certain Milady would leave early. But Xan's hours were uncertain, sometimes he'd hang around until nine or ten o'clock. When he wasn't included in a dinner evening. Tonight, however, he was off before Milady, all dressed up, and saying something about a banquet and a ball. Undoubtedly they would turn up at the same event. Our city isn't big enough to have two such affairs on the same night.

Once the two were safely away, I checked his room. The bed table light was on, Milady always leaves a light in the guest bedroom. Everything was as I'd hoped it would be. The unmade rumpled bed. The unkempt pillows. Bureau drawers left half opened. Clothes littering the floor. His droopy pajamas half on, half off the bed, one leg hanging down to the floor. It couldn't have been a better setting for Mimi's Jellicles. I could safely go downstairs to await my friend.

It was near to 9:30 that night when she and the brood arrived. In case some doubting Thomases should say, "Cats can't tell time," I should explain that there is a grandfather clock in Milady's entrance hall. It tells the hours with chimes, and the half-hour with a single bong. It is simple enough to count the chimes as they ring, and to know that the succeeding bong will note the following half hour.

I admitted the guests through my private door. Once all seven were inside, they followed me up the staircase to Xan's room. It took Mimi and me more than an hour to acquaint the kittens with the room, and the special hidey-hole each one would occupy while waiting for the signal to emerge. Mimi stressed the timing that each must adhere to, even as in a dance caper, to make this caper successful.

After the rehearsals, Mimi and I allowed the children to romp together like true Jellicles. In case your memory has lapsed, Mr. Eliot speaks of how they "dance a gavotte and a jig" and "jump like a jumping jack." Mimi's kits were as lively as any true Jellicle. It was near eleven o'clock—which was cutting it fine as sometimes Milady left a ball early—when I called time. Mimi then took each one to his position as Mimi and I had designated.

Xan's droopy pajamas were for Ruff Stuff. He was to wriggle into one of the pajama legs, the one lowest to the floor. Gruff was given a position in the toe of the bedroom scuff, half under the bed. Tuff Stuff had the place within the pillowcase on the pillow. A dangerous spot but exciting. And Tuff was aptly named.

Muffee was to clamber into the half-open bureau drawer and be ready to leap into Xan's hand if he reached for a clean pair of underpants. Otherwise to wait until Xan turned off his bed table light and dropped his head on the pillow. That was certain to bring on a violent reaction for which Tuff was eagerly awaiting. When such sounds—yowls is a better word for Xan's vocal explosions—were heard, Muff would leap from the drawer and scamper over to the bed to observe the melee more closely. And Fluff and EeNuff would scamper out from the skirts of the slipper chair and begin their hopping and skipping. By this time Xan would certainly be out of bed and they could use his leg for a Maypole. If Gruff and Tuff hadn't been discovered beforehand they would perform their famous leaps into the circle. All six could then play Ring around the Rosy with both Xan's legs.

It was near to midnight when Milady returned. She spoke to me as she passed the place where I was reclining at the top of the stairs. A place where I could watch Xan's door unobserved. I blinked at her and she said, "You should be asleep, Horatio. It's late.'' She looked weary, she was not accustomed to the midnight hour. She closed herself into her room, for her privacy. She always did, whether alone or with guests in the house.

Once her door was closed, I peered through the banisters and saw Mimi below in her designated place. Around the shadowy corner at the foot of the stairs. I knew she had made certain that Milady did not see her there.

We exchanged two blinks before retreating to our individual positions for the waiting.

I don't know exactly what time Xan returned. He has obviously had long experience in hiding this information. He can be quiet as a cat when he comes in at night, usually a little tossed, and smelling of the wine. It was no different tonight except that tonight I was waiting his return. It would have given me great pleasure to have tripped him atop the staircase. But it would have spoiled the entire scheme. I restrained my urge. He went into his room, closing the door as he does at night. To keep his morning sleep from being disturbed. Or perhaps he is afraid a cat might enter his room while he is asleep? As if any cat could stand the stink of him.

I moved to my position outside his closed door. From earlier observations of Xan's habits, it would not be long now. It wasn't. He doubtless shed his clothes to the floor as usual but did not put on his pajamas. He turned off the bed lamp. He must have bounced down on the pillow for he disturbed Tuff Stuff. And Tuff jumped out from the pillowcase right onto Xan's head.

Xan let out a yowl louder than ever a cat could. He was quickly out of bed it seems and out of habit found the half-hidden scuff for his foot. This did not please Gruff. Xan let out an even louder yowl as he felt the prick of a tooth or a claw on his big toe. Evidently he grabbed his pajamas to pull on so that he could leave this room, and Ruff Stuff made a slide out of Xan's leg.

By now Xan waited on no niceties. He didn't wait to even make a light. He banged open his door, still yowling and shouting and looking over his shoulder where all he could see were the little yellow moons bobbing about the place. Of course by this time Milady was awake. The noise would waken a stone image.

"What is the matter with you, Xan?" she addressed him. "Why are you yelling—waking everybody in the neighborhood, I'm sure."

He interrupted, shouting, "Look at that! Just look at that!" He pointed to his doorway. "My room is full of cats! Look at those yellow blobs of their eyes! They're getting ready to jump on me again!" He then turned on Milady. "You did this!" he shouted at her. "You did this on purpose! You put those cats in my room to get even with me because I don't like your damn cat."

(Needless to say, I had slunk out of the immediate area, choosing a darkling spot.)

"Nonsense!" Milady said. "You've been dreaming. You must have had too much to drink. Now stop making all this racket and go back to bed."

"Go back in there?" he yelped. "With all those damn cats? Never! You go in there, you like cats. I'll sleep in your room."

She advanced on him with her sternest voice. "You will not sleep in my room," she stated. "You will sleep in the guest room where you've slept these weeks. That is your room while you are in this house."

"I'm getting out of here right now," he shouted at her. He bolted into his room, made a light, and yanked his big travel bag out of the clothes closet. He began stuffing it with his things, clean and dirty, opening bureau drawers and dumping their contents into his bag. He filled a small travel pouch with his bathroom brushes, and medications for his face, and all the usual items. He didn't dress, he simply put his mac on over his pajamas. He took his wallet and keys from atop the bureau and stuffed them into a mac pocket.

Milady and I watched him from the hallway. Unobtrusively, Mimi and her Jellicle kits had taken off during the altercation. Xan came out of his room, still fuming, dragging the travel bag after him.

"I'm leaving," he informed her. "And I'll never come back here again until you stop running a Cat House." He stumbled down the stairs, the bag thumping after him on each step.

Milady and I had moved to the top of the stairs, the better to observe his departure. When he reached the lower hallway, she called down to him, "Don't bother to come back for what you've forgotten. I'll post whatever to your mother."

He ignored that and opened the front door. The car he was using stood in front of the house where he always left it at night. He didn't look back, he didn't say goodbye. He went out, attempting to bang the door after him. The door doesn't bang. It has one of those automatic closures which won't let it bang. He tried again and again, finally gave up and the door closed itself. Within a few moments, we could hear the car whamming away.

Milady was laughing. "He probably meant it to be an insult. Cat House!" She looked down at me and I blinked at her. She winked back at me. I'm sure she knew that I had a hand in what had happened tonight. "You can go to bed now, Horatio," she said, still laughing. "Goodnight," and she retired to her room.

Cat House. I don't know who or why they ever started calling a brothel a Cat House. When you think of it, it is quite an insult. A Cat House would be kept as clean and tidy as a cat keeps his or herself. It would have rectitude. It would not be open to any man who had the price. It would not be a Call House.

But I wonder if Xan even knew it was an insult. He wasn't very bright. He certainly wasn't dictionary-wise. But one thing is certain. He didn't come back to Milady's.

I should have gone right to sleep. It had been a long enough and busy enough day and night. Instead I found myself thinking about what I had accomplished. Not I alone. But with the help of my friends, Milady, Mrs. Odo, Mimi. A very successful time indeed. Xan was gone.

It didn't actually matter whether I went to sleep now or later. Unlike human people, cat people can go to sleep whenever they wish. Lying awake and trying to sleep, as Milady oftimes mentions to her friends, must be quite an annoying sensation.

Instead of sleeping, I began to ruminate about other conditions which might improve with a bit of planning. For instance, that yappy poodle up the street. To be sure, cats could not handle him. But dogs?

There are quite a number of dogs in the near neighborhood. Over in the next block there is an aristocratic tan collie with a slim white face. A very friendly dog. And two blocks down the hill is a Doberman pinscher, dark-skinned brown and black, built like a fine-honed athlete. Some people say that Dobermans are vicious. I've never found this to be true. It is only that they are impatient with clods. Three blocks beyond, there is a giant Great Dane. Imagine him looking way down at that blue hairbow which the yappy poodle wears atop of his head. Yes, *his* head. He is a dog, not a bitch.

I didn't have to go to sleep yet. I could stretch out on the hallway carpet and conjure up some new ideas. As Milady often says: Creative Procrastination can last just so long. She learned that phrase from her Doctor.

A dog wearing a blue hair ribbon!

Scat

·

Barbara Paul

Tess fiddled with the adjustment band of her earphones; there ought to be some way to make the things stay up without the top part pressing so hard on her head. She was getting a headache.

An elbow jabbed her in the side. " 'Scuse me," said Pauline.

Tess grunted *okay*. She'd sung with Betty before, but Pauline was a stranger. The sound booth the three of them were crowded into was so tiny there was no room for stools to sit on. They'd been standing in there for nearly two hours, with only one break.

"Let's *go*," Betty hissed.

The director must have heard her. "All right, girls," his voice said through their earphones, "let's try it again. Tess—bright-voiced, happy. Betty and Pauline, remember—no *doo-wah*. *Ooh*-ahh. Oooooh. Ahhhhh. It's what the customers are supposed to say when they see the new Scimitar 2000. Ooh, ahh."

"Why do they keep naming cars after weapons?" Betty muttered.

"Ready?" said the director. "Here comes your count."

The three women listened to the metronomic ticking fed into their earphones from the control room. On the eighth beat the taped music came in. On the sixteenth beat, they began to sing.

"Be good to your-seh-helf," Tess started.

"Ooh-ahh, ooh-ahh."

"Only the best for you-hoo."

"Ooh-ahh, ooh-ahh."

"Hold it," the director's voice cut in. "Problem here." The earphones went dead. They could see him in the control room, yelling at the engineer who was trying to concentrate on the panel in front of him.

"Does this happen a lot?" Pauline asked.

"Yes," the other two said together.

They were all silent a moment, and then Betty said to Tess, "You look like hell. What time did you get in last night?"

"Four. God, I hate these morning sessions."

"Me too, and I was in bed by eleven."

Pauline looked as if she wanted to ask a question, but just then the director's voice told them they were ready to go again.

This time they got it, much to everyone's relief. Later the announcer's voice would be dubbed in, then the whole thing fitted to the visuals. If the timing was off by even two seconds, the singers would be called back to lay down a new track. Tess made a good living that way.

The director thanked them all effusively and promised their checks would be mailed out the next day. The three singers left together, knowing they'd done their part to help persuade the American viewing public that it was well worth risking bankruptcy to own a shiny new Scimitar 2000.

Tess turned down Betty's lunch invitation, waved good-bye, and headed for the lot where she'd left her car.

She was yawning by the time she unlocked her front door; five hours between gigs simply was not enough. She dragged into the kitchen and opened a can of soup. Almost as an afterthought she reached into the cabinet and pulled out a can of cat food. Ocean whitefish with tuna, oh yummy. "It's here if you want it," she called out.

Tess took her cup of steaming soup into the bedroom where she kicked off her shoes and eased onto the bed. Ooooh, that felt good, ahhh . . . and immediately she heard Betty's and Pauline's voices in her head singing *Ooh-ahh, ooh-ahh*. She laughed. What else could one do except laugh? Nobody liked singing crap for a living, but it paid the bills.

She finished most of the soup—beef barley—and rested the cup in her lap. She lay back against the big reading pillow and felt herself drifting toward sleep. Then a movement caught her eye. The cat was just inside the bedroom door, licking his paw and washing his face. It was the closest he ever came to thanking her for his food.

"Hello, Hugo," Tess said tiredly.

Hugo didn't answer. He was a small gray cat, with a broken tail and a chunk missing out of one ear. His coat was growing back in nicely, though; when Tess's sister had first brought him home, big patches of Hugo's fur were missing, exposing ugly areas of raw, infected skin. One of his eyes had been sealed shut. And he'd walked with a limp.

Hugo had been a test animal in a cosmetics company's laboratory. God knew what they'd been trying out on him; but whatever it was, it had turned an ordinary alley cat into a vicious, semi-feral animal that saw every human gesture as a threat to his safety. Hugo had been rescued by PETA, the People for the Ethical Treatment of Animals, on one of their liberation raids. Tess's sister Debra, an ardent animal-rights activist, had been on that raid; Debra said they'd had to use a net to catch Hugo and drag him out. He'd fought and hissed and spat and clawed every inch of the way.

But then a couple of weeks later Debra learned she was being transferred to a new office her company was opening in Florida. It meant a promotion, and Debra had jumped at the chance. But uprooting the still maladjusted Hugo again so soon, at the same time she was house-hunting and learning a new job . . . it was too much for her. Debra begged her sister to take Hugo; and in a moment of weakness, Tess had said yes. But Debra hadn't been completely honest about Hugo and his problems; all she'd said was, "Don't ever, *ever* try to stroke his back."

She hadn't told Tess that Hugo hated human beings—all

human beings, no exceptions. At times it wasn't safe even to walk near him; the claws would lash out, ripping through cloth and skin. Yet even the one warning Debra had given her, Tess had managed to forget. On Hugo's first night with Tess, it had seemed the most natural thing in the world to stretch out her hand for a little cat-petting. Hugo had sunk his teeth into the back of her hand all the way down to the bone. She still bore the scars that little gesture of friendliness had cost her.

A light thump on the end of the bed startled Tess; Hugo sat crouched there, eyeing her suspiciously, ready to pounce at the first sign of danger. It was the only time he'd ventured onto the bed in the six months he'd been living with her. His eyes left hers and traveled to the cup in her lap.

Ah, it was the remains of the soup he wanted. "Still hungry, are you? It's all right, Hugo," she said soothingly as she moved the cup slowly toward him. "You can have it if you want." She drew back her hand and waited.

Eventually Hugo decided no trap was lying in wait and crept up to the cup. He finished the soup and licked the inside of the cup.

Tess smiled. "You like that, huh?" Her eyes slowly closed. She was almost asleep when she felt the lightest of pressures on her stomach. It felt like a cat paw.

She opened one eye. Hugo was testing her stomach while watching warily for any sign of reaction. Tess lay as still as she could, one arm draped across her waist. Taking his time, the cat oozed up onto her stomach and made himself comfortable. Hugo wasn't very heavy but he was warm; he felt good there. Tess was almost ecstatically pleased at this miraculous turn of events.

But the miracles weren't over yet. After a few minutes Hugo started nudging at her hand with his nose, gently, repeatedly. *He wants to be petted?* Tess wondered. Hesitantly she touched his head with the tips of her fingers; Hugo moved into the caress. To her surprise Tess found he liked to have his face stroked. A low rumbling noise began. It was the first time she'd ever heard him purr.

Breakthrough! Breakthrough! Tess grinned foolishly at the thought of falling asleep with a cat purring on her stomach. Especially *this* cat. It was true, a little love and kindness could—

But then she became aware the purring had stopped. Hugo was staring at her, making that kind of hypnotic eye contact only cats can manage. Hugo's own eyes were in what Tess thought of as his "attack mode." She pulled back her hand . . . but not fast enough. Hugo lashed out, his claws catching the side of her hand. Tess yelped with the pain; Hugo thumped down off the bed and disappeared.

"You stupid cat!" Tess yelled. "*I'm* not the one who hurt you!"

The pain was shooting all the way up her forearm. She went to the bathroom for antiseptic and a couple of Tylenol before returning to bed and trying to think herself into the proper frame of mind for sleep.

The Corner Bar wasn't on a corner and it was trying to be more than just a bar. It was located in a neighborhood of slum buildings and half-hearted restorations, nearly all the ground-floor space taken up by pawnshops, dry cleaners, cheap furniture stores, appliance outlets, greasy spoons. A small-time entrepreneur named Phil Maynard had bought the Corner Bar when it was a failing comedy club and was doing his best to turn it into a jazz spot. But there were problems.

The four-piece band was doing a set when Tess slipped in the back way. Lazy jazz, too early in the evening for anything else. Tess stood at a beaded curtain in a doorway and peeked out at the "stage"—just a small raised platform at one end of the room. The bass player had hair so blond it was almost white; he stared vacantly into space, his pupils jumping. Only nine-thirty and already flying. The other three members of the band, all black, were laughing at him. Tess suspected they laughed at her too; a black customer had once told her bluntly *White meat can't scat*. But Lester, the piano man, could follow anything she did. They got along.

"I want you to split your set tonight, Tess," a voice said in her ear. "Half before Tommy, half after."

She turned angrily; Phil Maynard, a beefy man with wiry black hair, was staring over her shoulder at the small audience. "That's a helluva thing to do to me, Phil! Why?"

He nodded toward the audience. "Joey LaCosta."

Oh. Tess's heart sank. LaCosta was an insider—they didn't like to be called "wiseguys" anymore—and everyone who knew him was afraid of him. Tess picked him out in the audience, sitting at a center table with two of his troopers. LaCosta had started dropping in to listen to Tommy Vincenza, an unsuccessful stand-up left over from the days when the bar was trying to make it as a comedy club. Tommy specialized in bathroom jokes. All of his jokes were old ones, and most of them weren't even funny. But Joey LaCosta liked Tommy's scatological humor; and what Joey liked, Joey got. When LaCosta had oh-so-politely mentioned that clinking glasses distracted him, Phil had got the message and stopped serving drinks while Tommy was on.

LaCosta didn't want to hear Tess; he'd put up with a little scat-singing while waiting for his man, but not a whole lot. "I'll split my set," Tess muttered.

"See those two guys over to the left by the wall?" Phil asked. "Cops."

Tess looked at them. "How can you tell?"

"I know one of 'em." He growled. "I try to run a nice clean club here and what do I get? Crooks and cops. I wouldn't have none of 'em if it wasn't for Tommy, but I can't get rid of him or LaCosta'll start leanin' on me." He rubbed a big hand across his mouth. "I'm gonna have to fire that bass player. Cops look at him and think we're sellin' drugs here and we're all in deep shit."

"Is that why they're here? They think—"

"Naw, they're keepin' an eye on LaCosta. Go get changed, Tess. Let's get rollin'."

"Why don't you put Tommy on now and let me do my set after?"

"Tommy ain't here yet. Go on, Tess."

She went to the communal dressing room, a small ex-storeroom to which a few mirrors and tables had been added. Tess climbed up on a chair to reach the gown she'd left hanging on the exposed water pipe that ran through the room. It was the same gown she'd worn the night before, but it didn't matter; the Corner Bar didn't attract the kind of customers that came back night after night.

And that too was Tommy Vincenza's doing. Music lovers would drop in for a little listening; but when Tommy got into his routine, always, every night, some of the customers would get up and wander out. Tommy turned people off. He was a throwback; people had stopped laughing at Tommy's kind of toilet humor years ago. All except Joey LaCosta. Joey La-Costa thought Tommy was a riot.

Tess had finished dressing and was fixing her make-up when Tommy walked in, carrying a blue airline bag. He was short, coming up only to Tess's shoulder, and almost as round as he was tall. A sixtyish man, Tommy had the bleary eyes and red-veined nose of a lifelong serious drinker; but his speech never seemed to be affected no matter how much alcohol he consumed. Before sitting down or saying hello, he pulled a bottle out of the airline bag, poured himself a shot, and downed it.

"Ah, that's better." He turned a bloodshot eye toward Tess and gave her a lopsided smile. "You're looking fetching tonight, m'dear!"

"Aren't you a little early, Tommy?"

"Yeah, I thought I might as well come on in. Didn't have anything else to do. Hey, Tessie, did you hear this one? How is the starship *Enterprise* like a roll of toilet paper?"

"I don't want to hear," she said firmly.

"They both circle Uranus and search for Klingons."

She just looked at him. And then changed the subject: "Did you know your number-one fan is here?"

"Mr. LaCosta, yes. Phil told me."

"You don't mind playing to insiders?"

"Mind? When he laughs, everybody laughs. I don't mind that at all."

"Then you don't want to keep him waiting, do you? Why not do your routine first tonight?"

"Ah m'dear, it's not that easy. You need to assimilate a certain amount of anaesthetic before you can go out and wipe the Mafia's ass." He poured another shot.

Tess gave up. She went and stood by the doorway with the beaded curtain until Phil was ready to introduce her. By then the customers had built up a good cloud of cigarette smoke. By midnight the haze would be so thick she'd have trouble breathing; not the best of conditions for a singer.

Phil went through his usual rigamarole of welcoming everyone, promising them *grrrreat!* entertainment and so on. "And now here she is," he finished, "the Corner Bar's own—Tess Ridgeway!"

A polite smattering of applause greeted her entrance. She glanced at the piano player and said, "Only half a set, Lester." Lester nodded, as if expecting something like that.

She might as well have been singing Greek folk songs for all the attention the audience paid. The two cops by the wall kept their eyes on Joey LaCosta. LaCosta was telling a story to his two troopers, a story that required much waving of the hands. The other customers were either listening to him openly or sneaking glances in his direction; an underworld celebrity was still a celebrity. The bar's one waitress moved among the tables, taking orders, delivering drinks. By the time Tess had gotten a few of the customers listening to her, her half-set was over.

Lester rolled his eyes in sympathy as the band members prepared to leave the stage. Tess charged off, snarled something at Tommy waiting to go on, and slammed into the dressing room.

A minute later the dressing room door opened and Cheryl, the waitress, came in carrying a drink. "Thought you could use this," she said with a friendly smile.

"Thanks, Cheryl." It was scotch, and it went down smoothly, caressing Tess's throat instead of burning; Cheryl had dipped into Phil's good stock. Tess grinned. "*Thanks*, Cheryl!"

Cheryl laughed and patted her blond frizz. "Tommy's feeling no pain. First time I ever saw him weave." She'd left the dressing room door open, and both women could hear LaCosta's *haw-haw-haw* booming out from the audience. "That must have been an especially gross one."

Tess took another swallow of the scotch. "If I were Phil," she said, "I'd buy Tommy a plane ticket to Los Angeles and then tell LaCosta he'd gotten an offer to go on TV."

Cheryl nodded. "That might do it. But Tommy could always come back."

"Yeah," Tess said glumly.

Both women were silent a minute . . . and then it hit them that the audience was equally silent. No applause, no Mafiaesque guffaws, nothing. Uneasy, Tess put down her drink. She and Cheryl stepped out of the dressing room to see what was going on.

They found Phil standing by the beaded curtain, staring out at Tommy, a look of horror on his face. "Is he out of his mind?" he asked. "Is the little twerp out of his fuckin' *mind*?"

Out on the stage, Tommy was sweating, playing to his one-man audience and straining for the laughs that just weren't coming. "There was a cop who was taking this wiseguy in for questioning."

Tess and Cheryl gasped.

"On the way they pass this little kid playing with a pile of shit. The cop says, 'Yucch, that's disgusting! What are you doing with that shit?' And the kid says, 'I'm making a cop.' The wiseguy thinks that's funny but the cop gets mad. So the cop says, 'That's terrible, why are you making a cop out of shit?' And the little kid says, 'Because I don't have enough for a wiseguy.' "

"Jeeeeeesus," Phil groaned. Out front—*dead* silence.

Tommy tried again. "Two other wiseguys, they're worrying about another member of the family, a cousin who walks with a kind of swish? So one day they follow him, and sure enough the cousin leads them straight to a gay bar. They watch as he looks over the action and finally picks out a comely-looking lad sitting at the bar. The cousin goes up to stand behind the lad and he says, 'Hi, there—mind if I push in your stool?' "

That did it. *"Basta!"* Joey Lacosta jumped out of his chair and pointed a finger at Tommy. "Who you think you are, you shit-for-brains? Hanh?" No one made a sound as La-Costa charged toward the now-trembling comic. "You stand up here and you make fun of my family? *My* family?"

"Mr. LaCosta, I—"

"I come to this shitty little club, I listen to you, I laugh at your jokes. I even slip you a nice tip now and then. And what do you do? You stand up here and mock me! You mock my family, you mock my business—what kind of way is that to show respect?"

"But Mr. LaCosta, I only—"

"You only what? I'll tell you what you only. You only insulted me, that's what you only. You insulted me in public."

"Oh no, that wasn't what I meant—"

"Shaddup. I'm thinking." LaCosta's two bodyguards moved up to flank him, in case he needed help in handling the dangerous Tommy Vincenza. Finally LaCosta said, "Awright. Here's what I decided. You gave me a lotta good laughs, Tommy, so I'm not going to do nothing this time. But if I ever hear you been telling these kinda jokes again, you know what's gonna happen, don't you? You hear me, Tommy? You hear what I'm saying to you?"

Tommy's voice came out in a squeak. "I hear you, Mr. LaCosta. But believe me, please, I meant no disrespect! I didn't mean anything by it!" He was talking to LaCosta's retreating back. "I thought you'd be pleased!" he called in one last attempt to mollify his former patron.

The three mobsters left; one of the cops got up and followed them. Phil ran out and dragged Tommy off the stage. Both men were panting. "Jesus Christ, Tommy, what's the matter with you?" Phil said to the quivering comic. "You got some kind of death wish or something?"

"Yeah, Tommy," Cheryl said, wide-eyed, "that was pretty dumb even for you!"

The comic looked so frightened and confused that Tess felt sorry for him. "But, but he said Mr. LaCosta *liked* jokes about the mob!" Tommy whimpered.

"Who said?"

"One of his boys. One of those guys here with him to-night."

Phil was thunderstruck. "And you believed him? You actually *believed* him?"

"Well, why would he tell me that if—"

"Because he was tired of coming in here. Because he wanted to make trouble. Because he was bored. Who the hell knows why? Jesus Christ, Tommy, how could you be so stupid? If you've brought the mob down on me, I swear to God I'll—"

"You can't fire me!" Tommy screeched. "You know you can't fire me!"

Phil stopped short. He licked his lips but said nothing.

"Wow," Tess said, "that must be some contract you have, Tommy. Who's your agent?"

Tommy was breathing heavily. "No contract. Phil and me don't need a contract. Do we, Phil?"

Just then the four band members came in from the alley where they went between sets to get away for a while. Lester took in the picture in one glance and muttered, "Back out-side."

"No, hold it," Phil commanded. "Go out there and play—*now*. Something lively, get their minds off what just happened. Go on, move!"

Not one of the band members asked what *did* happen; they crowded past Tess and Cheryl single-file through the beaded curtain.

Tommy had had time to think about LaCosta's threat. "J-Jeez, Phil," stammered, "wh-what am I going to do?"

"I'll tell you what you're goin' to do." Hands on hips, Phil glowered down at the little man. "Right now, you get the hell out of here. Then tomorrow you go to LaCosta and you apologize. Then you tell him exactly what you told me. Finger the goon, make trouble for *him*. And Tommy—don't come back here until you do it.''

"You can't fire me!"

"I'm not firing you, I just don't want you out on that stage until this business is settled. Y'unnerstand?'' Tommy nodded. ''All right, then, beat it.'' The comic dragged away, his shoulders slumping.

Tess stared at Phil, amazed that he was willing to let the comic come back at all. ''Tommy must have something on you.''

His face turned red. ''Mind your own goddamned business. Get out there and do somethin', help 'em out.'' He turned to glare at Cheryl. ''Why aren't you takin' orders?'' Cheryl ducked her head and hurried away. Phil looked back at Tess. ''I thought I told you to go sing!'' He pushed her through the beaded curtain.

The customers were still buzzing about the incident and not paying the slightest attention to the entertainers. Tess looked at Lester and shrugged. He shrugged back and played a couple of chords on the piano. Tess sang a few nonsense syllables, no particular song. He hit another chord, she sang *dah-doo-dah-diddley*. This went on for a minute or two; finally the crowd began to quiet down. Tess slid into *Icehouse Blues*.

Then something magical began to happen. Tess found her true voice and started singing the way she wished she could sing all the time. She built slowly, moving from slow song to less slow, picking up the tempo and pacing herself until the customers were yelling *Yeah!* at the end of each number. One part of scat singing was trying to reproduce the sound and phrasing of musical instruments; the brasses were easy, but this night Tess found she could actually do the wail of a saxophone. Occasionally she'd yield to one of the band members, dah-doo-diddling along in harmony as each one did his turn; even the blond hophead on bass had his inspired moment. Then came the climax of the set, and Tess threw back her head and gave it her all. She felt great; for one solid hour she'd been wrapped up in the kind of joy that came only from doing what she loved best and doing it well.

"Not bad, Babe," Lester said when she'd finished. It was the first compliment he'd ever paid her.

Offstage, a laughing Phil gave her a big hug. Cheryl was there too, excited and holding out a drink that Tess didn't need this time. But she took it anyway, thanked them both and headed for the dressing room.

She was pacing in the cramped little room, trying to walk off her adrenaline high, when a knock came at the door. It was the cop who'd stayed after LaCosta had walked out.

"Hi, I don't want to disturb you," he said, smiling, "but I just had to tell you that was the absolutely best scat-singing I have ever heard."

She said thank you and then laughed. "And how many scat singers have you heard?"

He grinned back at her. "Only three or four. You're not exactly mainstream, you know."

"I know. For most people, scat's a nostalgia thing. But it'll never die out completely. It's too much fun."

"Still, if you can earn a living at it—"

Tess made a face. "Nobody can live on what Phil Maynard pays. I have another job. You know those voices singing away in the background of TV commercials? Sometimes that's me."

He hesitated and then said, "I haven't introduced myself. My name's Graham Burke."

Tess nodded. "Pleased to meet you, Graham." She waved her glass in the air. "I'd like to offer you a drink, but this is all I've got."

"That's all right, I'm on duty anyway. I'm a police detective."

"I know. Why did you stay behind when your partner followed our visiting mobsters out?"

"He'll contact me if he needs me," Graham Burke said shortly. "Tell me, how did you get started in this kind of singing?" Big smile.

Warning bell; he hadn't answered her question. "You're watching someone here, aren't you?" she guessed.

The smile disappeared. "I can't talk about that."

"Which means yes."

An awkward pause developed. "Well, thanks again for some great singing." He smiled wryly and left.

Tess's good feeling had vanished. The police were keeping the Corner Bar under surveillance. Immediately she thought of the coked-up bass player—but why hadn't they just arrested him, if drugs were what they were looking for? Could LaCosta have some connection with the club other than Tommy Vincenza? Then she remembered that Tommy had something on Phil, something strong enough to force him to keep Tommy on the payroll even though the comic attracted the kind of customer Phil wanted to avoid. Phil? The police were keeping an eye on Phil?

With an effort she put it all out of her mind. She had two more sets to get through, and it would take some doing to match the pitch and intensity of the last one. Tess had to conserve her energy; it would be hours before she could climb on the chair to hang her gown on the water pipe and go home to Hugo.

Tess slept until noon and got up then only because Hugo was scheduled to get his shots at two. The cat was prowling about and hissing, mad because she wouldn't let him out. Tess stayed out of his way.

She should never have let him become an outside cat in the first place. One day she'd caught him shredding her living room drapes with his claws. She'd opened the door and yelled *Scat!* and chased him out, secretly hoping he'd run away. But no such luck; Hugo kept coming back to the one place in the world where he could count on a safe place to sleep and something to eat.

One of Tess's dates had tried to pet Hugo when she wasn't looking; Hugo had bitten and scratched so violently that she'd had to drive the man to the emergency room of the nearest hospital for treatment. The doctor told her to get the cat declawed; Tess said that would leave him defenseless out of doors. Her date had been more blunt: *Have him put away.* Hugo was not a pet, he pointed out; he was a savage creature that she was foolishly harboring and that would one day turn against her.

But Tess couldn't bring herself to have the cat destroyed. Instead, she'd called the ASPCA. They told her they'd take Hugo, but he'd probably be put to sleep; people wanted to adopt kittens, not cats. So then she asked the vet who treated Hugo to help him find a new home. Dr. McInerny had been politely discouraging, saying he couldn't in good conscience foist Hugo off on anyone.

So she was stuck. Tess was just going to have to put up with him and pray that sooner or later he'd come around.

She started getting ready to take Hugo to Dr. McInerny's office. An Ella Fitzgerald tape was playing, buoying Tess up a little; Ella always made it sound so easy. Tess took the portable kennel out of the closet, being careful to close the bedroom door so Hugo wouldn't see it just yet. Hugo hated the kennel; he hated to ride in a car, he hated being taken to a different place, he hated all those dangerous humans in the vet's office. Sighing with resignation, Tess got out a pair of welder's mitts that came all the way up to her elbows; she always hated this part.

It was a battle. But no matter how fiercely Hugo bit and clawed at the protective mitts, Tess held on and finally got him into the kennel. The first obstacle was over. Tess turned off Ella Fitzgerald and carried Hugo to the car.

He yowled all the way. Inside the vet's office, he switched to a low menacing growl, ready to take on anything that moved. The assistant was ready for him, though; she was wearing animal handler gloves when she took Hugo out and held him on the examination table.

"Don't touch his back," Tess reminded Dr. McInerny.

"I remember," he said. Swiftly he gathered up the fur over Hugo's collarbone, inserted the needle, and it was done. "Do you know how male lions kill each other?" Dr. McInerny asked as the assistant wrestled the spitting, scratching cat back into the kennel. ''They kill each other with a bite to the spinal cord. Hugo still feels threatened by what the experimenters did to him and he's literally watching his back. We don't know his full history—it could be a long time before he comes to trust you.''

''So be patient?'' Tess asked wryly.

''So be patient.''

On the ride back Hugo didn't make a sound. He crouched into a small ball and stared out of the kennel, never taking his eyes off Tess. At home he didn't run away and hide as he usually did but instead stayed close to Tess, following her from room to room. When she plopped down to read the paper, he sat on her feet. He looked so small and vulnerable huddled there that her heart went out to him. When later she went into the kitchen, he went with her, staying underfoot all the time. When she sat at the table to eat, there was Hugo, sitting on her feet again.

Then she got it. He was *anchoring* her there, trying to keep her from going away, from abandoning him.

''Oh, Hugo,'' Tess said with a sigh. ''Whatever am I going to do with you?''

That night Tess found Phil behind the bar, grinning and pouring a drink for Tommy, who looked happier than she'd ever seen him. She perched on the bar stool next to the comic and said, ''You must have patched things up with your pal Joey.''

Tommy raised his right hand with two fingers crossed. ''We're like that, m'dear, we're like that.''

''Tommy told him about the goon who caused all the trouble,'' Phil said.

''He believed you?'' Tess asked Tommy.

''He sure as hell did! This trooper—his name's Alfio— seems like he'd given Mr. LaCosta grief before. Mr. LaCosta said, 'Alfio, I told you the last time, if you pulled any more stunts I was gonna have you sweeping the floor of one of our factories!' He went on talking like that—like I wasn't even there listening! Then he told Alfio to get the hell out and he'd deal with him later.''

"Well, hallelujah," Tess said with a smile.

"Yeah, ain't it great?" Phil looked pleased, but Tess thought he must be of two minds about this turn of events. Happy that the insiders were no longer mad, not so happy that they'd be coming back to the Corner Bar.

"And Tessie, you know what he did next?" Tommy said with a note of awe in his voice. "He apologized to me! Joey LaCosta apologized to *me*! And he gave me this." He showed her his left hand, a ring glittering on his little finger. "I never had a pinkie ring before in my life," Tommy said in that same tone of awe. "Those are real rubies, you know. Took it right off his own hand and gave it to me.''

Tess shook her head but didn't say anything; Tommy's gangster-worship could lead to no good end. Cheryl came up to the bar to get an order filled and Tess asked her, "How are they tonight?" Meaning the customers.

"Lethargic, kind of," Cheryl said. "I don't think these are the same people who were here before. I mean, I don't remember these faces. Nobody from last night.''

"Probably afraid of an encore."

"Wouldn't you be?"

Tess looked over the small crowd. Not much talk going on; most of the customers were just sitting staring into their glasses. An unusual number of solitary drinkers, some of whom looked as if getting blind raging drunk within the next few hours was the only goal in life worth pursuing. Lester and the other band members came straggling out and started getting ready to play. "At least we won't have to worry about LaCosta again for a while.''

"Oh, didn't I tell you?" Tommy interposed, still admiring his ruby ring. "Mr. LaCosta's coming back again tonight. To show there are no hard feelings, he said.''

Tess and Cheryl exchanged a look. "Wonderful," Phil said tonelessly.

Tommy was feeling good, his bleary eyes more open than

Tess had ever seen them. "Say, girls, did you hear the one about the—"

"I've got to change," Tess said quickly and slipped away from the bar.

"A customer wants me," Cheryl announced and darted off.

Ah well, Tess thought as she made her way back to the dressing room, *he still has Phil to listen to him.*

Poor Phil.

Halfway through Tess's set, Joey LaCosta and his two shadows came in. One of the two had been there the night before, but the other was a new face, a replacement for the troublemaking Alfio.

The mood of the crowd had changed. Friday was always the Corner Bar's best night, and the lethargy that characterized the early drinkers had disappeared altogether. The customers were talking cheerfully, drinking, even listening to Tess. Graham Burke and his partner were sitting at their same table by the wall; Tess hadn't noticed them come in. She was singing only peppy songs, since that seemed to fit the mood of the crowd, and the band was bouncing right along with her. Cheryl was busy, even looking a little harried; Phil ought to think about bringing in extra help on the weekends. When Tess finished her set to noisy, good-natured applause, she threw Graham a wink; he responded with a smile and a wave.

When she pushed through the beaded curtain, she was surprised to find Tommy wasn't waiting to go on. Phil usually introduced the comic, but tonight he was out front pouring drinks as fast as he could. The band members started coming off the stage for their break. "Tommy's not here," she said to Lester.

"Dressing room," he mumbled and headed straight for the alley.

"All right, *don't* help me look for him!"

He didn't. None of the band did. They were in too big a hurry to get to the alley and do whatever they did there between sets.

Muttering to herself, Tess made her way to the dressing room. The door was closed, generally a sign that someone was changing clothes. She pounded on the door with her fist. "Tommy! You're on."

No answer.

"Come on, Tommy! They're waiting." She opened the door and drew back as an unexpected stench made her gag. She pushed the door the rest of the way open . . . and found Tommy.

He was hanging by the neck from the water pipe that ran through the dressing room, the rope knotted high under his right ear. As if in a trance Tess moved toward him, drawn by the strangeness and unbelievableness of what she'd walked in on. She saw the comic's hands had been tied behind his back. As if hypnotized she stared at his hands, eventually realizing that his briefly owned but highly prized pinkie ring was missing. Finally the smell drove her back; in his last moment of life, Tommy had fouled himself.

Outside, she closed the dressing room door and leaned against it, a tightness in her chest making it hard to breathe. Then, without warning, a surge of fear swept over her. Someone who killed people was *here*, right here. Right now.

She ran out front as fast as she could and screamed at Detective Graham Burke that Tommy Vincenza had been murdered.

A Lieutenant Iverson had arrived to take charge of the case, which should have warned Tess right there: police lieutenants normally did not personally investigate the slayings of third-rate comedians in shabby night spots. Graham Burke had dashed after Tess following her startling announcement, while the Corner Bar's customers all suddenly remembered appointments they had elsewhere. Graham's partner had had the presence of mind to restrain Joey LaCosta, which meant his two troopers had stayed behind as well.

Lieutenant Iverson—balding with protruding eyes and big teeth—could be the kindly uncle or the threatening authority figure, whichever the occasion called for. He'd huddled with

Graham when he first arrived and put off asking questions until the Crime Scene Unit had arrived and completed the search for physical evidence. Taking pictures, dusting for prints, putting things in little plastic bags. Finally Tommy's body was cut down and carried away in a body bag. Only then did the tightness in Tess's chest begin to ease.

Graham stopped by the table where she was sitting with Cheryl and placed a hand on her shoulder. "You holding up all right?" She nodded. "The Lieutenant wants you to tell him about how you happened to find Tommy. He'll be over in a minute." She nodded again.

The customers' mass exodus had narrowed down the number of suspects considerably. They sat at the tables between the bar and the stage—Tess, Cheryl, Phil, the four band members, and Joey LaCosta with his two ever-present musclemen. Right behind LaCosta in a posture of guardianship stood Graham's partner, a fair-haired man named Stefanovich. A number of uniformed officers were still present. Lieutenant Iverson looked as if he wanted to make a speech but settled for walking over to Tess and Cheryl's table. "Which of you is Tess Ridgeway?" he asked.

"I am."

He sat down opposite her. "I'm sorry to put you through this, Ms Ridgeway," the kindly uncle said, "but I want you to tell me how you came to find the body."

Tess told him. She told how Tommy had not been waiting to go on as usual and she'd gone to the dressing room to get him and found him dead. She mentioned the missing ruby ring. She said she didn't touch anything but came straight out front and told Graham Burke.

Graham's partner, Stefanovich, cleared his throat. "She told everybody else as well," he said. "She just shrieked it out."

Tess glared at him. "I do not *shriek*."

Iverson raised his eyebrows. "That's when all the customers took off? Yes. Where was the band during all this?"

"Out in the alley."

"In the alley? Really." He turned to face the band members, each of whom was sitting at a different table. "What were you doing in the alley, fellows?"

"Breathin'," Lester muttered.

"Oh my, we got a wisemouth here. Now listen—"

"No, man, that's what we were doin'—breathin'," Lester insisted. "Gets mighty smoky in here."

"Isn't that the truth," Cheryl said with a nod.

The police lieutenant looked unconvinced, but he didn't pursue it. "When did you last see the victim, Ms Ridgeway?"

"Oh . . . it was right before I went to get changed. He was showing me his ring. Lieutenant, this wasn't just an ordinary robber, was it?"

"Not a chance. The killer didn't even try to make it look like a robbery—the ring must have been an afterthought." He turned and addressed the room at large. "Who was the last to see Tommy?"

There was a silence, and then Phil said, "I guess I was. He was sittin' here at the bar until Tess started her set, then he went back to the dressing room."

"Did you see him go into the dressing room?"

"Well, no, I was behind the bar."

At that moment Joey LaCosta heaved a much-put-upon sigh. "Lieutenant, how long am I gonna have to sit here listening to this?"

The kindly uncle changed into the authority figure. "Until I'm satisfied you had nothing to do with this killing. And LaCosta—I'm not easily satisfied."

"Why would I kill the guy? I liked him!"

"When was the last time you saw him?"

"I didn't see him at all tonight. Tommy never came on 'til the bird finished singing."

Chirp chirp, Tess thought.

Iverson turned back to Phil. "Had Tommy already gone back to the dressing room by the time LaCosta got here?"

Phil thought back. "Yeah, he had."

"That's right, Lieutenant," Stefanovich interposed. "Me

and Burke, we were right behind LaCosta. Tommy wasn't out here.''

Iverson nodded, clear at last on the sequence of events. "We're going to take your statements individually now. Mr. Maynard, I'd like to use your office.''

Phil shrugged. "Sure.''

"Lieutenant,'' Tess said, "are you finished with the dressing room yet? My street clothes are in there, and . . .'' She gestured to the sparkly gown she was wearing.

"We're not quite finished, but—Burke, do we have any female uniforms on the premises?''

"I'll see.'' Graham left and returned almost immediately with a short black woman. "This is Officer Dodson.''

Iverson said, "Dodson, go with Ms Ridgeway while she changes her clothes. Make sure she touches nothing other than her personal belongings.''

"Yessir.'' Officer Dodson followed Tess out of the room.

But when Tess got to the dressing room, she hesitated.

"The body's been removed,'' the policewoman said gently.

"I know. I still don't want to go in there.'' But she made herself do it.

Tommy's last stench lingered slightly; the dressing room had no windows for airing the place out. Tess slipped out of her gown and decided to take it home rather than hang it back up on the water pipe. She put on jeans and sneakers and was pulling a sweater over her head when the door banged open and two cops walked in.

"Hey!'' yelled Officer Dodson. "Knock first!''

"It's all right, I'm ready,'' said Tess. She gathered up her gown, her raincoat, her purse.

"Sorry,'' said one of the cops, as they both set about their business—business that was noticeably different from the careful, even finicky approach taken by the Crime Scene Unit. These two looked under tables, pulled out drawers and checked behind them, shone a light in the ventilator shaft.

"What are you looking for?'' Tess asked.

"Scat.''

"What?" Indignantly.

Officer Dodson explained. "Scat. Heroin. Wanna play word association? Joey LaCosta, scat."

"But, but he wouldn't have any heroin stashed here," Tess objected as she and the policewoman left the dressing room. "The Corner Bar's not part of LaCosta's operation. The only reason he ever came here was to listen to Tommy." *Which he wouldn't be doing anymore,* she suddenly thought. Probably the only good thing to come out of the comic's death.

"Still gotta check," the black woman said. "LaCosta's got a partner we can't finger, and LaCosta keeps coming back to the Corner Bar."

"That's why the police have been watching the place?"

"C'mon, let's go. My sergeant says I talk too much."

It was more than an hour before the police got around to taking Tess's statement. By then all four members of the band had left. Phil and Cheryl were straightening the place up, Phil washing glasses as fast as Cheryl could carry them from the deserted tables. Lieutenant Iverson and Graham were drinking coffee that Phil had made for them, letting Stefanovich take a crack at LaCosta in Phil's office. LaCosta's two bodyguards were gone, ordered by the police to wait outside.

Lieutenant Iverson stood up when he saw Tess coming, back to the kindly uncle again. He smiled, showing his big teeth, and pulled a chair out from the table. "Ms Ridgeway?"

"I'm awfully tired, Lieutenant," Tess said. "I really would like to go home."

"Just one more question. Please?" He gestured to the chair.

She sighed and sat down. Not even so much as a friendly grin from Graham Burke; he was all business.

"Now, Ms Ridgeway—may I call you Tess?" Iverson asked. "Tess, we've run into a roadblock. Frankly, we can't find any reason why someone would want Tommy Vincenza dead. The picture we get is of a vulgar, harmless clown who was no threat to anybody. Is that the way you saw him?"

"Pretty much."

"Did you ever see him in the company of Joey LaCosta outside the Corner Bar?"

That's two questions. "I never saw either of them outside the Corner Bar, together or separately."

"Hm." Cheryl started inching over toward their table, wiping her hands on a towel; Iverson saw her coming but pretended he didn't. He said, "Do you know any reason at all why he might have been killed, Tess?"

Cheryl was by their table. Tess glanced up at her and said, "No, I don't."

"Yes, you do, Tess," Cheryl blurted out. "Tommy was blackmailing Phil!"

"Jesus Christ!" Phil yelled from behind the bar.

"You were there, Tess," Cheryl insisted. "You heard it too."

Graham was looking from one woman to the other. "Tess?"

Tess gritted her teeth and said, "I heard Tommy insisting that Phil couldn't fire him, and Phil never denied it. That's all." She turned to the waitress. "Cheryl, you don't really believe Phil killed Tommy."

"Of course not! But if Tommy was squeezing Phil, he coulda been squeezing somebody else as well, couldn't he?"

Iverson was leaning back in his chair, his hands folded comfortably over his well-padded middle and his protruding eyes half shut. He directed a big-toothed smile in the direction of the bar. "Mr. Maynard! Why don't you come join us?"

Phil muttered something under his breath and took his time getting there. Graham drew up chairs for Cheryl and Phil, making five people who were crowded around the small table. Phil sat there glowering at Cheryl. "You're fired."

She flapped a hand at him. "No, I'm not. Phil, don't you see? If we don't help them all we can, they're going to go on thinking the Corner Bar's part of LaCosta's scat operation. You don't want that, do you?"

"She has a point," Tess said mildly.

There was silence for a moment, until Iverson sat up

abruptly and rubbed his hands together. "Well! Now that you've all decided to cooperate with the police, let's hear it. What did Tommy have on you, Mr. Maynard?"

"It has nothin' to do with what happened tonight."

"Let me be the judge of that, please. Well?" Phil didn't answer. "Mr. Maynard, do I have to point out that you are our only suspect?"

Graham leaned toward Phil. "Let's put it this way, Maynard. You tell us right now, or we're taking you downtown and booking you."

"Shit." Phil looked as if he wanted to punch someone. "All right. Tommy found out I paid off a building inspector. Bastard wouldn't let me open without a kickback."

Iverson made a tsk-tsking sound. "Corruption in city government, will it never end? We'll want the name of the inspector and the particulars. But how much was Tommy soaking you for?"

"I paid Tommy union minimum and not a penny more," Phil said hotly. "You can check the books!" Then some of the anger went out of him. "All Tommy ever wanted from me was a stage and a spotlight."

Iverson nodded. "But as long as you provided him with that stage and spotlight, he continued to attract a criminal element to your place of business, did he not?"

"*I didn't kill Tommy!* I didn't like his routine and I sure as hell didn't like seeing LaCosta in my place, but . . ." Phil held his hands up helplessly. "But that's just not reason enough to kill him."

Tess agreed, and Lieutenant Iverson looked as if he did too. Cheryl said, "I know you didn't kill him, Phil."

"Oh gee thanks, Cheryl. That means a lot."

At that moment, Joey LaCosta came charging in from Phil's office. He stopped by Lieutenant Iverson and said, "I'm leaving. I cooperated with you guys, but now I'm through cooperating. You got nothing on me, and I'm leaving. You want to talk to me again, see my lawyer." He walked out without waiting for an answer.

Stefanovich had followed him out. "I'm sorry, Lieutenant, I just couldn't hold him any longer."

Iverson waved a hand dismissively. "We have nothing to charge him with anyway. Unless it turns out that he and Mr. Maynard here are in partnership."

"For Christ's sake, *I'm* not LaCosta's partner!" Phil snarled. "You gotta look in your own department for that!"

The heads of all three policemen snapped toward him. "What do you know about that?" Iverson barked.

"Only that LaCosta is partners with or is payin' off or has *some* connection with a cop."

"*How* do you know that?" Graham asked.

Phil turned his hands palms up. "Tommy liked to brag. He was puttin' the squeeze on the cop." He snorted. "And you say I'm your *only* suspect! Tommy was a threat to whatever arrangement LaCosta had with the police. LaCosta musta sent one of his goons back to the dressing room to take care of it."

Graham shook his head. "Stefanovich and I kept our eyes on LaCosta all evening. No one left the table from the time we got here until Tess came running out with the word about Tommy."

"That's right, Lieutenant," Stefanovich said.

"Who's the cop?" Iverson demanded.

"Dunno," Phil answered. "Tommy wasn't givin' away his meal ticket."

"It's all a bunch of horseshit anyway," Graham said in disgust. "Everyone loves to think *dirty cop*."

"Well, well." Iverson scratched his balding head. "It seems our harmless comic wasn't so harmless after all."

They went over it again, and then again, Iverson urging Phil to remember Tommy's exact words. Tess stopped listening; she was so tired she was drooping.

Graham noticed. "Lieutenant, would it be all right if we let the women go home? It's late."

"Of course, how thoughtless of me," Iverson agreed immediately. "I thank you for your help, ladies. You go on home now."

"I'll walk you to your car," Graham said to Tess. Stefanovich picked up the cue and offered his services to Cheryl.

Outside, the air was damp as well as chilly. "Where are you parked?" Graham asked.

Tess had to think. "Down here. Left side of the street." They walked in silence for a moment or two. "You can't seriously suspect Phil," she said. "All he's guilty of is bribing a city official, and he was more or less forced into that."

Graham smiled sourly. "I wish I had a dollar for every time I've heard a felon confess to a lesser crime to divert suspicion from a larger one. Nope, Maynard's our best bet."

"Well, I think you're wrong. Here we are, my car's right over—oh, no! Awww, *no!*"

The car had been stripped. All four tires were gone. The trunk had been sprung and the spare taken as well. The hood was up; the thieves had helped themselves to the battery plus a few other parts. They'd taken her tape deck, radio, and her Jack Teagarden tapes. They'd even taken the boots and umbrella she kept in the back seat.

"Thieving sonsabitches," Graham muttered. "Let me call it in and then I'll drive you home."

He followed her inside when she unlocked the door. Hugo was nowhere in sight, she was glad to see; the last thing she needed tonight was a cat attack. By the time Tess had left for the Corner Bar earlier that evening, Hugo had fully recovered from the trauma of his visit to the vet and was back to his normal nasty self.

Tess dumped her gown, her raincoat, and her purse on a chair and collapsed onto the sofa. She was feeling numb; the cannibalizing of her car had capped the day perfectly. It would be a day to remember, all right.

"Do you need a drink?" Graham asked her. "Or coffee? How about something to eat?"

She shook her head. "Shouldn't I be saying those things to *you?*"

"I don't want anything. But you're looking kind of down."

She laughed shortly. "Why should I feel down? Everything's peachy keen. I sing trash during the day for money so I can go into that crummy bar at night and sing a kind of music that had its heydey over sixty years ago. I live with a cat that hates me. I'm involved in a murder. And my car has just been stripped. Why should I feel down?''

He gave her a small smile. ''Where do you keep the booze?''

''Kitchen.''

He went into the kitchen and fixed her a drink. ''You have a cat?'' he said, handing her the glass. ''I like cats. Where is she?''

''He. Around, someplace.'' She took a sip; scotch again, but not the smooth stuff Cheryl had brought her at the Corner Bar. Tess put the glass down; she didn't want the drink. She caught a glimpse of a small, gray, furry face peeking around the doorjamb; Hugo was watching Graham, checking out this intruder into his private space.

''Tess, I think you need to get to bed. I'm going to leave you my card, and I want you to call me if things get too bad. Will you do that?'' Graham started feeling through his pockets. ''I can never find my card case when I want it.''

While he fumbled through his pockets, Tess watched Hugo ease around the doorjamb into the room. He hid behind a potted plant, his eyes still fixed on Graham. ''Just write it down for me,'' she said.

''No, I got it here someplace. Oh, *hell*.'' He went over to a table and started emptying his pockets. A notebook, loose change, keys, two ballpoint pens, a pocket knife, a ring.

A ruby ring. Tommy's ruby ring, the one LaCosta gave him and he'd been so proud of.

Graham? Graham Burke? Tess turned her head away quickly.

But she hadn't been quick enough. Graham heaved a long, sad sigh. ''That wasn't too smart of me, letting you see the ring,'' he said. ''But it wasn't too smart of you, letting me know you'd seen it.'' He gathered up his belongings and put them back in his pocket. ''Ah, Tess, Tess! I didn't want this to happen.''

CAT CRIMES

They stared at each other, the air electric between them. "You killed Tommy," she said in a high tight voice. "*You* are LaCosta's cop?"

A muscle in his face twitched; he didn't like that way of putting it. "We all have our own ways of surviving. Tommy was getting to be a problem. That was his way of surviving, you know—collecting for not talking. LaCosta's not what you'd call discreet. He gave just enough away that Tommy was able to put two and two together. I couldn't let it go on, Tess."

She pressed the flats of her hands against her temples. "You actually put that rope around his . . . why did *you* do it? That seems more like LaCosta's line of work!"

"LaCosta didn't know. If he'd found out a little prick like Tommy Vincenza could put the screws on me—well, it could queer our arrangement. And I'm not going to let *anything* queer our arrangement."

She understood. She took a breath and said, "What are you going to do?"

"I got to figure this out. I don't *want* to kill you, Tess."

"Then don't! Do you really think I'd say anything if I knew it would get me killed?"

"Keep quiet for a minute, will you?" He lowered himself onto an armchair opposite her, tense and stiff.

Tess jumped up and started pacing, trying desperately to think of a way out. Absently she noticed Hugo crawling on his stomach toward Graham. The damned cat was *stalking* him. *Atta boy, Hugo! Come charging to the rescue!* She was having trouble concentrating.

"You aren't going to try anything foolish, like running for the door?" He took his gun out of his shoulder holster and held it on the end table to his right.

"No." She stopped her pacing and picked up a pewter box that was said to have belonged to Billie Holiday; musical notes were engraved on the top. She opened and closed the lid nervously, the box's weight giving her something solid to hold on to. "Graham, let's try to work something out. I—

108

I'll go out and commit a crime and you can take pictures and—''

"Don't be foolish!'' he snapped.

"But there's got to be another way!'' She opened and closed the lid of the box. *I am actually standing here thinking about attacking an armed man with a pewter box.* "I'm not Tommy Vincenza. I'm not going to make trouble for you.'' If she could just get to the phone . . .

He grunted, didn't answer. Hugo was crouched under the end table that Graham was resting his gun on.

Tess saw the exact moment he decided to kill her. The tension disappeared, replaced by a kind of euphoria. The deciding was the hard part, not the doing. A loose sort of smile appeared on his face, and he said, "I'm sorry, Tess. I really am.''

She knew there was no point in trying to talk him out of it now. "You're a stupid man, aren't you?'' she said sharply. "Solving your problems with violence—the first resort of the stupid man. A surefire sign of failure.''

He just laughed, rather enjoying the situation now that he'd made up his mind she had to die. "Ah, Tess, I don't have to justify myself. All I have to do is figure out *how*. Why don't you put on some music? I like music while I'm thinking.''

"Go to hell.''

He didn't seem to hear her. "Perhaps an accident? Nope, Iverson would see right through that. I guess you'll have to go the same way Tommy did.''

Maybe she could throw the box at him and run for the door. He was almost ignoring her; Tess the person had already ceased to exist for him. He just smiled that loose smile and stretched out his legs, crossing them at the ankles. He looked completely relaxed.

Hugo emerged from under the table and started sniffing at his feet. "Why, here's your cat! Hello, kitty.'' He switched his gun to his left hand and reached his right down toward Hugo. Hugo hissed. "What's the matter with him?''

"He's . . . shy.'' Tess swallowed. "He, ah, he loves to have his back stroked, though.''

"Most cats do." He put his hand on Hugo's back.

Tess made her move. The minute Hugo sank his teeth into Graham's hand, she raised the pewter box in the air and brought it down as hard on the detective's head as she could, cutting off his yelp of pain and surprise. The gun fell to the floor, and Graham toppled forward on his face. Hugo bolted from the room.

Phone. Call for help. But Graham was moving, groaning and trying to get up on his hands and knees. Tess felt a flash of panic. This wasn't the way it happened on television—he was supposed to pass out long enough for her to call the police! She hit him again. He fell forward again, still groaning. She dropped the box and picked up his gun. She pointed it at him, wondering if she would have to shoot him.

No, this wouldn't do. *Call the police, call the police!* She put the gun on the table and started looking through Graham's clothing; she found the handcuffs tucked into his belt in the back. Tess jerked his arms around behind him and cuffed his wrists together. That done, she just sat down on the floor, *plop*. It took her a couple of minutes to stop trembling.

Then she made the call.

By the time the police took Graham Burke away, he was fully conscious, demanding medical attention and loudly denying his guilt. He even went so far as to accuse Tess of murdering Tommy and then planting the ring on him. The police seemed wholly unimpressed.

Lieutenant Iverson stayed behind. "Are you sure you're all right, Tess?"

"I'm fine." And she was, now that it was over. "I don't see how he did it. He was sitting there all evening, right next to his partner—what's his name, Stefanovich."

"I imagine Stefanovich will tell us that Burke left the table to go to the men's room at least once. Stefanovich was there to watch *LaCosta*, remember, not his partner."

"And you had no idea Graham Burke was connected?"

Iverson heaved a heavy sigh. "We were sure LaCosta had

some cop in his pocket. That's why he's still walking around free. We could never catch him with the goods—he always seemed to know where and when we were going to show up with a search warrant. We'll get him now, though. But to answer your question, nothing pointed to Burke in particular."

Tess nodded. "Why'd he take the ring? Simple theft?"

"No, he recognized it as LaCosta's. He was trying to divert attention away from his partner. That was his job, protecting LaCosta. Remember how quick he was to alibi him? Burke was trying to throw suspicion on Phil Maynard."

"Where is Phil? Did you arrest him?"

"Oh, I sent him home hours ago," Iverson said. "The man was clearly innocent."

For the first time in hours, Tess smiled. "Lieutenant, you are a treasure."

"That's what I tell my wife every night." Iverson smiled back, big-toothed and friendly. "Well, good-night, Tess. Lock up tight."

"I will." When he was gone, Tess stood in the middle of the living room for a few minutes, doing nothing, thinking nothing, enjoying the silence. It had been an ugly night.

Then she started a systematic hunt for the cat. She found him in her bedroom closet, crouched down behind the shoe rack. Tess sat on the floor outside the closet, trying to make herself less menacing. "Hello, Hugo," she said softly. "You don't even know you saved my life tonight, do you?"

The cat stared at her, not moving.

"You certainly earned your right to live here, you know . . . not that you need to. You *have* the right. But I thank you just the same. Can I get you something? Sardines? Lobster? A gallon of whipped cream?"

Hugo hissed.

Tess didn't mind. "That's all right, Hugo, you take your time," she said. "I'll wait."

Blindsided

•

William J. Reynolds

By the winter of '87 I had two seasons in with the Royals. Then, late that New Year's Eve eve, drunker than I should have been wandering through a part of Kansas City where I shouldn't have been, I got mugged. They took my gold wristwatch, my credit cards, forty-eight dollars in cash, and eighty-six percent of the vision in my right eye. If there's one thing a pitcher needs as much as a good arm, it's depth perception, and with mine gone so was my major-league career. Any league, for that matter.

The Royals offered to put me on staff, but I wouldn't have any of that. I had a couple of small endorsement contracts that weren't affected by my injury, but I walked away from them. I walked away from Carolyn, too, and moved back north. Dad and my brother, Gates, still farmed the old place, but that had never been for me. All there had ever been for me was the game, and now that was gone.

I looked around for a place, but there wasn't much available that wasn't a foreclosed farmstead. Not much rental housing in town, either. Then the Egyptian, the only remaining movie house in town, closed for good. I'd spent half my youth in the Egyptian: as a kid, on the main floor, soaking up bad Westerns and even worse World War II flicks; as a teenager, in the balcony, trying to cop a feel from Anita Van Otter or Lenore Hamaker. Whatever happened to wire-reinforced underwear?

On an impulse, I bought the Egyptian. It was bigger than I had realized. Besides the main auditorium, there were two floors of office space above and a full basement below, with half a dozen dressing rooms—the Egyptian had been built for vaudeville—and mazes of storage rooms bulging with all kinds of movie and stage junk. The auditorium was in good shape, so I left it alone and began gutting out the top floors to convert to living space. It was shaping up to be a lifetime project. That was all right with me.

The winter passed. I spent most of my time alone, working on the Egyptian. When spring came, I helped Dad and Gates with the planting. Dad's opinion was that the people who put lights on farm implements did so for a reason, so we were usually out in the field until ten, eleven, or later.

After one such session, one warm night that May, I got back to the Egyptian at around midnight. The headlights of my Jeep illuminated a figure on the bench under the wide marquee, as if someone was waiting for the box office to open. It's unusual for people around here to be out so late, but I wasn't worried; it's even more unusual for people around here to get mugged. I climbed down from the jeep.

The figure on the bench stirred as I approached. "I thought you'd packed up and moved away," Lenore Hamaker said. "I've been sitting here almost two hours."

"I was out at my dad's," I said. "Sorry you had to wait. You should have called."

"I've been calling," Lenore said. "All I ever get is your damn machine. Don't you ever listen to it for messages?"

"Not usually," I admitted. "I haven't felt much like talking to anyone." I especially hadn't felt like talking to Carolyn. There wasn't anything I had to say to her.

"That's what I figured," Lenore said. "That's why I decided to just come on over. Aren't you going to ask me in?"

"I hadn't planned to. Lenore, it's late, I'm tired . . ."

"I brought you a house-warming present." I hadn't noticed the big carton on the bench until Lenore waved a slender hand at it. "Not even *you* are rude enough to turn away someone who's been sitting out in the cold, dark night for two hours to give you a house-warming present, Carve Straka.''

"It's seventy-three degrees, Lenore.'' I sighed. "Come on in, then.''

"What girl could refuse an invitation like that?''

I unlocked the glass doors to the lobby. The neon tubing over the concession stand in the center of the lobby provided the only light. In it, Lenore's hair looked redder than it was. Usually she wore it loose, letting it fall in gentle waves to her shoulders. Tonight, though, she had pulled it back in a low ponytail. It emphasized her strong features, her wide eyes and high cheekbones, her mouth and the small, almost cynical smile that always seemed to hover there. I touched her cheek. "Haymaker,'' I said, mispronouncing her name the way we always had in school. Back then it used to make her boil. Tonight she only smiled.

"I never thought I'd see you again, Carve. I was sorry to hear about what happened down in Kansas City.''

"Them's the breaks,'' I said. I moved away from her. "I'd buy you something, but the concession stand's closed.'' The Milk Duds, Junior Mints, and Jujube boxes behind the glass were just for show. The fountain was dry.

Lenore had set her carton on the ticket-window counter when we came in. Now she pointed at it. "Aren't you going to open your present?''

It was a heavy-cardboard carton. The Sioux Nation logo peeked out from layers of various kinds of packing tape. At the moment, though, the lid was held in place by a length of yellow twine tied in a shoelace knot. I slipped the knot and removed the lid.

"Cats,'' I said.

"You're welcome,'' Lenore said. She reached in with both hands and pulled the two cats out of their bed of straw. They were not much more than kittens, skinny, with paws and ears they had yet to grow into. One of them was a marmalade tiger, the other a tortoiseshell. They mewed and fidgeted in Lenore's hands. "I brought them out from my barn,'' Lenore was saying. "I've got more than I need out there anyway, and I figured if you didn't need pets, you could at least use the pest control. This old place's got to be loaded with mice."

"Yes, but we stay out of each other's way," I said. I had forgotten about Lenore's being a cat fancier. When we had been together, years ago, she always kept two or three in the house, as pets, besides however many were around her parents' farm to keep the rodent and serpent population under control. Evidently her taste hadn't changed.

She held the cats out and I gave them perfunctory scratches behind the ears. We always had cats around the farm when I was growing up, too, but they were strictly outdoors animals—mousers, not pets.

Lenore set the cats down and they started to explore.

"Well, thanks," I said.

Lenore shrugged in that way she had. "I figured no one else'd think to give you a couple of mousers."

"No one else has given me anything. They've pretty much kept their distance."

"Word around town these past few months has been that's how you wanted it."

"Word around town's been right."

A long silence followed, broken by Lenore saying, "So. Do I get the nickel tour?"

"Sure," I said. "I guess we can skip the balcony. You're familiar with that." She slugged me lightly on my right biceps. I took her upstairs first, showed her where I was knocking down walls and rearranging the old floorplan, turning cramped offices into open living areas. At the moment, the top floors were nothing but plaster dust, exposed lathing, and jerry-rigged electrical wiring, but I told her how I wanted the layout to go and how I wanted to get a kind of mezzanine effect from the third floor, opening the ceiling right to the roof, where I wanted a skylight. "An architect friend of mine is going to come down from the city and tell me how much of my plans are balderdash," I said.

We ended up downstairs, in the basement, where I had cleaned out the two largest dressing rooms, knocked a hole in the wall between them, and set them up as my living quarters. "Too hot and dusty to live upstairs," I told Lenore, offering her a chair.

She sat, and smiled at me. I located a couple of beers in the half-size fridge in the corner, and passed one over to her. "Happy days," I said before downing half of my bottle.

"Old ones," she said, "or days to come?"

I said nothing.

Lenore took a sip, then said. "I'm sorry about what happened, Carve, to you and me. I never meant to hurt you. I never *meant* anything, things just happened. You were gone and Jerry was here, and . . ." She shrugged.

"I never blamed you," I said. It was only a little lie. "I was off at college, then off chasing around the minors. I never expected you to wait or anything." That, too, was only a little lie.

"I thought I would wait," Lenore said. "I meant to. I don't know what happened."

I did. I was gone and Jerry Denholm was here. After my brother, Gates, Jerry had been my best friend in the world. Pretty soon he was Lenore's best friend. Pretty soon Lenore was pregnant. She and Jerry got married. Lenore miscarried. The marriage bumped along for another year after that. Last anyone had heard, Jerry had gone up to the city to make his fortune. That was four years ago. I got the story from Gates. Gates had been seeing a little of Lenore these past couple of years.

"Gates tells me you're an artist these days," I said to change the subject.

"Yeah, I guess. When the Penney's store closed, I needed to find some work. I'd always painted, you know, oils and watercolors, and I started hauling them around to all the arts-and-crafts shows in the area, church bazaars, sidewalk sales, all that kind of thing. Two years ago, a magazine called *Heartland Artist* did this little article about me and two, three other women painters in the region. Next thing I know, this art-gallery owner in the city is calling me, says he saw my pictures in the magazine and do I want to put together a show at his gallery. I figure he's crazy, but we do the show and he sells every painting! Now I've got to come up with a bunch more pictures, 'cause he wants another show this fall.''

"That's great," I said. "I'd like to see that article some time.''

She looked a little surprised. "All right," she said, and smiled.

Time is a funny thing. You come back to a place after a long while, time gets all knotted up, bent and twisted back over and around itself. Everything is the same and everything is different, including yourself. I rattled around the Egyptian all winter half expecting to bump into my eighteen-year-old self coming around the corner from the opposite direction. I would not have been the least surprised if it had happened.

I was not the least surprised that Lenore somehow was in my arms, with her mouth against mine and her sweet fragrance all around me. Time had folded back, contracted. It was now years ago, and this was the most natural thing in the world.

And then time snapped straight again, and I pulled away from her. "Gates," I said. "You and Gates are together now . . ."

"Not like that," she whispered in the stillness. "We're just . . ."

"Just good friends," I said. Lenore giggled, and I kissed her again.

Toward mid-summer, things slow down on the farm. Most of the work is for the weather to do. We had good corn weather that year: hot, sunny, and humid. Dad and Gates busied themselves with general maintenance around the farm, painting, shingling, fencing, all the things they wouldn't have time for come autumn. I went back to work on the Egyptian, rising early and trying to get as much done as possible before the day's heat came on full-blast. The upper floors had never been properly air-conditioned. I had junked most of the ancient window units that had been propped here and there, and after I had gotten a good look at the building's wiring, I was almost afraid to run the two or three I had saved. There were some big old industrial-strength auditorium fans down in the storage rooms, and I dragged them upstairs, oiled them up, and put them to work. They didn't cool the air much, but at least they kept the dust in motion.

The cats made themselves right at home. After weeks of steering wide of me, they now seemed to be in competition to see who could be the most underfoot the most often and make the greatest mess. I started out calling them each Cat, then switched to Fred and Barney, and lately had been calling them Sturm and Drang. I had majored in physical education, but my minor had been lit. The cats weren't bad company, but I wasn't sure about how they helped with the mouse problem I hadn't thought I had. Before, my mice were heard and not seen. Now, Sturm and Drang seemed to think that I wanted to inspect every rodent they killed. I did not.

I spent a lot of time with Lenore. In the afternoons, when it got too hot to work on the Egyptian, I'd tool out to her place, a little farm she owned just north of town on the old highway. Oliver Creigh and his son rented most of her land; Lenore kept enough to let her feel isolated. On those hot days we'd sit in the shade out back of the house. She would paint and I would sit and read. I was starting in on all of the books I had promised myself I would read someday when I had the time. We'd have the radio going, but if a ballgame came on I'd switch over to CD and play some rock 'n' roll from when we were kids.

I never brought my calculator along, so I don't know how many cats she had around the place. Three shared the house with her: Amber, Pirate, and Leapy Lee, so named because of his habit of coming up behind you and leaping from the floor to your shoulder. Unfortunately, Leapy Lee was no high-jumper. He'd make it about halfway, then dig in and climb the rest of the way. My back still has the scars.

Besides the house cats, Lenore had another score or more who lived in and around the outbuildings. Some of the braver ones would venture up to the patio to see what we were doing those hot afternoons. Lenore had names for them all, but how she could tell them apart is anybody's guess.

More often than not, the long afternoons would turn into long evenings, and the long evenings into short nights.

It was a Friday morning, eight o'clock, and Hugh Claussen was leaning on the bell next to the service door in the alley out back of the Egyptian. I was up, had been for hours, working on my mess. I hadn't spent the night at Lenore's; my architect friend was coming up today and there were a few things I wanted to do before he showed up. I went to the back of the building, leaned out one of the big energy-inefficient windows, and called down two stories, "What do you want, Huge?" We had always called him Huge, though he wasn't especially.

"I want you to let me in," Huge said.

I went downstairs, through the auditorium, and popped open one of the two big exit doors on either side of the stage. Huge came in. His sheriff's uniform, light blue with navy trim here and there, was rumpled and wrinkled. Dark rings of sweat stained his underarms and the middle of his back. His eyes, deep in his craggy face, were red. He needed a shave.

I said, "You look like hell, Huge."

He said, "There someplace we can talk?"

I looked around at the empty theatre. "Probably be safe here."

He sighed, and sank heavily into a front-row seat. Huge was my age, but at the moment he looked thirty years older. The dim light from the tiny lamps down the side aisles was enough to show that—that's how bad he looked.

Huge ran a hand through his hair and said, "Goddammit, Carve. I know life's kind of kicked you in the shins lately. That's why I hate like hell to have to tell you. Lenore's dead."

The four-foot-high wall at the front of the stage was behind me. I kind of staggered back into it and leaned on it for support. "What?" I stammered, stupidly.

"Been out there since two this morning," Huge said. "Whoever it was, Carve, he beat her to death. Killed one of her cats, too, even. Goddammit, what kind of man does a thing like that?''

"What time?" I said.

"Well, sometime between eleven and about one-thirty— but that's only on account of we know she was on the phone with Liz Gunderson until eleven, Liz told us, and it was one-thirty when Bill Reeves found . . . found her." Reeves was one of Huge's men. "Bill was on his regular patrol, coming back in on the old highway. Lenore's lights were on, which wasn't unusual—she painted all night sometimes—''

"I know."

"—but Bill could see from the highway that her front door was wide open, and that *was* unusual, it being so hot and Lenore's having central air. He thought he'd better stop and see whether she was okay. She wasn't. Found her dead on the living-room carpet. Her and the cat. Goddammit."

"How?" I said.

He looked at me oddly. "Told you: beat to death. Actual cause of death was probably broken neck—we'll know for sure later on today—but she was probably unconscious before that happened. From the bruises—you sure you want this, Carve? Okay . . . From the bruises, I'd say someone smacked her good half a dozen times. In the face. Someone good and strong." Huge sized me up a little. I'm good and strong. He seemed to let go of that thought, though, and went on: "My guess is, first one knocked her out, or pretty damn near. Then the son of a bitch got down on the floor with her, on his knees, straddling her, and gave her another five, six clouts for good measure." He rubbed his eyes.

I said, "Was she . . ."

He looked at me. "No, Carve. No, she wasn't raped."

I nodded.

Huge cleared his throat and looked at the illuminated clock over the stage-left exit door, and said, "Carve, do you know where your brother is?"

"Gates?" I said, although I have only the one. "Why?"

"He wasn't out to his place. Your dad said he hadn't seen him today. Hadn't seen him since last night."

I took in some air. "Wait a minute, Huge—"

"When Bill Reeves was going out on patrol along the old highway, about eleven-thirty, Gates's pickup was in Lenore's driveway." He looked away from the clock dial and into my face. "Goddammit, Carve—"

"All right," I said.

Gates had come by at around seven to help me tape some drywall. I led Huge upstairs by the narrow staircase the movie-going public never saw, and we found Gates in the big dusty space that I foresaw as my living room. He was sitting on an Igloo cooler drinking iced coffee from a plastic cup. Plaster dust, glued to him by sweat, made him look pale, but actually by that point of the summer Gates was as brown as a nut. My "little" brother was several inches taller than me, broad-shouldered, with long ropy muscles from the base of his neck down his arms and back, where the plaster dust was rivered with sweat. He and I shared the same light brown, not-quite-curly hair and our mother's dark, wide eyes.

"What pulls you out so bright and early, Huge?" Gates said. I went over and retrieved my own iced coffee from a windowsill. Even at that hour of the morning, it was too damn warm for hot coffee.

Huge looked at me, cleared his throat, looked at nothing in particular, and said, "Lenore Hamaker was killed last night."

Gates took a long time before he said, "What do you mean, killed?"

"I mean someone killed her." For the first time, he looked directly at Gates. "Where were you last night, Gates? Between eleven and one, one-thirty?"

Gates looked at me. "Is this some kind of joke?"

"Huge doesn't think so," I said.

"Home," Gates told the sheriff. "Me and dad worked until about nine, then I went back to my place and did some work around there until, I don't know, eleven or twelve, then I hit the sack."

"Goddammit," Huge said. He got up and went over to one of the windows, looking down at the street below.

Gates looked at me, asking with his eyes. I said, "Bill Reeves saw your truck in Lenore's driveway last night."

"Oh." Gates studied the cup in his hands. Then he sighed heavily. "All right, I was there. I went out a little after eleven, I suppose."

"Why'd you lie about it," Huge said.

I said, "Maybe you want to talk to old Johansen before you say anything, Gates."

"I don't need a lawyer. I didn't do anything." He turned toward Huge. "I lied because I was embarrassed. Everyone around knows that Lenore and I were kind of, you know, together. And we haven't been for a while." His eyes darted toward me, then back at Huge. "I was sort of hoping to get things going again." He fiddled with the cup. "Guy doesn't need everyone in the county knowing about something like that," he muttered.

"I'm sorry, Gates," I said. "Lenore told me it was no big thing between you two."

He put on a lopsided smile. "I suppose that's how she looked at it."

Huge said, "So you went to talk to her. Then what?"

"Not much. I told her I wanted to get back together with her. She told me she wasn't interested. She was in the middle of a painting she was working on, so she asked me to leave and I did."

Huge came over to Gates, grabbed him by his right wrist, and lifted. The back of Gate's hand was all banged up and swollen, red welts beginning to turn into blue bruises, skin torn away from the first two knuckles.

Huge said, "Whoever killed Lenore did it with his fists, probably."

"Come on, Huge," I said. "Gates's hands are always banged up—he's a farmer, for chrissake."

Gates took his hand back. "Me and Dad've been working on this old tractor—you know, Carve, the old White? Been trying to get it running again, just for the hell of it. The hood on the thing lifts out on either side, and the spring-hinge on the left side isn't too reliable—as I found out last evening, when the hood came down on my hand. Lucky I didn't break it.''

"And you were alone when this happened, too," Huge said.

"As a matter of fact."

"Goddammit."

I said, "Look, Huge, what's the story here? You going to charge Gates or what?"

"What law school'd you graduate from, Carve?"

"The one that teaches you to put up or shut up."

He gave me a hard look, then nodded and went back to looking out the window. "You got a hair-trigger temper, Gates, everyone knows that. Shoot, I've known you since you were a pup, I've seen it myself. I still remember your beating the crap out of Danny Freitag—"

"Huge, that was in high school," Gates said. "I didn't hit Lenore. I never would've hurt her."

"Danny Freitag said some dumb-ass thing—I don't even remember what it was, and you probably don't either—and you went off like a bomb. I don't think you even knew what had happened until we pried you off'a him." He faced Gates. "Could be that you had words with Lenore, she said something that got under your skin"—Gates had his head down, shaking it emphatically—"and you saw red. Popped her a good one, then couple-three more for good measure. Didn't even know what you were doing, maybe." He paused. "Voluntary manslaughter, that'd be, probably. Not murder."

"I didn't do anything. She was fine when I left her."

"What time?"

"I don't know—twenty minutes after I got there, I suppose. Quarter to twelve, maybe. I didn't pay attention to the time."

Huge was silent for a long time, until I said, "Well?"

"We collected some physical evidence from the scene. I sent it down to the state crime lab about an hour ago. They'll have some results for us in a week or two. Then we'll know more." He looked at Gates. "You weren't planning on leaving town in the next few days, Gates, were you?"

"Matter of fact, yes, Huge," Gates said. "I *live* out of town."

"You know what I mean," Huge said.

The service was the following Tuesday. The little church was hot and sticky. Though early, it was that unreal, hazy sort of summer day where the heat just hangs in the air at eye-level, making everything shimmery. Lenore's mother had driven over from Ames, where she was living with Lenore's sister. Barda Kirkover, who was Lenore's paternal aunt and who had taken a good stab at teaching Gates and me piano when we were boys, was there, up from the Good Sam home. A lot of people we had grown up with; I hadn't realized so many of them were still around town. And Jerry Denholm, Lenore's ex-husband, was there too.

For some reason, I was surprised to see him. But not half as surprised as when he turned up at the Egyptian later that afternoon. He had a six-pack in his hand and a foolish look on his face. "A peace offering," he said, holding up the six-pack.

I let him in.

His hair was thinning and his gut was thickening, but otherwise he was the same old Jerry. My used-to-be next-best friend.

It was too hot to be working upstairs, but I was anyway. He followed me up and perched on a windowsill while I went back to the wall I was wrecking. The radio was blasting, the fans were whining, and the cats were poking around the debris. It was too hot for them up there, too, but they were intent on figuring out what the hell I was doing.

Jerry watched the cats for a while, drank some of his beer, and then finally said, "You know, I never meant to steal Lenore from you, Carve. Things just happened."

"Lenore said almost exactly the same thing."

"If it's any consolation, calling it quits was Lenore's idea."

I stopped what I was doing and looked at him.

He nodded. "I was interested in making it work. I loved her, Carve. I'd've never married her if she hadn't gotten pregnant, but I did love her and I wanted to stay with her. But she said it had all been a mistake from the start, and she wasn't interested in trying to patch it up.'' He shrugged. ''Well, what can you do—it takes two, right?'' He tried a laugh that didn't quite come off. ''That's when I left.''

I went over and took one of the beers. ''So what've you been up to?''

''I moved up to the city, you know, kind of bounced around there for a while. I work for a publishing company now, selling ad space for half a dozen various magazines they do.'' He took a drink. ''I was sorry to hear about your accident.''

''When three guys jump you and beat the living daylights out of you, it's not what I'd call an accident,'' I said. ''But thanks. I was surprised to see you at the church this morning. How'd you hear about Lenore?''

''Oh, I keep in touch with the old home town,'' he said, smiling. ''I still take the *Ledger*, even.''

''The *Ledger* hasn't come out yet this week.''

He gave me a look. ''My mom still lives here, Carve. She called me. Nothing mysterious about it.''

''Sorry,'' I said.

''That's all right. I understand. If my brother'd been accused of murder, I'd be looking around for another suspect too.''

''No one's accused Gates of anything,'' I said quickly.

''Well, the *law* hasn't accused him. The sheriff's waiting on some results from the state crime lab.''

Suddenly Jerry was laughing. ''What's so funny?'' I said.

''I was just thinking of old Huge Claussen trying to handle a homicide investigation. Lost dog, yes; parking ticket, no problem—but murder?'' He went into a fit of laughter, and pretty soon I did too. When we were about recovered from it he wheezed, ''Goddammit,'' and we were lost again.

Time folded back on itself. Pretty soon we were playing *remember-when* and *whatever-happened-to*, trying like hell to make up for the lost years and doing a fairly decent job of it. I found Jerry a pair of gym shorts and, stripped down to them and his sneakers, with me similarly dressed, and both of us still sweating like butchers, he helped me get the south wall finished and ready for painting. Later, we took turns cleaning up in the shower next to my temporary living-room, then grilled a couple of steaks on my electric broiler. More beer disappeared, more old memories reappeared, and it was late before Jerry said he had to get going.

I was fairly drunk—drunker than I'd been since that night in Kansas City last winter . . . I reached up unconsciously and rubbed my right eye, as if I could massage the vision back. In another line of work, the loss of vision would have been little more than a nuisance. It was like having a piece of gauze draped over my eye. Except when I wear the special one-lens glasses I'm supposed to wear when I drive. Then it's like having a slightly thinner piece of gauze draped over my eye.

Through my good eye I watched Sturm and Drang clean off the dinner plates. Drang finished first. He hopped down from the makeshift counter, washed his chops for a good long time, and then sauntered over past my armchair. He gave me his oh-do-you-still-live-here look, sniffed at the catnip-laced scratching post I'd shelled out forty bucks for at Coast-to-Coast, and then proceeded to claw the hell out of the side of the sofa.

Too tired and too buzzed to care, I watched the latest in-stallment of the long, slow death the cats apparently had in mind for my furniture. Drang honed his front claws to his satisfaction, then lifted his hind legs, dug in with his back claws, and climbed over the arm of the sofa, eventually set-tling in on a cushion.

Some contact closed, some connection was made in the back of my head. I felt as if several cups of strong black coffee had been piped directly into my bloodstream.

Rummaging around in all the junk I had accumulated over the summer, I found the copy of *Heartland Artist* with the article about Lenore. Then I made a call to Directory Assis-tance. It was getting late, but I went ahead and called the city anyway. After a longish conversation, I called Directory again and got another number, then made another toll call.

When I finally set the phone down, I didn't have anything that a prosecuting attorney would call proof, or even good, convincing circumstantial evidence, so there was no point talking to Huge Claussen. Not yet, anyhow.

But I did call Bill Reeves, the deputy who had found Lenore, and had him answer one question.

Fully awake then, fully sober, I went back upstairs and made a lot of racket until the small hours of the morning.

Gates was already on hand when Jerry showed up at the Egyptian late the next morning. Like my brother, Jerry had come dressed to work. I had told them, when I called each of them early that day, that I needed help removing a wall.

"Hope you're not as hung-over as I am this morning," Jerry said to me when he had finished greeting Gates. He did look a little fuzzy around the edges, and his eyes were red and bleary.

"No," I said, "I was stone sober by the time I hit the sack. I had a lot of calls to make to the city."

Jerry gave me an odd, querying look. I glanced over at Gates—he was to my right and behind me, perched on a paint drum, so I had to twist my head around like an owl to see him. My brother gave me a similar, questioning look. I hadn't told Gates what I was up to this morning. I'm his big brother; every so often I have to do something to impress him.

"Good news, buddy," I said. "You're off the hook." Then I turned back toward Jerry.

"Hey, great," Jerry said. "You mean ol' Huge actually came through for once?" I didn't say anything, and Jerry's smile got a little raggedy. Maybe it was last night's beer. "What're you giving me the eye for, Carve?" he said. "Something I don't know?"

"Something you do know, I think."

Jerry frowned and looked at Gates. There was no way Gates could enlighten him, so I went on:

"Last night, after you left, one of my cats proceeded to rip the hell out of my sofa. Nothing unusual there; I'd've been more surprised if he'd decided to use the scratching post. But it got me thinking—reminded me of something I didn't even know I knew." I pulled *Heartland Artist* out of the back pocket of my cut-offs. "There was an article about Lenore in this magazine a couple of years ago. The author's a freelancer in the city. I found her number and called her last night. It took a little doing, but I finally got her to tell me that she'd come up with the idea for the article when a friend of hers kept pestering her about this woman artist he knew. The friend's name was Jerry Denholm. The artist's name was Lenore Hamaker."

Jerry said nothing.

"Then I called Harold Everson, who owns the gallery that handled Lenore's work. I didn't have to prod him at all. He told me right away that Lenore's paintings had been brought to his attention by a magazine ad rep he worked with all the time. Everson had the impression that the rep had really been pushing Lenore, sending tearsheets of the *Heartland Artist* article to every gallery in the city, talking her up every time he visited or phoned one of his clients. We know that ad rep's name, too, don't we, Jerry?"

"You make it sound like something criminal, Carve," he said. "All I did was try to help Lenore with her painting career. She really was good, you know—Everson wouldn't have taken her on otherwise."

"I know that. What I don't know is why you made it your business."

"Why shouldn't I? I was in a position to help—I knew the publications, the writers, and the galleries. Why shouldn't I help Lenore? I loved her. I told you yesterday, Carve, she left me, not the other way around. It was never my idea."

"No," I said. "But I think it *was* your idea to get Lenore started on a promising career, and then let her know she had you to thank for it. Was she supposed to fall into your arms, Jerry, sobbing in gratitude, and beg you to come back to her?"

Jerry looked away. "Something like that," he said. "But it'll never happen now."

"I don't think it ever would have happened," I said. "I

128

think you were down here last Thursday night. I think you went out to see Lenore—late, after Gates had left—and sprang your little surprise on her. She didn't react the way you expected. Knowing Lenore, she probably was a little ticked off that you'd tried to manipulate her. My guess is she sort of said thanks-but-get-lost. And then you let her have it.''

"No," Jerry said.

"It's going to be another scorcher, Jerry," I said. "You want to take off your shirt?"

"What?"

"I noticed it yesterday, but it didn't really click until my cat went to work on my furniture. When we were working up here and you had your shirt off. Your back's covered with scratches, Jerry."

"Really?" There was sweat on his upper lip now. But then, the room was warm. "Guess I'm not used to manual labor."

"The scratches were there when we started work," I said, "and they weren't brand-new ones. Looked to me like they were about a week old."

"What makes you such a fucking expert?" Jerry said. His voice wavered, from anger, fear, or some other emotion.

I said, "Lenore's cat Leapy Lee mistook my back for the north face of the Eiger, too, Jerry—more than once. He was smart enough to come up on my blindside, too, the little bastard. My guess is, while you were talking to Lenore last Thursday night, Leapy Lee came up behind you and clawed his way to the top. You were already mad, because things weren't going the way you wanted with Lenore, and when the cat dug in you lashed out, sending him flying. I checked with Bill Reeves, and Leapy Lee was the cat they found dead of a broken neck. Now you were really seeing red—you turned on Lenore."

"No," Jerry was saying.

"And then you ran. Understandable, I guess. What I don't understand is your letting Gates take the heat. Were you really going to let him go to prison for you, if it came to that?"

"You've got it wrong, Carve—"

I shook my head. "Here's what we're going to do, Jerry. We're going to get on the horn and get Huge Claussen over here. And you're going to tell him the story, all of it."

"Listen, Carve—"

"If you don't feel like talking to him, Gates and I will be happy to help you work up to it, won't we, little brother?" I had hoped Jerry would break down and confess, like they always do on TV—partly because I didn't have any "smoking gun" to wave in his face, partly because I didn't really want to have to beat a confession out of him. I knew that wouldn't play well when the thing got to court. But right now I was more interested in getting my brother off the hook than in helping a prosecutor make his case, so if we had to knock Jerry into a cooperative mood, then that's what we'd do.

I was turning toward Gates, who had been silent throughout. Then everything went white. Then everything went black.

"He blindsided you."

"In more ways than one," I said. I sat up on the floor, and immediately regretted it. My head felt like a bass drum, one currently in use. "You call Huge?"

"No. I was more worried about you. You dropped like a rock and didn't move."

"But you weren't so worried that you called a doctor," I said, and grinned. I regretted that too.

"The phone's downstairs, and I was afraid to leave you alone."

"Shoot," I said, "a beanball hurts worse." It was only a little lie. "Help me up," I said, putting out my hand. The room rocked a little, then settled back down.

"You gonna be all right?"

"Eventually," I said. "We better call Huge. But first—I owe you an apology, Jerry."

He grinned bashfully. "Forget it."

"Not likely. Where'd I screw up?"

"When you fingered me for killing Lenore," Jerry said. "You were pretty much on the money right up to the thanks-but-get-lost part. Including the cat climbing up my back—only I didn't hurt the damn cat; Lenore peeled him off me. They were both alive when I left, Carve. I got in my car and drove back to the city. I didn't want everybody in creation to know my big fat scheme was a big fat nothing and Lenore just plain didn't want me. That's why I never said anything about being down here Thursday. As far as Gates—well, for all I knew, he *had* killed Lenore. Sorry, Carve.''

I nodded my aching head, then went downstairs to call Huge Claussen.

"What happens now?" Jerry said when Huge was done swearing at me.

"Damned if I know," I said. "I guess I better go talk to Dad, before he hears it from someone else."

It was quiet out at the farm. The midday heat hung in the air, and you kind of had to wade through it to get from here to there. Even the horseflies weren't very energetic.

Dad's half-ton Dodge pickup was parked in the shade of the garage out back of the house. I figured he'd be in having lunch, but the house was empty. I checked the garage. His Reliant was where he always kept it. The big red combine was down by the old shed, so he wasn't out in the field. Maybe he was tinkering with something in the shed . . .

I didn't run, but I walked quickly.

First thing I saw was that the doors were closed, the side door and the big overhead door on the south end. Closed and locked: the oversized padlocks hung in their hasps, glinting in the noontime sun.

Then I saw Gates's pickup, parked around back of the shed where it couldn't be seen from up by the house.

The pickup was empty.

I turned my attention back to the shed and was about to holler when a voice came from behind me—so quiet as to startle.

"Yeah, he's in there."

I turned. Dad came out from behind the rickety, disused

corn crib just south of the shed. He carried his rifle, business end toward the ground.

"I wouldn't've expected him to come back here."

"He needed some money, I guess. And he planned to leave his pickup here and take my car—figured no one'd be on the lookout for that."

"Probably right." I glanced toward the shed. "He alive?"

"Well, of *course* he's alive," Dad said with disgust. "I wouldn't have had to lock him in there if he was dead, would I? I came home for some lunch. Could tell from the way he came shootin' out the back door that something was wrong. I got out of the truck, asked him what the problem was. He pushed on by me and headed for the garage. I saw my car keys in his hand." Dad hefted the rifle. "Got the shooter off the rack in my truck, went into the garage, and asked him again what was wrong. He was more talkative that time."

"And then you locked him up. You call Huge?"

"Nope. Figured I'd wait and see whether you were dead or not. See how much trouble the boy was in."

"Enough," I said. "Better call Huge. Give me the key first."

"You want the gun too?"

"I won't need it."

He paused, then nodded and handed over his big, heavy keyring. He started up toward the house. I thought he looked old. It was the first time I'd ever thought that about my dad.

I went in through the side door. It was dark in there, gloomy, but still hot. Gates was along the far wall, sitting on the bare dirt with his back against the curved wall, in one of the few uncluttered parts of the big old Quonset. He stood up slowly and slapped dirt-dust from his jeans. He came up to me.

"You okay?" he said.

"No thanks to you."

"Yeah. I'm real sorry, Carve." He held out his right hand.

I took it, then yanked him toward me and cuffed him along the ear with my left fist. Gates staggered back, tripped over Dad's air compressor, and went down to the dirt. After a minute or so, he climbed back to his feet, shaking his head. "I guess I had that one coming."

"You had worse than that coming," I said, "but my head hurts too much. What was the big idea anyhow?"

"Slugging you and running like that?" Gates shakes his head. "I don't know. When do I ever know? I just *do* stuff, half the time I have to undo it later on. You know that." He looked away from me, toward the row of filthy little windows across the overhead door. "No undoing this one, is there?"

"No. For once, you can't run away from it. The cards have been dealt, you gotta play the hand." The words left a sour taste on the back of my tongue even as I said them. What had I been doing for six months now except running away from the hand I'd been dealt?

Gates looked at me, as if he knew what I was thinking. But he only nodded, and said, "What will happen to me?"

"Shoot, I'm no lawyer, thank God. Huge probably called it pretty close—voluntary manslaughter. You didn't mean to kill her, did you?"

"God, no, Carve—you know that. I was crazy about Lenore. But she was done with me, she made that plain. Then that fool cat came flying at me—I saw it out of the corner of my eye and just kind of swung out, you know. I never expected to hit it, but I did and it went down and didn't move. Then Lenore was yelling and crying and everything, and I clouted her one just to get her to shut up. I—I don't know what happened after that. But she was dead." He looked at the back of his bruised hand.

After a while I said, "Dad went up to call Huge. Before they get here and everything gets crazy, let's go call old Johansen. He'll know what to do—probably know a good defense lawyer for you. My guess is that trying to cover it up and run off like you did isn't going to help you any. I don't know, with plea bargains and prison overcrowding and slick lawyers and all that, but I suppose you're looking at a little time down in the state pen. Still, look at the bright side."

Gates gave me a look, the kind of look that indicated he

was wondering just how badly he'd scrambled my eggs back at the Egyptian.

I grinned and said, "They've got a baseball team at the pen."

Dad had already phoned Johansen, who'd been doing the family lawyering for longer than anyone could remember, and Johansen said Gates should surrender himself down at the sheriff's office. It would look better later. He also promised that someone would be there for Gates within the hour, even if it had to be Johansen himself. I wouldn't have minded seeing that; I don't believe I had ever seen old Johansen except behind that big cherrywood desk of his, in his office in Watsonville. I wasn't even sure he had legs.

I waited for Gates out in the Jeep while he and Dad had a few words in the kitchen. Then Gates came out, got in the passenger side, and we drove out of the yard. Dad was standing in the front window when we came around the house to the front road. I gave the horn a couple of toots.

Later on I went back to the Egyptian. There was that wall I wanted to take out, but I found myself downstairs in my old armchair, beer in hand, listening to the radio. The Beach Boys—"Wouldn't It Be Nice?" Sturm and Drang were on the concrete floor, on their sides, legs out, like they'd been steamrollered. These hot days are hard on the fur-coat set.

The song ended, and the local station switched over to the regional net, which was broadcasting a Royals game.

I started to get up to switch it off, then stopped and settled back into the chair. Time folded back on itself. After a while I picked up the phone from the floor and dialed Carolyn's number.

The Last Temptation
of Tony the C.

.

Christopher Fahy

He couldn't believe she liked this halfassed town any better than he did—she simply refused to admit it, the stubborn bitch. Why the hell had he stuck with her all this time? Why hadn't he ditched her ages ago, before they left Paris?

Because she'd had money and even a shot at a job back then, that's why. And he had been lonely, she'd wanted some company on her travels—so here they were.

The job was supposed to be at the Peggy Guggenheim, but when they got down to Venice they learned it was gone. The bastards had hired some other artist, another American, right off the street instead. They figured that Tara had changed her mind, they said. Just because she was two weeks late. The bastards. The news didn't faze her, though: She had money. And jobs opened up at the Peggy G. all the time, she said, and if they could hang around for a little while, she'd score for sure.

So they hung around for a month, and nothing came up, and prices were high—not as high as they'd been in Paris, but high—and drugs weren't easy to get, so they split for Florence. They stayed in a little hotel in the center of town, saw Dante's tomb, Giotto's tower, the paintings at the Uffizi and lots more stuff—and he'd actually had a desire to pick up a brush. Nothing strong, not as strong as the urge for some good cocaine, but a definite twinge. They found some

135

grass and some decent speed, one balanced the other out pretty good, and they ate good and slept good too.

In Vienna it wasn't so good, it rained a lot, and Tara had stomach cramps—from something she ate in Florence, no doubt. She was crabby and wouldn't sleep with him, and stayed at the pensione while he roamed the museums and walked the gray Danube's banks in the dreary rain.

In Berlin they had one whale of a fight. She had talked about going back to New York, as she missed her cat (her mother who lived in Queens was keeping it), and he'd told her she liked her goddamn cat better than him. "Well, Tony, I've known Sugar longer than you," she said in her lazy, sleepy way, with that curl of her upper lip he had grown to hate. "And she's nicer than you, and she doesn't blow all my money on drugs the way you do."

Her money. Sure. Like her CEO daddy had nothing to do with it, right? And she'd known from the very beginning he wasn't a saint. Well that was the last straw, that wiseass remark, and he'd stormed out into the street and hit the bars. Got away from lil' ol' Tara a while. Tara, Jesus, what kind of a name was that? The name of that mansion in *Gone With the Wind*? Her real name was probably Mary or Sue. That Southern accent—give me a break. When she'd grown up in Queens?

In one of the bars, quite late in the day, he'd found a dude who sold him something, and after a night that was lost forever he'd woken up in a tattered room with a headache the size of a house. He'd found Tara (Linda? Jane?) back at the hotel, drinking hot chocolate and reading the *Trib*, just as cool as could be. And the look in her eyes said quite clearly: You goddamn fool.

Then Amsterdam. Warm sunny days, bike rides, cheap tasty Indonesian food, cheap drugs—who could ask for anything more? Except maybe the turn, the change he had come to Europe for, the change that would break through the blockage that numbed his desire to paint. Every so often he got just a flicker, like back there in Florence, but nothing that said: This is it!—Like it used to in Omaha and his first days on Riverton Street. That change hadn't come.

And it sure wasn't going to come in Amsterdam's opposite, *this* friggin' place, zero city, he thought as he rounded another bleak corner. The weight of these buildings, their dark brown baroque facades, crushed the juices right out of his soul. How could anyone ever paint in a burg like this? The Avenue Louise was sleepytime, the Grand Place medieval glitz, the cops wouldn't even let you stick your sore feet in the public pond. Everything was *verboten* here. Bunch of tight-assed bourgeoisie. Whatever happened to Bruegel's peasants, dancing around with their dicks sticking up, swilling beer, eating platters of pig? They were rednecks, yeah, but at least they had *life*. *These* schmucks. . . . And as for drugs—a billionaire couldn't buy a joint in this goddamn hole.

Why had he ever left Amsterdam? Now *there* was a city, a place where folks knew how to *live*. The kids smoked cigar-sized joints in the public parks while they waded around in the ponds, and nobody said boo. Cocaine, acid, smack, you could get it all. And the town even gave you clean needles! To go from that freedom to this was too much, too much. But when Tara had ''done'' the Van Gogh Museum, the Rijksmuseum and cruised the canals, it was time to move on, she said. To this. Verbotenville.

And now it was starting to drizzle again. Same thing as Berlin and Vienna. His hair was already wet, Jesus, where *was* this place?

When he looked up again, he saw it: *Musée Royaux Des Beaux-Arts*. Not bad-looking. Huh.

He stopped for a moment and reached in his pocket and took out a foil square. Looked around—no cops—then opened the foil and popped the two pills in his mouth.

He'd gotten the pills in Amsterdam, and this was the end, sad to say. He'd done one yesterday and it wasn't bad: brought a bright clean edge and a mellow cool. A little too mellow, actually, and that's why he'd taken a double this time. Try to sharpen things up a bit.

As he walked through the entrance door, his depression deepened. Ahead he saw ornate gold frames and stern portraits of soldiers and kings.

Am I really ready for this? he asked himself.—Then shrugged, bought a ticket and went inside.

A portrait by Jan van Eyck, 1434. Lotta water under the bridge since those days, man. Porcelain people: they looked like they'd shatter to bits if you knocked them down. Hands and fingers so white, so thin. Big nose on the dude, and the cuffs on the chick's robe two feet long. Good technician, van Eyck. The grain in the wood floors, amazing.

Stuff by Aertsen and van der Goes, and some others that left Tony cold. Good old Rembrandt, of course. Soldiers. Yeah, it was good—but *soldiers*?

On to a Bruegel—a famous one—*Landscape with the Fall of Icarus*. Old Ick is head down in the water, drowning, and who gives a damn? Life goes on. Hey, you fly too close to the sun, you fry your tailfeathers, right? And here was one of those peasant paintings, the dancing, the drinking—and what was that stuff going on in the corner? Somebody getting roughed up, getting robbed. Even back then, man, the world was royally screwed.

Then Rubens. He'd had a good deal: sketch out the compositions and paint the heads, get your lackeys to do the rest. Rake in the dough and keep most for yourself. Tony scowled at the canvas. Were all broads big mamas back then? Or was that all that guys liked to see in the buff?

Another room. Franz Hals. His smiling peasants had never made Tony joyous, not in the least. It was something about their teeth. He squinted. Ugly teeth, mean ratlike teeth. He thought: The pills are kicking in.

After Hals he had just about had enough. He was crossing another gloom-packed room when a triptych on a table caught his eye. He stopped.

A Bosch? No kidding. He hadn't expected that. Even though Bosch was Belgian, the Prado had most of his stuff, though God knew why. Tony had seen it his first trip to Spain.

He looked at the brass plate attached to the painting's frame. ''Attributed to Hieronymous (Jeroen) Bosch, c. 1508.''

Attributed to. Well it looked like the real thing, all right. Good old Hieronymous, Jerry the B., as they used to call him in art school. Now *there* was a painter, there was a guy who *knew*.

The triptych was smaller than most—each panel was only about two feet high and a foot across—and was darker than other Bosches that Tony had seen. Or was that the effect of the drugs? Couldn't tell. He squinted, leaned close.

The first of the panels, the one on the left, was brighter than the other two, with a lovely lush garden and naked slim people (no Rubens heavyweights here). Way off in the distance, however, some bad shit was coming down: an ugly knot of insectile limbs was rolling across the green hill.

In the next scene—again, pure Bosch—things were radically falling apart. Some poor naked dude pulled a huge wooden wagon that overflowed with green corpses; an arrow was buried between his shoulder blades. Another nude guy slumped against a stone wall while a huge fish with legs stuck long pins through his neck. There was one of those giant pathetic tree-men, fishing boats stuck to his severed limbs, and his broken-egg body was chock full of fat priests and nuns doing something obscene. Fishlike birds with thin murderous bills and the legs of humans sailed through the dark blue sky, as crowds of milk-pale people below were nibbled by monster rabbits. Above it all, Jesus sat on a cloud, shrugging and raising his arms as if saying: Hey man, I mean what can you do with these fools?

The third panel depicted all hell breaking loose—quite literally. The sky was a flaming red cauldron of sparks, and people were being devoured by cow-sized rats. A fat yellow pig had one sad skinny dude by his ankles, and dipped him head-first into lava. Another doomed sucker puked bilious green bubbles, out of which black roachlike insects came crawling to feast upon babies' eyes. Not a fun time at all.

Tony wished he had waited till later to do those pills, whatever the hell they were. He wasn't feeling the same way he'd felt when he'd done them before; and now that he thought of it, these had been different, a different color, red, not blue, like yesterday's. Old Bosch was plenty without added zip, these golden haloes, these buzzing sounds, these shimmering wavy lights, and he thought: Maybe Jerry the B. used to take something too, like mushrooms or something, whatever they had in those days. Whatever, he'd gone all the way. You bet. It was almost as if he had actually been there, had actually visited hell and come back with the news. Or maybe to him the everyday world looked like this, like the underworld. Maybe that was it.

Despair sank its talons in Tony's heart. That vision, that singular way of seeing—what did it take to achieve it? He was starting to think—no, he'd thought for a while now—that he'd never be able to break through like that, make it over the edge.

He stared at the painting, that hellish third panel, and thought: Fantastic! I'd give *anything* to be able to see like that, take *anything.* . . .

Shaking his head in awe, he turned away—and suddenly realized something.

He was all alone in this room. There was nobody else in sight, not even a guard.

He looked back at the painting, then up at the sign on the wall. *C'est interdit à toucher les peintures.* Well, that was the same everywhere, no museums would let you touch paintings, that went without saying. But how delicious to touch one right here in Forbidden City!

He looked around quickly—left, then right—then caught his breath and did it: reached out and touched the right panel, the blazing inferno—specifically, a snarling cat—with the tip of his right index finger.

Ow! Gasping, he jerked his hand back.

An electric shock! The bastards had wired the paintings! Real sweethearts in charge of this place, oh yeah, the least they could do was tell you the damn things were juiced! He looked at his stinging, tingling hand, and his fingers were yellow and green.

He'd done some stuff in Santa Fe that had made his hand look like that, some peyote—or maybe mescaline. Made him puke like a dog all night and half the next day. Not *that* again, he said to himself. Man—

A guard was in the doorway now. He'd come out of nowhere, poof, like a friggin' ghost, and stood there scowling. Had he seen? Had the painting set off an alarm? Couldn't be—or the guy would be on him for sure.

He was one weird dude, that guard, one *mean*-lookin' dude. His hair stuck up in silver spikes and his yellow-green teeth looked like fangs. His hands were black, with blue-black nails, like a friggin' gorilla's hands. I am *outta* this place, Tony said to himself.

As he started to walk, the floor seemed to ripple. The paintings, especially their golden frames, seemed to shine with an inner light. Not bad, he thought. Looks like I'll get something out of this stuff after all.

On the street, though, the light hurt his eyes, and his pupils contracted with sudden sharp pain. The rain had stopped, but the sky was still brooding and gray. Good thing the sun's *not* out, Tony thought, I'd be damn near blind.

The street was deserted—except for a guy at the end of the block, on the corner, waiting for the light to change. The light was huge, a blood-red sun, even this far away. Tony squinted against its glare.

It shifted to splintery emerald green and the guy crossed the street. He was hunched down, bent, was wearing gray, and looked for all the world like a giant bird. His nose was as sharp as a sandpiper's beak, and his arms in his floppy gray cape looked like wings. And—what? Did he actually lift off the ground and fly a few feet?

This stuff was *bad*, even worse than that Santa Fe crap or that junk he had done in Chicago with . . . yeah, Drusilla. A chick with a name like that, he shoulda known better. Drusilla, Tara—how come he always got stuck with these weirdo women?

When he reached the corner, his feet felt soft on the curb, soft and light. His whole body felt light, like he might float away if he didn't watch out, or like if he jumped—

He tried it; jumped. And got up. He got *up*—into slam-dunk range. Impossible, he thought. There isn't a drug in the world that could—

Someone was staring. She (*was* it a she?) stood in one of those dark baroque doorways, her thick eyebrows furrowed, skin doughy and pale, her huge eyes like lumps of black coal. Okay, so I jumped, Tony thought. So what is it, a crime? Is jumping forbidden too? As he finished this thought, those black eyes blinked, and a serpent's red tongue darted out from the woman's blue lips, sprouting spirals of flame.

Whoa!

He walked in the other direction. Bad stuff, and how long was it going to last? The Santa Fe garbage had taken three days to metabolize—and this shit seemed stronger than that.

It dawned on him then that he wasn't walking—not walking, but *capering* down the street. I don't want to do this! an inner voice said, I am making a fool of myself! But he couldn't stop.

They stared. The whole lot of them stared. They were naked or wrapped in rags, their eyes burning, beaks clacking, their vicious horns slicing the air. He snarled at them as he capered by and they shrank back or slashed with their claws.

Whoa!

Shaking their fists, they spat as he passed. "I don't speak your friggin' language!" he tried to say, but it came out all garbled, a jumble of noise.

His shoes were suddenly killing him. He tore them off quickly and dropped to all fours. That felt better, much better, yes.

Which way was home? Down here, this street? Yeah, down—

When he turned the corner, the world was fire. Flames poured from the roofs and windows of towering flat wooden buildings. The heat was unbearable. Christ! Where the hell were the fire trucks?

In the flickering darkness between two tenements, crowds of naked people screamed as coals rained down on their flesh. Lizard men with slick skin and long snouts lashed another nude throng with black whips. Further along the cobblestone street giant weasels chewed people's thighs. Much worse than Santa Fe, Tony thought. *Much* worse.

Then it hit him: It wasn't the pills.

He had touched the painting—had touched the forbidden painting and caused all this. The painting had been the gate, and he, Anthony Catalano, a sinner—

No! Tony said in his mind, his skin flooded with sweat, it's just the pills!

—And a bird rushed at him, huge and blue. It brandished a thick black stick in its claws and the funnel-like hat on its head spouted purple-green smoke. Its beak went wide, snapped shut again, went wide, and the clamor that issued forth from that scarlet gash made Tony's blood run cold. He tried to scream, Stop! but the sound that came out was a hiss. The bird was on him, stretched its neck—

And Tony charged it, biting its leg. It screeched, flapped its sandpaper feathers at Tony's hot head. He ran—and ran, past grinning goats and toads with red coats and black tongues.

His stomach suddenly cramped with a horrid pain. He moaned and squatted, pushed—and out of his heat came steaming eggs which cracked and spewed forth monster crabs that clicked their claws and pursued. He ran. Had to get back to Tara, the room, lock the door, call a doctor—

He craned his head and the street was full of them, after him, all of them, lizards and fish-men, men with diaphanous wings and bright scissors where fingers should be. Foxes with beaks and long ears that hung down to the ground, giant snakes with the faces of men. The sky was roiling with sulfurous clouds and his breathing was filled with brimstone, he couldn't go on—

And suddenly here it was! This was it, this was it, his

building! He yanked on the heavy entrance door, ran inside, slammed it shut.

And if she was a demon too? he thought as he crouched in the shadows, fighting for breath. If this hell was the way things really were—and touching that painting had merely allowed him to see it? No, he told himself, that can't be it, she'll help, she will, she *has* to help.

He raced up the high dark stairs, turned right, and there was the door to the room. He pounded on it. Tara! Tara! he tried to shout, but the noise he made, it sounded like—

"Did you have to shoot him?" she asked, looking down at the hallway floor. "Did you have to *kill* him?"

"Ah yes," the policeman said in his heavy accent. "He was dangerous. Quite dangerous, he bit one of us in the leg. He was wild, wild."

"It seems such a shame," Tara said.

The policeman shrugged. "He maybe had some kind of sickness? We'll have him examined."

"What kind of a cat is he, anyway?" Tara asked.

"I don't know," the policeman said. "I don't know cats."

"Such an ugly thing. Those teeth, those claws . . ."

With a look of disgust the policeman said, "I don't want to touch him, I'll send a man out right away." He nodded. "Sorry for all the trouble, madame. Goodbye."

"Goodbye," Tara said.

Brushing her stringy hair away from her eyes, she went back inside. The thought of that cat made her naked toes curl. So ugly-looking, so mean. They had plenty of weird things back in Queens, but they didn't have cats like that.

She went to the window and looked at the street. Still gray, still raining. Depressing.

Yeah, Tony was right, this city could get you, could bring you down bad. It was time to move on again.

She'd tell him that as soon as he came home.

Buster

·

Bill Crider

When the phone rang, Hack Jensen, the dispatcher at the Blacklin County Jail, picked it up on the first jingle.

"Sheriff's office," he said. "Hack speaking." He listened for a second. "Yes'm," he said. "Yes'm, Miss Onie. Yes'm." Every time he said "Yes'm," he nodded his head. "Yes'm. I'll tell him right now. Don't you do anything. He'll be out there before you know it."

Because of the dispatcher's respectful tone, Sheriff Dan Rhodes, sitting at his desk on the other side of the room, didn't need to hear Miss Onie's name to know that Hack was speaking to someone even older than himself. Hack was somewhere in his middle seventies, but Miss Onie was well over eighty.

Hack said "Yes'm" one more time and hung up the phone. He turned to Rhodes. "That was Miss Onie Calder. She says you better get out to her house quick. Says somebody's killed Buster."

Miss Onie lived in a two-story house on the far northwest side of Clearview, an area of town that had once been fashionable but that was now occupied mostly by tumbledown old homes with weeds growing high in the yards and trees that had not been trimmed for years. Her house was different from the others in the neighborhood only because it was bigger.

Rhodes parked the county car in front and walked up to the door. There were weeds springing up through the cracks in the sidewalk, and a young hackberry tree was pushing through a place on the edge of the porch where several boards were missing. There were high wooden columns on the porch, and their paint was cracked and flaking away, like the paint on the outside walls and window frames.

Rhodes banged on the screen door with the heel of his hand. The door rattled in the frame, making a considerable noise. When Miss Onie didn't appear immediately, he kept on banging. He knew that her hearing wasn't particularly good.

The door behind the screen was half wood and half glass, and Rhodes could see into the hallway. After a minute or so, he saw movement in the house and someone approached the door.

"Is that you, Dan Rhodes?" Miss Onie called out in a high, thin voice.

"Yes, ma'am," Rhodes said. "It's me."

He heard the sound of a deadbolt being pushed back and the door opened. Miss Onie stood behind the screen. She was about five feet tall and must have weighed a good hundred and sixty. She wore thick glasses and had her gray hair piled up in a bun.

She pushed on the screen and Rhodes moved out of the way. "Come on in," she said. "Buster's in the kitchen."

Rhodes went in the house and Miss Onie closed the door behind him. The place was a fire chief's nightmare.

To Rhodes' right, there was a stairway leading up to the second floor. The steps were piled high with old newspapers and magazines, some of them bundled together and tied with string, some of them simply sitting in loose stacks. Rhodes recognized the distinctive yellow spines of hundreds of issues of *National Geographic*.

The hallway was like the stair, and Rhodes had to turn sideways to make his way down it. There were stacks of newspapers, magazines, and other paper items. Rhodes saw a copy of the Clearview newspaper dated November 5, 1943, on top of one stack. On the top of another was a 1953 calendar from Calder's grocery.

Rhodes hadn't thought of that particular store for years. It had closed sometime around 1960, when Miss Onie's husband had died, but Rhodes could suddenly remember buying baseball cards there when he was a kid. He could still remember the smell of the gum that came with the cards.

The gum was flat, pink, and brittle, and he wished that he had about six pieces of it right now, strapped in front of his nose. The smell in Miss Onie's house was incredible.

Part of the reason was that Miss Onie never opened the windows of her house. Winter or summer, spring or fall, the windows remained tightly closed. So the smell had built up over the years. It was a combination of mustiness, age, and cats.

It was the cat smell that was the strongest, and it was clear to Rhodes why that was so.

Cats were everywhere.

There were yellow cats, gray cats, and black cats. There were calico cats and patchwork cats. There were big cats and middle-sized cats, along with a few kittens. There were tomcats and pussycats. There were cats that had a vaguely oriental look and cats that looked like they had just come in out of the alley.

Rhodes didn't try to count them. There must have been forty or fifty of them.

They scratched at the fraying carpet on the stairs and at the peeling wallpaper. They seethed around Rhodes' legs, purring and meowing, bumping their heads against him, rubbing against his ankles. They walked down the hallway atop the magazines and papers. They peered at him from between the balustrades of the stairway. Cat hair floated in the air all around him and danced in front of his eyes.

He sneezed.

"Bless you," Miss Onie said.

Then they were in the kitchen, which was relatively free of clutter, except for a mound of cereal boxes that reached nearly to the ceiling in one corner and a line of bowls of dry cat food alternating with bowls of water along the baseboard.

On the cracked Formica top of the cabinet by the sink there was a package of something wrapped in foil. Pinkish liquid ran from the foil, and there were two cats on the counter lapping at the liquid with their tongues.

"Naugh-ty boys!" Miss Onie said, shooing them with her hands. They jumped lightly from the counter, landed on the floor, and mingled with the other cats.

"You know better than to play with Mama's lunch," Miss Onie said. She turned and looked at Rhodes. "Pork chops," she said.

Rhodes looked at the cat hair wafting all around and settling on the foil and wondered if he would ever eat pork chops again.

"Where's Buster?" he said.

"Over there," Miss Onie said, pointing at her kitchen table.

The table was made of oak and might have been attractive if it had ever been polished. On its dull surface lay the body of a huge ash-colored tom. The cat was stiff as a poker, its eyes open and glassy. As Rhodes looked at it, two other cats—not the same two who had been at the pork chops—levitated themselves up onto the table. They sniffed at Buster's mortal remains without much enthusiasm and then jumped silently back to the floor.

"Poisoned," Miss Onie said. She brushed at her cheek, where there was a red patch of a rash of some kind.

Rhodes wasn't surprised to see the rash. He found himself itching in all sorts of unlikely places, and he refrained from scratching only with a powerful effort of will.

"You're sure about that?" he said. "That Buster was poisoned, I mean?"

"It was that Ralph Ramsdell," Miss Onie said. "He's the one done it, because of Tuggle bein' such a bully. But that's not my fault. I can't help it if one of the boys is a little rowdy, can I? You know what they say."

"No," Rhodes said. "Maybe you better tell me."

"Boys will be boys," Miss Onie said, looking down at Buster. "That's what they say." She brushed at her eyes. "Buster was such a good boy, too, nothin' at all like Tuggle, so I don't see why Ralph Ramsdell—"

"Maybe you better tell me about Tuggle," Rhodes said.

"Oh. Well, he just came here a few weeks back." Miss Onie looked around at the cats churning around the kitchen, some of them meowing, some of them purring, some of them not making a sound. "I swear, I don't know why cats keep comin' here. Just seems like this place attracts them, somehow."

"I guess some places are like that," Rhodes said. He sneezed.

"Bless you. I guess so. Anyway, Tuggle came here in bad shape. He'd been declawed on his front paws, couldn't climb a tree or anything. I thought he'd be happy here with the boys, but he's a real roisterer, that one. Goes out all the time, picks fights with the neighbor cats, especially that big orange one that belongs to Ralph Ramsdell. It's a real sight to see, the way he does. He can't fight with his front paws, but he rolls on his back and just works those other cats over with his hind feet. The fur flies, let me tell you."

Rhodes was about to ask how Tuggle could get out when a dark blur smashed through the bottom of the kitchen door and shot through the room.

Rhodes looked at the door and saw that a flap built into it was still swinging.

"Tuggle!" Miss Onie said to the fleeing cat, now being pursued out of the room by about half the population of the kitchen. "Is that mean Mr. Ramsdell shootin' at you again?"

"Shooting?" Rhodes said.

"He's got him one of those BB guns," Miss Onie said. "He likes to use it on the boys. But he didn't stop Tuggle with it, and that's when he started putting out the poison. I want him stopped, and I want him arrested for the murder of Buster!"

"I'll see what I can do," Rhodes said.

* * *

Rhodes stepped off Miss Onie's back porch and sneezed. Then he took a deep breath of the crisp fall air. It was quite a relief.

He looked across the back yard at Ralph Ramsdell's detached garage. Ramsdell's house faced the street that ran perpendicular to the one running in front of Miss Onie's house; the garage was between the two houses and to the back.

Rhodes walked over to the garage. The fall sun felt good on his back.

"You in there, Mr. Ramsdell?" he said when he was nearly to the garage.

"Who wants to know?"

Rhodes stopped just outside the garage. "This is the Sheriff, Mr. Ramsdell. Dan Rhodes."

A short, skinny man came out of the shadows, walking along the side of what looked like a 1949 or 1950 Dodge that was backed into the garage.

"What can I do for you, Sheriff?" the man said. He was wearing a pair of jeans faded almost white, a blue work shirt, and a pair of black suspenders.

"I wanted to ask you about Miss Onie's cats," Rhodes said.

"Sonsabitches come over here botherin' Al," Ramsdell said. "All the time. Can't leave him alone. He come in the other day, bleedin' like a stuck pig. Damn left ear split right down the middle. I never woulda thought so much blood could come from a split ear."

"Al's your cat?" Rhodes said.

"Short for Alley. Anyway, those damn cats been pickin' on him for a couple of weeks. I told her if it didn't stop—"

"By 'her' you mean Miss Onie."

"That's the only 'her' around here. Anyway, I told her that if it didn't stop, I was goin' to Wal-Mart and buy me a gun. I warned her, Sheriff, fair and square. But it didn't stop, so I got me the gun."

"You want to show it to me?" Rhodes said.

Ramsdell turned and walked back into the garage. While

he was gone, Rhodes heard a car door slam. He turned and looked out at the street. A black Ford Ranger was parked there, and a man was walking toward Miss Onie's house.

Then Ramsdell was back, carrying a small rifle.

"Here it is," he said. "Just a BB gun."

Rhodes put out his hand, and Ramsdell gave him the gun. It was a Crossman Powermaster 760.

"Single shot," Ramsdell said. "You got to pump it ever' time you shoot it."

"Did you just use it?"

"Damn sure did. That big tabby come over here lookin' for trouble, and he found it. Shot him right square in the butt. I'll teach him to come over here tryin' to beat up on my cat."

"Where is your cat, by the way?" Rhodes said.

"In the garage," Ramsdell said. "He likes to sleep on top of the car."

"I don't guess you ever thought about using anything more lethal than a BB gun on Miss Onie's cats, did you?"

"Hell no," Ramsdell said. "What do you mean by that?"

"Miss Onie says you poisoned Buster."

"Who the hell is Buster?"

"One of her cats."

"Well, I didn't poison whatshisname, Buster, nor nobody else. I got me a BB gun, but you can't kill a cat with a BB gun. Hell, Sheriff, I don't want to kill 'em. I *like* cats. I just want to keep 'em off poor old Al. A BB won't hurt 'em, maybe sting a little is all."

There was a soft thump, and Rhodes looked into the garage. An orange cat was walking along the hood of the old Dodge. Ramsdell reached out and rubbed the cat's head. The cat started to purr.

"This here's Al," Ramsdell said. "Look here. You can see where those damn cats split his ear."

Rhodes looked. The ear was split, all right.

"I sure wouldn't want anything happenin' to Al," Ramsdell said. "He's about all the company I got."

"And you wouldn't hurt anyone else's cats, either?" Rhodes said.

Ramsdell sighed. "I sure wouldn't," he said.

"That Ralph Ramsdell's a liar and the truth's not in him," Miss Onie said.

She had the pork chops sizzling in a heavy black pan, and the cats were milling around and yowling. It had been stuffy in the room earlier, despite the cool fall weather outside. Now, with the pork chops smoking in the pan, it was even worse. Miss Onie had rolled up the sleeves of her dress.

There was a young man with dark hair sitting at the table. Buster was gone.

"This is my nephew, Robert Calder," Miss Onie said over her shoulder when Rhodes entered the kitchen. "Robert, this is Sheriff Rhodes."

Robert got up and extended his hand. Rhodes shook it.

"Glad to meet you, Robert," Rhodes said, releasing the nephew's hand. "What happened to Buster?"

"Oh, I took him outside," Robert said. "Couldn't have him cluttering up the kitchen, not when somebody's fixing lunch and all."

"Where is he?" Rhodes said.

"Out in my truck," Robert said, smiling. "Don't worry, Sheriff. I won't dump him on public property."

"Dump him!" Miss Onie said, turning from the stove, a two-pronged cooking fork in her hand. Rhodes noticed that there was a large purple bruise on her left arm. "I thought you said you were going to give him a decent burial."

"I am, Aunt Onie," Robert said. Noticing that Rhodes was looking at the bruise, he added in a lower voice, "Aunt Onie fell down last week. I've been trying to get her to hire someone to stay here with her, but she won't hear of it."

"I didn't fall down, and don't you say so," Miss Onie said. "I just bumped into the cabinet. And I don't need anybody here pesterin' me in my own house. Sheriff, did you arrest that Ralph Ramsdell?"

"Not yet," Rhodes said. "He didn't seem like the kind of man to go around poisoning cats."

Miss Onie shook her head. "Well, he is. Anybody'd shoot at a cat with a BB gun would just as soon poison him as not. And you'd better do something about it."

"He has a cat of his own," Rhodes said. "He likes cats."

"Ha," Miss Onie said. "He just got that cat to chase mice. He doesn't like mice, either."

"I don't guess you have much of a problem with mice, yourself," Rhodes said, looking at the swarming cats.

"Robert takes care of that," Miss Onie said. She turned back to the stove and prodded at the pork chops. "Got to cook these things well done, or you might get that disease, tricky-nosis. I've had some of the symptoms, lately. Been meanin' to get myself checked by the doctor."

"Now, Aunt Onie," Robert said. "You know you don't have trichinosis."

"Ha. Shows what little you know about it. Wouldn't be eatin' these pork chops right now if I had anything else in the house."

One of the cats, a mostly white calico, stood on its hind legs and pawed at Miss Onie's apron. "You stop that, Sassy," Miss Onie said. "You can't have any pork chops." She swung the cooking fork down, and the cat dropped to the floor and sat looking up at her.

"I got plenty for visitors, though," Miss Onie said to Rhodes and Robert. "Either of you want me to set you a plate?"

"No thanks," Rhodes said. He wasn't so much afraid of getting trichinosis as of getting a hair ball. "I have to be getting back to the jail."

"I have to go, too," Robert said.

"You better not leave here without arrestin' that Ralph Ramsdell, Sheriff," Miss Onie said.

"I'll have to do a little more investigation first," Rhodes said. "I'll just leave by the back door."

He let himself out and once more took a deep breath of

153

the clean air. Then he walked out to the black pickup that was parked by the side street to wait for Robert.

"Poor old Buster. Stiff as a poker."

Rhodes turned and saw Robert Calder standing beside him, looking down at the carcass of the cat that lay in the pickup bed.

"Not that Aunt Onie will miss one cat, more or less," Calder said. "Lord knows what she sees in them."

"They keep her company, I guess," Rhodes said, thinking of what Ramsdell had said.

"They do that. But, Lord, the smell in there. I think she's getting a little senile, to tell the truth. Falling down and not wanting to admit it, talking to those cats like they could understand her. It's not normal, Sheriff."

"That's a mighty big house," Rhodes said. "Does Miss Onie live in all of it?"

Calder leaned forward, resting his arms on the side of the pickup bed. "Just a few rooms. The rest of the place is closed off."

"What about the cats? Do they have the run of the place?"

"Nope. They can go in and out through the flap in the back door, but they don't get into any of the upstairs rooms."

"What's in the rest of the place?" Rhodes said. "I mean, is it like the downstairs?"

Robert laughed. "Just about. I guess Aunt Onie never threw away a thing in her life, or Uncle Josh, either, when he was alive. What anybody'd want with all that old junk is a mystery to me. Cereal boxes, newspapers, magazines. God knows what-all she's got in there."

"Nothing will get chewed up by mice, though," Rhodes said. "Not with all those cats around. But then, from what Miss Onie said, I don't guess she holds with having the cats keep down the mouse population."

Robert looked for a moment as if he didn't quite know what Rhodes was talking about. Then he smiled. "Oh. You mean what she said about me taking care of the mice. I just bought some mouse bait for her. Since she doesn't let the cats out of those downstairs rooms, she has to use something else for the upstairs. You know how those old houses are. Mice come in about this time of year, looking for a warm place to stay.''

Rhodes didn't really know, not ever having lived in one, but he could imagine. He reached into the pickup bed and poked Buster's stiff carcass with his index finger.

"I'll just take the deceased with me," he said.

"You don't have to do that, Sheriff," Robert said. "I'll take care of it."

Rhodes picked Buster up. "Can't let you do that," he said. "You never know. Buster might be evidence. I'll see that he gets a good burial." He stuck the stiff body under his arm.

"What about Ramsdell?" Robert said. "What are you going to do about him?"

"We'll see," Rhodes said.

He forgot all about Ramsdell when he got back to the jail, however, because there had been what the newspapers liked to call a "daring daylight robbery" of a convenience store.

" 'Cept this one was a little different," Hack said.

Lawton, the jailer, was leaning against the wall, eager to join in. "That's the truth, Sheriff. There ain't never been one like this."

That was the way it always went. Hack and Lawton would talk around the subject for as long as they could, trying to make Rhodes ask about the specifics of the crime. He resisted as long as he could.

"Teenagers," Hack said. "You never know what they'll think of next."

"*I* know what they'll think of next," Lawton said. "Same thing they always think of. You prob'ly think about it a lot too, seein' as you're sweet on Miz McGee the way you are."

Hack's face got red. "You take that back," he said.

"I didn't mean anything by it," Lawton said. "Besides, you were the one that brought it up."

"I wasn't talkin' about *that*. I was talkin' about the way teenagers come up with these new ways to steal things."

"Well, it was a new one all right," Lawton said, nodding.

"All right," Rhodes said. He couldn't stand it any longer. "What was new about it?"

"The turtle," Hack said, getting it said before Lawton could.

"They stole a turtle?" Rhodes said.

"Nope," Lawton said. "They used one as a weapon."

"You're making this up," Rhodes said.

"Not a bit of it," Hack said. "They went in the Quik-Sak carryin' a snappin' turtle. Big ol' mossback, accordin' to the clerk. Must've weighed twenty, thirty pounds. Said if the clerk didn't empty the register, they'd get the turtle to bite off his fingers."

"Coulda done it, too," Lawton said. "I seen one of them things once, he bit a tree limb right half in two. That thing must've been three inches around."

"I don't doubt it," Hack said. "I remember one time—"

"Never mind that," Rhodes said. "What about the robbery?"

"Oh," Hack said. "Well, natcherly the clerk gave 'em all the money in the register. Wasn't but about thirty bucks. Ruth Grady responded to the call, and she ought to be able to catch 'em. They drove off in an old Chevy, and the clerk got the license number."

"But did he get it right?" Rhodes said. He'd dealt with eyewitness reports of license numbers before.

"I expect he did," Hack said. "Anyway, Ruth'll know whether she stops the right car or not."

"Yeah," Lawton said. "Not too many people carry snappin' turtles around with 'em nowadays."

"They took the turtle with them?" Rhodes said.

"Sure they did," Hack said. "You don't think they'd leave a dangerous weapon like that lyin' around, do you?"

Rhodes shook his head. "No," he said. "I don't guess they would."

"I almost hate to tell you," Herman Talbert said. "You sure you don't know where they are?"

Talbert was the owner of Clearview's only baseball card shop. Rhodes had stopped by to talk about the old cards he'd thought of that morning in Miss Onie's house.

"I don't have any idea," Rhodes said. "I traded a lot of them for comic books, I think."

"You don't have the comic books, either, I bet," Talbert said. He was young and enthusiastic, with brush-cut black hair and eyes that sparkled behind his glasses. "They might be worth more than the baseball cards."

"Read them to pieces," Rhodes said. "No cards, no comics."

Talbert shook his head in sympathy. "Happens all the time. That's why they're worth so much. A 1952 Topps Mantle card, now, in like-new condition, that would be worth in the neighborhood of ten thousand dollars all by itself."

Rhodes whistled. He'd had no idea.

Talbert picked up a slick magazine with a photo of Bo Jackson on the front from on top of his counter. Below the glass Rhodes could see colorful cards in plastic protectors with small price stickers on them.

Talbert opened the magazine and located the page he was looking for. He ran his finger down a list and said, "According to this month's Beckett, that Mantle card would go for eight thousand. Of course, you'd have to find someone willing to pay that much."

"How hard would that be?" Rhodes said.

"Not as hard as you might think. Of course none of the others from that year are worth near that much, except maybe the Willie Mays."

"What if somebody found a whole box of cards from that year?" Rhodes said.

"You mean just a box of loose cards? That would depend on their condition."

"No," Rhodes said. "I mean a box of unopened cards, still in the packages, gum and all."

"Holey moley," Talbert said. "I have no idea. A lot. A whole lot." He looked at Rhodes over the tops of his glasses. "You don't know where to find anything like that do you?"

"No," Rhodes said. But he wasn't sure he was telling the truth.

"Warfarin," Dr. Slick said. "That's what killed Buster."

Rhodes had not given Buster's body a burial of any kind. He had taken it to Slick, one of Blacklin County's veterinarians, for an autopsy.

"Warfarin," Rhodes said. "Pretty easy to get hold of."

Dr. Slick nodded. "Sure is. Used in a lot of rat bait."

"How fast would it work on a cat?" Rhodes said.

"Not too fast, unless he got a lot of it at one time. Cats wouldn't normally eat enough of it. You leave it out for rats and mice and they eat it over a period of time. It doesn't work instantly."

"So it wouldn't be the kind of thing you'd use to kill a cat," Rhodes said.

"Nope. There's lots of better things for that."

"That's what I thought," Rhodes said.

Robert Calder lived in a run-down house not too far from his aunt's. He was in his driveway looking under the hood of his pickup when Rhodes stopped by late that afternoon.

He looked up when Rhodes approached and wiped his hands on a red rag that had been hanging out of the pocket of his jeans.

"Hey, Sheriff," he said. "What can I do for you?"

"I want to talk to you about your aunt," Rhodes said.

Calder turned around and slammed down the hood of the truck. "Brake fluid was low," he said, turning back to Rhodes. He wiped his hands again. "What about my aunt?"

"She didn't fall," Rhodes said.

The sun was going down and there were long shadows across the scraggly lawn. It was much cooler than it had been in the morning, and Rhodes thought they might have a freeze that night.

Calder stood there looking at Rhodes, but he didn't say anything.

"You told me Miss Onie got that bruise on her arm from

a fall," Rhodes said. "She didn't. She bumped into the cabinet, just like she said."

Calder tossed the red rag on the pickup hood. "She has a little trouble remembering, like I told you."

"A little," Rhodes said. "That's why she writes things down."

"What things?" Calder said.

"Things like falls, or bumping into cabinets. She does that so that if she wakes up hurting one morning, she'll know whether she needs to worry or not."

"I don't get it," Calder said. "You mean she keeps a diary?"

"Sort of. She showed me where she wrote it down."

Rhodes pulled a small spiral notebook from his back pocket and flipped back its yellow cover. He flicked back the pages until he came to the one he was looking for.

"Here it is. 'November fifth. Bumped into kitchen cabinet. Left arm.' "

"Maybe she didn't fall, then," Calder said. "I thought she did."

"Then there's that rash on her face," Rhodes said.

"I didn't see any rash," Calder said.

"Not to mention the trichinosis."

"I don't know what you're getting at, Sheriff. My aunt doesn't have trichinosis."

"I know it," Rhodes said. "She's being poisoned."

Calder leaned back against the hood of the pickup. "You've lost me, Sheriff. Trichinosis, diaries, rashes. I don't think I can do anything for you, after all."

"You might tell me why you dropped by your aunt's house every day at meal times."

Calder pushed himself away from the pickup and started walking toward his house. "I go by to check on her, make sure she's all right. You know how it is, an old lady living alone. Something could happen, and she'd need help."

Rhodes followed him. "I asked Miss Onie about Buster, too. He ate table scraps. He was the only cat that did. He

159

refused to eat the dry food, and Miss Onie humored him even if she didn't think table scraps were good for him.''

"I didn't know that," Calder said. He had reached his front door.

"I didn't think so," Rhodes said. "Anyway that rat poison you'd been putting in the food, Buster got too much of it. It's a good thing he did. Otherwise you might have gotten away with killing Miss Onie."

Calder turned. "Sheriff, why would I want to do that? Why would anyone want to do that?"

"Baseball cards," Rhodes said. "Cereal boxes. Dixie cup tops. Comic books. Old coffee cans. Miss Onie's got all of them. The upstairs is knee-deep in them. She and her husband kept everything from the store that didn't sell. They couldn't bear to part with anything, so they just stacked it away. She took me on a little tour about an hour ago. It's all still there. And it's all worth a lot of money."

"Even the cereal boxes?" Calder said.

"Even them. People will collect anything."

"I could have had any of it for the asking," Calder said.

"No you couldn't," Rhodes said. "Miss Onie said you did ask. She told you it was all in her will."

"That damn will."

"I have to agree with you on that one," Rhodes said. "I never did understand anyone who would leave everything to a bunch of cats."

"Everything," Calder said, shaking his head. "The house to be left just as it was. Sheriff, it was a pure waste."

"Maybe," Rhodes said. "But that was no reason to kill anyone. You could have challenged the will in court when the time came."

"I wasn't going to kill anyone," Calder opened the screen door and reached inside.

Rhodes's hand clamped around Calder's wrist as Calder tried to bring the shotgun out and up.

"You won't be needing that," Rhodes said. "You don't want more trouble than you've already got."

Calder relaxed his grip and let go of the shotgun. "I guess you're right. Besides, I don't think you can get a conviction."

"We'll see," Rhodes said. "You never know what a jury will do. They might think killing that cat is worth fifty years."

"I never meant to kill any cat."

"That part, I believe," Rhodes said.

Almost as soon as they got Calder booked and printed, Ruth Grady came in with the two suspects from the convenience store robbery.

"Caught up with them on the old Obert Road," she said. "You'll have to send somebody for their car."

"I'll drive you out there after we've got these two taken care of," Rhodes said. "You can drive it back."

"No sir, not me."

"Why not?" Rhodes said.

Hack laughed. "I bet I know. Snappin' turtle."

"That's right," Ruth said. "I never saw anything like that, not close up. It looks like something out of a book on dinosaurs. *I'm* not getting in that car."

"You better not shoot it," Hack said. "We got us a sheriff who can solve animal murders real quick."

Ruth looked at Rhodes. "What's he talking about?"

"Never mind," Rhodes said.

Catnap

·

David H. Everson

"**I** don't do divorce," I said firmly. "It's my New Year's resolution."

This year and every year, I thought, as I leaned back in my swivel chair and glanced out my dust-streaked office window at the silver Capitol dome. I often do that just to remind myself of who signs the checks that pay the bills at Midcontinental Op and Associate. There are a lot of jobs I don't *have* to take, as long as the Speaker remains major domo under the dome. When and if he loses his Democratic majority—bite my tongue—and I lose that connection, well, resolutions were made to be broken.

My name is Robert Miles and I'm a private eye with a difference. My mean streets are the corridors of power in the Illinois Capital. Call what I do for the Speaker of the Illinois House of Representatives opposition research.

"That's not—" the woman in my client's chair started to reply.

Crack! Boom! Outside, there was a sudden series of muffled explosions and the pale blue winter sky was dotted with red bursts around the Capitol dome.

"Oh, my goodness," she said, putting a hand to her face.

"Don't be alarmed," I said. "That's not Saddam Hussein. They're just testing the fireworks for the First Night celebration. Been doing it all day." I fiddled with some papers on my desk, anxious to get out of this interview. "All my friends who own one say divorce gets nasty and personal."

And so does politics, I thought.

It was the middle of the afternoon, December 31, 1990. I had been about to close up shop for the year when she had peeked in my half-open door. "Robert Miles?" she had asked.

"Guilty."

"The private detective?"

I had nodded.

"How exciting."

I had stifled a yawn. "Can I help you?"

"I certainly hope so. My name is Sylvia Ransome." She had taken a deep breath. "I've never done anything like this before."

"Most folks haven't. How can I help you?"

She had danced around the issue for several minutes until I had concluded from her repeated trashing of her husband—"that bastard"—that it must be divorce. So I had made my statement of principle.

Now she seemed to welcome the distraction of the fireworks. She pointed at the window and said, "Of course you're going to First Night. It's such a Springfield *happening*."

Springfield happening. Classic oxymoron, I thought. "Of course I'm not. Prior commitment." Actually, I did have plans for New Year's Eve. Stay off the streets. I was going to pop a bowl of corn and watch a video of Art Carney and Lily Tomlin in *The Late Show*; then I was going to continue rereading Robert B. Parker's *Early Autumn*. "I don't do happenings either," I said.

First Night is Springfield's attempt to provide a wholesome nonalcoholic outing for the entire family on New Year's Eve. Another one of those goofy ideas which give me a pain in the keister. Billy Joe Barstool was not going to be deterred from drinking and driving by G-rated entertainment.

Sylvia sighed and gave me a look of civic reproach.

I started to get up. "I'm sorry," I lied. "I've got to be closing up."

She put up a hand. "Divorce is not my problem. I *have* the divorce."

I sat back down. "Oh." Hard information. Progress. Of a sort.

She was in her mid-forties, I guessed. Her hair was ebony—dyed?—with a white streak right up the middle. Her eyes were gray, her eyeshadow dark. She was wearing about three more coats of paint on her face than I cared for. She had draped some kind of fur over the back of the chair. She wore a pink wool suit, white hose and black pumps. Now she picked up a black purse and said, "Do you mind if I smoke?"

Another strike against her. "No," I said. "Can you give me some better idea of what you want me to do?"

She made a production out of it. Fit the cigarette into a filter, fired up a gold lighter and lit up. She inhaled and then blew smoke out her nostrils. "The problem is that Hank—that bastard—has kidnapped Callie. I'm sure of it. To get back at me."

"Hank is your ex?"

She nodded. "Dr. Henry Ransome. The no good son of a bitch. You see, I got a good financial settlement. A very good one. I deserved it. He was nothing when I met him. I put him through med school. He's an oral surgeon. It's been like pulling teeth—no pun—to get him to live up to the agreement. Now he thinks he's found a way to strike back." She noticed the quarter inch of ash on her cigarette and looked around in vain for an ashtray. I pushed an empty Coke bottle across the desk for her. Her face betrayed distaste but she flicked ashes into the bottle. In the background, there was another explosion of fireworks. She flinched again. "I want you to get her back."

I was thinking that custody battles were an extension of divorce and thus I could invoke my New Year's resolution. But for some reason—probably because my job is asking questions—I said, "How old is Callie?"

She shut her eyes for a second and counted to herself. "I've had her for almost five years," she said.

Had her?

"Hank never paid any attention to her when we were married. I'm very worried. She has special needs. Her diet. She has to be combed every day."

Combed? "Did you adopt her?"

"Of course."

The hunting dog in me was taking over. "Can you give me a description?"

"I can do better than that." She got a photograph out of her purse and handed it to me. I looked at it. Of course. It was a color Polaroid of a calico cat with a black patch over the right eye. I closed my eyes for a second. "I don't do pets," I said. "I don't have many rules, but I draw the line in the kitty litter at catnapping cases."

She frowned. "I don't understand. Is this too . . . trivial?"

"It's not that. Look, as far as I'm concerned, custody battles over children or pets are a logical extension of divorce work. It puts me in the middle of a war zone. Which I don't do willingly."

"That's irrational."

"Makes sense to me."

"You seem to have more cases you won't take than those you will."

"That's why they call it self-employment. Try Land of Lincoln Investigations," I said. "They're in the book."

She sniffled a little, then got huffy, then sniffled some more. But I was a rock, so she finally gave up and left.

I fiddled around with the files for a few minutes, then shut my eyes for a quick . . . catnap. The phone buzzed. I almost decided to let the answering machine pick up. Then I thought, what the hell. It might be Mitch or Lisa. I grabbed it. Mistake. Fast Freddy Martin said, "The Man wants to talk to you."

"On New Year's Eve?" I said.

"Hey, the Man works three hundred sixty-five or more

days a year. If you're going to exceed in this business,'' Fast said, ''you have to get with the program.''

''Yes, mine furor,'' I responded.

Let's face it. One of the costs of working for the Speaker is that I have to swallow a little white wine now and then. Fast Freddy is the Speaker's John Sununu. The guy who delivers the bad news—in the fractured English which I call Fastspeak.

''Robert,'' the Speaker said, ''I need a favor.'' He sat ramrod-straight in his royal blue chair behind his immaculate desk, toying with his small silver gavel. A single yellow legal pad and three well-sharpened red pencils rested in front of him. We were in his spacious office on the third floor of the Capitol. Outside, I could see the reflection of the street lights off the snow on the Capitol grounds.

I nodded. ''Of course.'' Half of my gross comes from political investigations contracted for by the Speaker. Which meant I didn't have to do divorce work. I owed him, big time.

''Ah—'' He seemed embarrassed. At a loss for words. A first in my presence. ''Sylvia Ransome,'' he said. He paused. ''She's from a prominent Springfield family. The Porters. She called—'' He paused again, put the gavel down and made a steeple with his hands. ''I understand—'' He coughed.

I rolled my eyes, knowing what was coming.

He leaned toward me. ''I understand you spoke with her earlier today.''

I nodded.

''You refused her case.''

I nodded.

''Robert, I'd like for you to reconsider.''

''Why?''

''Because her father—Bill Porter—has been a major contributor to the Fund for a Democratic Majority,'' Fast Freddy snapped.

''I see,'' I said. I looked at Fast. ''Since I'm paid out of that account, you figure she already *is* my client.''

"Robert," the Speaker said softly.

I turned back. He lasered me with his pale blue eyes. I had to strain to hear him. "I would consider it a personal favor if you would reconsider. Talk to her again."

I dipped my head slightly. "That's a done deal," I said, knowing that I would end up taking the cat caper.

I walked briskly home to my apartment on the near north side, where I was greeted at the outside door by Clockwork Orange. Clockie is the marmalade-colored male cat who consents to room and board with me. He's a real scrapper, a down and dirty alley-fighter. Both of his ears had notches from previous fights. I knelt down and stroked him. As far as I could tell, he hadn't added any battle scars today. "Clockie, lad, you know anything about calicos?" I asked. "All I know is that they are always female."

He walked back and forth between my legs, his striped tail forming a question mark. I knew the meaning of his query.

"Okay, let's see what's for supper," I said.

The next morning I drove my 1981 Toyota Tercel down to Auburn for New Year's Day. My associate, Mitch Norris—formerly a major-league catcher and now a part-time scout for the Cardinals—and I watched the Hall of Fame bowl game on his forty-inch screen in his spotless living room. Clemson punched the daylights out of Illinois. "The fightless Illini," Mitch groused.

I was starting to tell him about the cat caper when the phone rang. Mitch got it. "For you," he said. "Lisa."

I frowned. Lisa's my wife, the woman I share a no-fault separation with. (I told you, I don't do divorce.)

"Yo?" I said. "How'd you track me down?"

"Process of elimination. New Year's Day. You're either at home or at Mitch's—overdosing on bowl games. Rob, I think you're terrible."

"You called to tell me that?"

"What would Clockie think?"

"Cats don't think."

"Ha! How could you not free that poor little oppressed animal?"

I made the connection. She was talking about the calico. That woman was putting on a full-court press. "You know Sylvia Ransome?"

"Of course. She comes from a family whose roots go back to Lincoln. She's a former student of mine." Lisa teaches American Studies at Lincoln Heritage University.

"Sometimes I think almost everyone in Springfield has Lincoln connections and is one of your former students. Not to worry. She's already pushed the right button."

"The Speaker?"

"Yes."

"Rob, I have to confess, I told her to call him. I was just following up."

Lisa is an absolute tiger on follow-through.

"And a happy New Year to you, too," I said.

"Stop by on your way home. I'll make it up to you."

At Lisa's, I was greeted at the door by a gigantic St. Bernard dog. He licked my hand. "What's this?" I said.

"One of my colleagues is on sabbatical and I'm taking care of Otis."

Otis? "Turn on the TV. I want to catch the end of the Notre Dame-Colorado game."

"Fat chance," she said.

The next day I drove through a snow storm to meet with Sylvia Ransome at her ritzy condo on West Washington. At the door, she looked down at my wet Nike court shoes. "Would you mind removing those?"

"No problem." I slipped out of them.

She led me into the living room. I was almost blinded. The walls, carpet and furniture were all white. There were large mirrors on three of the walls. A picture window overlooked a patio covered with snow. I felt like I had stepped in an arctic whiteout.

She noticed my reaction. She made a half-turn and held out her hand, palm up. "I redecorated last week. You're looking at a cool ten thousand dollars," she said proudly. "My analyst suggested it as therapy for the divorce." She smiled. "Callie will scarcely know the place when you bring her back. I'm so glad you've reconsidered. Please sit."

I sat on the edge of the couch to contaminate as little of the room as possible. "The Speaker and Lisa are a dynamic duo. I need to establish some basic facts."

"Of course."

"Are you certain that Hank took the cat?"

She nodded. "Absolutely."

"Cats have been known to . . . wander away."

"Callie is an indoor cat. She *never* goes out."

"I see. Then how did Hank get her?"

"Waited until I was not home, let himself in and stole her. He took some of her toys, too."

"He has a key?"

"With all the redecorating, I haven't had the time to get the locks changed."

"Why didn't you go to the police?"

She widened her eyes. "I want to avoid the bad publicity."

"Do you know where he's living?"

She laughed harshly. "With his slut in her crummy apartment on South Sixth Street."

I thought of four ways to get Callie back. In ascending order of escalation, they were: reason, trickery, breaking and entering and intimidation. Within the intimidation category, I had a choice of Mitch—if minor mayhem was involved— or Big House Bellamy—if the big stick was needed. Bells was a local enforcer that I used when I needed to upgrade my firepower.

I decided to follow old Hank around for a day or so to check out his routine and temperament. The first day on the job was Thursday. He went to his practice on West Wabash by the White Oaks Mall at 8:30 A.M. and stayed till 5:30 P.M. Then he drove back to the apartment and, after an hour, he and the "slut" left and went out to dinner. Then the fun couple hit several of Springfield's trendier night spots: Play It Again Sam's; Boone's; Chantilly Lace. Ditto the next day and evening. If necessary, I decided to do the B&E the next time they went out.

But Saturday, I caught a break. The temp was zero, not counting the wind chill. I was parked outside the brownstone Hank shared with the slut, listening to George Strait on the local country radio station, when Hank came out and got into his light blue Honda Prelude. Just in case we missed it, his vanity license plate said: P-LUDE 2. A sticker on his bumper said Oral Surgeons Satisfy. Another touted a local health club.

We drove the snow-packed streets over to MacArthur and turned south. He turned in at the Town and Country shopping center. I noticed that *The Russia House* was playing at the cinema, appropriate for the Siberian temperatures in Springfield and my playing tag with Hunt. I parked in front of the National Food Store and followed him inside. I pushed a shopping cart with a balky wheel along behind his. He picked up two six-packs of Perrier, lots of fruits and vegetables, Tender Vittles and Kitty Litter.

That's a clue, I thought.

Let's try reason, I thought.

I walked over to him. "You have a cat?" I began.

He was maybe six-three and looked like he worked out. Actually, he looked like he might be on steroids. He had short reddish blonde hair in a brush cut. He looked at least ten years younger than Sylvia. He stared at me for several long seconds, like maybe I had uneven and discolored teeth.

"I just got one," I continued. "A novice. I'm wondering whether canned food or—"

"Fuck off," he said.

So much for reason.

Trickery.

On Monday, I put on a pair of dark glasses, shoved a nondescript cap on my head and drove out to the pet store in

White Oaks Mall. I purchased a pet taxi and a dozen red roses in a vase at a flower shop. Then I drove to the apartment on South Sixth. I almost slipped on the icy front steps. I rang the bell. After about a minute, a green-eyed blonde in a red velour lounging suit answered. "Yes?"

I grinned. "Flower Power Incorporated delivering posies and poesy for you."

She smiled at me. Her teeth were whiter than white. "Oh, those are beautiful. Poesy?"

I tried to look around her, but all I could see was a long dark hallway. "I'm supposed to recite a poem," I said, my teeth chattering. "It's part of our service." I nodded at the hallway, indicating that the front step was not the appropriate place for a love poem.

She beamed. "How romantic. Please come in."

Flowers do it every time. What if I was Ted Bundy, I thought. She led me down the long hall to the living room. The apartment was long, laid out like railway cars. The living room was the middle car. I took a quick survey of the room. Large-screen TV. Lots of throw rugs on the oak floor. Traditional dark wood furniture. Bingo. A calico cat was lying in the window, sunning herself.

She clapped her hands. "Let me hear the poem."

I cleared my throat. "Roses are red, violets are blue, hand over the calico and these are for you." I knew my poem wasn't Vachel Lindsay, but hey, I made it up on the spot. I shoved the vase into her hands and turned toward the window.

"What is this?" she snapped.

I took off the dark glasses. "The flowers were a ruse," I said. "I'm here for Sylvia's cat."

She did a double take and then she narrowed her eyes. "Get the hell out of here, before I call the cops."

I shrugged. "Go ahead. You're holding stolen property."

"Huh?"

I walked over to the cat and fingered her collar. I read the silver identification disk. The cat nipped at my finger. Sharp

171

teeth. "This says she belongs to Sylvia Ransome. The lady wants her cat back. No trouble, no charges filed."

The blonde stared at me and then laughed. She lifted her left arm, pulled up the sleeve and showed me a long scratch from her wrist to her forearm. "I've just come from the doctor. I had to take a shot so I wouldn't get an infection. That *thing*—" she pointed to the cat—"scratched the hell out of me. That bitch can have *her* bitch back as far as I'm concerned. Hurry, get her out of here before Hank gets back."

I hustled out to the car, grabbed the pet taxi, brought it back in. I put it down and went over and stroked under Callie's chin. She rolled over on her back and purred. I tickled her stomach.

"Stop fooling around," the blonde said. "Hank might come home at any time. He has a hell of a temper."

"What are you going to tell him?"

She rolled her head back and forth. "You overpowered me."

I picked Callie up and carried her over to the pet taxi. I tried to nudge her in. She hissed and tried to twist out of my arms, but I forced her into the cage. She fussed all the way out to West Washington.

"Shut up," I said. "You *can* go home again."

Wrong.

Sylvia held Callie in her arms and baby-talked to her. Then she put her down. The calico walked regally over to the side of the new white couch, stretched and put her front paws on the arm of the couch. *"No!"* Sylvia shrieked. "Don't even think about it." She picked the cat up again. "Mommy's baby's going to have to be declawed. I didn't mind when you tore up Hank's stuff, but Mommy has all new things." She put her down.

Callie stared at Sylvia and then sauntered toward the kitchen.

"You are a miracle worker," Sylvia said to me. "Tell me all about it."

I did. Without editing.

"That bastard. That slut." She grinned. "A real ugly scratch?"

I nodded.

Sylvia almost purred. Callie had returned to the couch, eyeing it. "No, baby," Sylvia said. She picked up the cat again. "Did they teach you these bad tricks?"

Eventually, she put the cat down and wrote me a check. As she handed it to me, Callie started to scratch the couch.

"No!" Sylvia shouted. She ran over and batted the cat a good one. Callie raced off down the hall.

As I left, I said, "Get those locks changed."

"Satisfactory, Robert," the Speaker said, when I reported. "I owe you one."

"Thanks Rob," Lisa said when I called. "I owe you one."

"I'll think of something," I said.

A few days later, Sylvia Ransome called me at the office. "He stole her back," she said.

"How? Didn't you get those locks changed?"

"I did. But I wasn't home and he talked his way past the manager. Said he was picking up some of his clothes. Can you get her back?"

I sighed. I knew I should refuse, but I couldn't stand the Speaker-Lisa tag-team approach again. "I expect I can," I said. Where was I on that scale, I thought. Oh, yes. Breaking and entering.

Mitch agreed to be the lookout and drive the getaway car. That evening, we waited down the block in Mitch's Chevy Celebrity until Hank and the blonde went out on the town. Then I used a credit card to open the door to the apartment. I carried Callie out to the pet taxi where she promptly relieved herself.

"Nothing stinks like cat piss," Mitch said, firing up a cigar.

He drove me out to Sylvia's apartment. When I handed

the calico over to her, I said, "This is the end of the line. Finito. Endgame. It's your job to keep her now."

"Of course," she said. "I'll send you a check."

"Write it now," I said.

She did.

A week later, I got a call at the office from Sylvia Ransome. "Mr. Miles?"

"She's gone again? I told you—"

"That's not it," she said. "I've been thinking it over."

"Huh?"

"I may have been hasty."

"What do you mean?"

"I've been selfish. I want you to take Callie back to Hank," she said. "It's not fair for me to monopolize her."

"What happened? She throw up on the rug?"

"Yes. And she tore my couch to shreds before I could get the little bitch declawed. My drapes are ruined. Plus she refused to use her box. You know what that means. Are you sure that Hank's slut hates the cat?"

"It goes way beyond hate."

"I'll pay you twice what I did for you to get her to give her back."

I sighed. It was against my better judgment, but I knew I'd get the old one-two punch from the Speaker and Lisa if I didn't agree. "Okay," I said.

I called the apartment. The slut answered. "It's the roses-and-poetry guy. Let me talk to Hank," I said.

"Oh, Henry," I heard her call out.

He came on the line. "What do you want?"

"Sylvia has thought is over and she wants you to have Callie."

"No fucking way."

"What about joint custody?"

"Fuck off."

* * *

Well, let's try intimidation.

I drove to the Right Stuff, a bar on North Eleventh. The House is part-owner. Maximum Security Face Johnson was tending. He glowered at me. No one could remember the last bar fight when Max was tending. I think even Big was intimidated by Max.

"Big?" I said.

"Out of town."

"Oh? Like to pick up a quick hundred?"

"Doing what?"

"Just be yourself," I told him.

We tracked Hank to his health club.

"What the hell?" Hank said, trying to get up from the weight bench. Max held him down easily with one arm.

"This is Max Johnson," I said. "You may have read about him in *Police Beat*. When he was in the joint, a honky dentist yanked his wisdom teeth without any painkillers. He purely hates honky dentists. Do you get my drift?"

Hank gulped. "I'm an oral surgeon."

"A distinction without a difference to Max."

"That's a threat."

"That's a vow. Now, will you take Callie back?"

"What?"

"Sylvia's changed her mind."

He shook his head. "Cindy would kill me. No way, Jack."

"Max . . ."

Max pushed down on the weights.

"Okay, okay, I'll take the little bitch."

Then I thought it over. Did I really want that on my conscience? Did I want Lisa interrogating me about Callie's welfare? Did I want visitation rights?

"Forget it," I said. "You renounce all claims to the cat?"

"Yes."

I got a similar agreement from Sylvia. Then I called Lisa. "You owe me," I said.

"I do."

I told her what I wanted.

"I'd love to take her," she said. "But you forget one thing."

"What's that?"

"Otis."

"Cats and dogs can learn to live together."

"Rob, I just don't think it would work."

I set the pet taxi down in my living room. "Clockie," I called, "come meet your new roommate. Here's a chance to learn all about calicos."

Callie hissed.

Last Kiss

•

Douglas Borton

Gray was in no particular hurry to leave Craig Allen's house. The killing had been nearly silent, and he doubted that any of the neighbors had heard a thing. He figured he had time to take care of a few little details.

The first order of business was cleaning up the mess he'd made. Experience had taught him that it was a good idea to conceal evidence of a murder whenever possible. The longer it took the police to catch on, the colder the trail would be.

A sudden soft patter drew his gaze to the front windows. He watched as the glass was speckled with fat silver raindrops like beads of mercury. The squares of sky framed in the sash bars had turned an unreal shade of purple; distant palm trees shivered in gusts of wind. Somewhere thunder cracked.

Gray smiled. He'd always liked the summer thunderstorms that rumbled over the peninsula, bringing relief from the choking heat and the omnipresent August dogflies. The storm was a good omen, he was sure. The fates were on his side.

He lifted Allen's limp body off the couch and laid it gently on the hardwood floor, then examined the sofa. The damage wasn't too bad. A large burgundy splotch had discolored the center seat cushion, but other than that, he saw only a few random spatters here and there. The usual thing. He could take care of it in no time.

Under the kitchen sink he found a stash of cleaning supplies, next to a wastebasket stuffed with yesterday's St. Petersburg *Times*. Grinning, he retrieved the paper, unfolded it, and savored the headline: PINELLAS COUNTY KILLER CLAIMS NINTH VICTIM.

Number nine had been an elderly widow named Eleanor Ritter, who'd lived alone in a musty, dust-silvered house in Dunedin, just north of Clearwater. Gray had done her nearly a week ago, but her body had turned up only the day before yesterday, in a marshy tidal flat out on Honeymoon Island. Then all the local news outlets, which had been focusing on the summer heat and the Annual Fishathon and other such trivial nonsense, had redirected their attention to its proper object: himself. He'd been featured in every newscast, every paper, every radio call-in show.

Oh, he was famous, all right. A regular celebrity. And he loved it. Show business was his life.

Whistling, he filled a bucket with tapwater and detergent, carried it back to the living room, and set to work scrubbing off the stains, pausing frequently to wring out the sponge. The water in the bucket darkened to a muddy pink.

While he worked, he thought about his secret pastime and the pleasure it gave him, the dark, intoxicating thrill of taking an innocent life—the life of a victim selected by purest chance. It was, in fact, the element of chance, of randomness, that most appealed to him; any sort of logical motive would have made his hobby drearily pedestrian.

He never knew in advance that he would do it on a specific day. He would simply awaken and *feel* it. There were certain magical mornings when he could smell death in the Gulf breeze blowing through the lace curtains of his bedroom window, mornings when the distant cries of sea birds became the pleading voices of the damned.

It was on such mornings that Gray would hop in his battered Plymouth Horizon, roll down the windows, and cruise the sunlit streets for hours, driving up and down U.S. 19, cutting east or west on intersecting avenues, exploring the residential neighborhoods of St. Petersburg or Largo or Seminole. Finally he would ease to a stop in front of a particular house and say with a snap of his fingers, "That's the one." He could never say why any given house was the one. He just knew, that was all.

The late Craig M. Allen's house was a one-story bungalow on a quiet side street in St. Pete Beach. After choosing the house, Gray had parked two blocks away to ensure that his car would not be connected with the crime.

Approaching the bungalow on foot, he'd noticed a newspaper lying on the front steps, sealed in a plastic bag to protect it from the coming rain.

The newspaper bothered him. If anyone were home, the paper would surely have been picked up by—he checked his watch—eleven-thirty A.M. And this was a weekday; whoever lived at this address might not be back till six or later.

Gray frowned. He would have to get inside the house somehow and await his quarry's return. The ambush itself would be fun, but the waiting would be hard.

He was still contemplating the long, frustrating period of inactivity ahead when from inside the house rose a man's angry shout.

"Dammit! Dammit to hell!"

Glass shattered.

Gray's frown vanished. Somebody was home, after all.

He walked briskly up the path, mounted the front steps, and pulled on the rubber gloves he always wore. Then he rang the doorbell.

"Go away!" the same muffled voice screamed.

Gray leaned his fist on the buzzer.

"Fuck you! Fuck *everybody*!"

Gray shook his head, dismayed. He detested foul language. In his darker moments he often reflected sadly on the deteriorating moral standards of today's world.

Once again he rang the bell. This time he got no answer at all. It seemed the man simply was not in the mood for company.

He considered his options. He could sneak around to a side window and break in, but that would be messy and slightly risky; the guy might have a gun or something. Of course Gray himself was armed—he had a sweet little Luger .22 buried in one of the deep pockets of his raincoat—but he didn't want to use it; guns just weren't . . . well . . . aesthetic.

He decided on a different approach. In other, similar situations, he'd learned that a person was more likely to open the door when addressed by name.

Flipping up the lid of the mailbox, Gray found today's mail, which, like the newspaper, had yet to be picked up. Three envelopes in all. Two were addressed to Craig M. Allen; a third bore the name of a certain Ellen Norris.

"Mr. Allen?" Gray called out.

An endless stretch of silence. Then the man's voice quavered in answer.

"Yeah?"

Gray expelled a breath.

"Mr. Allen," he said smoothly, "I live over on the next block. Don't believe we've ever met. My name is—" he hesitated for a microsecond—"Dougherty. Kyle Dougherty. I've got a package for you. They delivered it to my address by mistake."

"Oh, the hell with it. Hell with it. Hell with it."

Gray detected a definite slur to Craig Allen's words. The man was drunk. Yes, stupid with liquor, tossing obscenities around, smashing things, and acting less than polite to his newfound neighbor, Mr. Dougherty, who'd been nice enough to bring over a misdelivered package on a stifling August morning damp with the threat of rain.

"I'm sorry, Mr. Allen. Couldn't quite catch that. Look, would you mind letting me hand this thing over to you? I've got to get to work."

If that didn't do it, Gray would break the door down. He was losing his patience.

"Okay, okay," Allen groused. "Hang on."

A moment later the door swung wide. Gray gazed at a man in his thirties, not too far from his own weight and build—broad shoulders, thick neck, strong legs—details that were easy enough to observe, since Allen was wearing nothing but a pair of eyeglasses and Jockey shorts. His eyes were sleepless and grief-haunted, bruised by purple crescents. He weaved briefly as if the floor were moving under him, then got a grip on the door frame for balance. His breath smelled like kerosene.

"So where is it?" Allen mumbled, looking around for a package.

"Right here," Gray said, and brought up his right foot, fast, driving the toe of his boot into the man's gut. Allen staggered backward, wheezing. Gray stepped through the doorway and shut the door behind him. There was a soft snick as the latch bolt slid into its socket.

Allen tried to speak. Only a low gurgle came out. Gray grabbed him by the arm and pitched him onto the nearest article of furniture, a battered couch leaking crumbs of stuffing out of its cushions. The springs groaned.

"Jesus." Allen shook his head groggily, finding his voice at last. He looked up at Gray, his filmy eyes swimming behind thick lenses. "Hey, man. That . . . that hurt."

Gray smiled. Slowly he withdrew the hammer from his coat pocket.

He had purchased the hammer at a hardware store in Tarpon Springs seven months ago, shortly before he began pursuing his hobby. It was a big hammer, more than a foot long, the largest one the store carried. Its wooden handle was as thick as two of Gray's meaty fingers. The cleft claw was enormous, jutting out savagely like the beak of some huge predatory bird. The business end of the hammer, its face and neck, consisted of a knob of blue steel, now pitted and scored; to Gray it always felt vaguely erotic when he fisted his hand over it. He liked to rub that cold steel cylinder and feel the short hairs of his groin bristle and itch.

Slowly, rhythmically, Gray slapped the hammer against his open palm. Each new blow made a dull meaty whack. It was the sound of steel striking flesh, and he liked it.

Craig Allen stared at the hammer, his lower lip trembling.

"Look, pal," he whispered. "I won't give you any trouble. You . . . you can take anything I've got. No problem."

He did not seem quite so soused anymore, Gray noticed. Funny how terror had a way of sobering you up faster than a cold shower ever could.

"There's plenty of stuff here for you," Allen went on, babbling now. "A pretty good color TV and a boombox and—"

"Shut up."

Allen shut up.

"I don't want your stuff, as you call it. I simply want to ask you a couple of questions."

"Questions?"

"Yes, Craig. Questions. First of all, just out of curiosity, why are you hitting the sauce before noon? You some kind of a lush?"

Allen lowered his head. Oddly he seemed almost ashamed of himself, as if for a moment his fear of the stranger in his house rapping a hammer against his open hand was overpowered by simple social embarrassment.

"No, it's not like that. See, I woke up this morning and found out my girlfriend had walked out on me. Left a note and everything. Just like in the movies." He ran a shaky hand through his hair and flashed a friendly, helpless, slightly goofy smile. "Guess I went a little nuts."

"Guess so," Gray agreed. "Don't you have a job to go to?"

"I'm enrolled at the Vo-Tech Institute, but I just couldn't hack it today. I'm learning how to repair air conditioners. I figure in Florida there'll always be a demand, you know?"

"Good plan. Now let me ask you another question. Do you know who I am?"

"Huh?" He was plainly baffled. "No. 'Course not. How could I?"

"Many people know me," Gray said softly. "People I've never even met."

"I don't get it."

"Have you ever heard of the Pinellas County Killer, Craig?"

Allen stared at him, his face a waxwork display. Then he

swallowed once. Gray watched his Adam's apple slide up and down in a slow, heavy motion.

"That's who I am," Gray continued, his voice very quiet, barely audible over the conch-shell roar of blood in his ears, that high, tuneless music he always heard at these moments. "What they call me anyway. My real name is considerably less dramatic. Would you like to know my real name?"

"No. No, please, don't tell me. Please."

"Leonard Gray." He smiled as Allen shut his eyes briefly. "Of course, having imparted that information to you, I'll have to make certain you don't pass it along to anyone else."

Allen hitched in a breath. His eyes were locked on the hammer as it rose and fell, rose and fell.

"No, man," he whispered. "Come on. Don't."

"Sorry, Craig. Looks like this just isn't your day."

Gray swung the hammer up. Allen let out a warbling yell and launched himself half off the couch. Sober, he might have caused Gray some serious problems; but alcohol and self-pity had slowed him down and left him weak, so it was easy enough to shove him back onto the sofa, then bring down the hammer in a deadly arc that sent its blunt end smashing into his face.

Allen's glasses exploded in a spray of plastic bits. The first high fluting note of a scream escaped his lips, and then Gray caught him in the throat with the hammer's claw and tore his larynx out. He beat the man again and again, crunching bone, laughing, till finally Allen lay still, his near-naked body spangled in red, a bloody harlequin.

Gray dropped the hammer and stood leaning over the couch, breathing hard. Then slowly, almost reverently, he knelt and took Allen's head in his hands, cradling it gently. He kissed his victim's forehead, his eyes, his cheeks.

"Thank you, Craig," he whispered between great gulps of air. "Thank you so very much."

He kissed the corpse one last time, as always, on the mouth.

Gray smiled now, remembering the kill and above all that

last kiss, the final tribute he paid to each of his victims. He liked to think of it as a goodnight kiss.

After half an hour he'd gotten out the worst of the stains. He surveyed his work and nodded, satisfied. As a final touch, he knelt by the corpse, lifted its head, and sponged up the small pool of blood that had formed on the floor while Allen lay there observing the clean-up procedure with his sightless, glassy doll's eyes.

The only unfinished business was the small matter of hiding the late Mr. Allen's remains. In daylight, even in this downpour, it would be too risky to remove the body from the house and dispose of it in the Gulf as he'd done with Eleanor Ritter, but he could at least stash the corpse in an attic or cellar, where it might not be found for several days. By then, even if some of the neighbors had chanced to see him or his car, their memories would be safely hazy and indistinct.

Still mulling over possible places of concealment, Gray emptied the bucket into the kitchen sink. There was a bad moment when he was afraid the blood-red water wouldn't go down; the drain was sluggish, partly clogged. Then gradually the water level lowered, till the last of the evidence spiraled away with a gurgle and hiss.

He returned to the living room, clapping his hands busily the way people do after completing a tedious but necessary chore, and that was when he saw the cat.

A black Siamese, huddled under an occasional table directly across from the couch. No doubt it had been there the whole time.

It must have seen everything.

Gray approached the table and got down on hands and knees.

"Here, kitty, kitty."

The Siamese stared back at him with round, frightened, deeply green eyes.

Gray extended a gloved hand. The cat shrank back, hissing, showing its fangs. Gray frowned.

"Not very friendly, are we?"

184

He reached into his pocket and pulled out a short coil of rope, an item he always carried with him when he was on the prowl; vaguely he'd imagined that it might come in useful for binding a victim's hands. He flicked the rope at the kitty in short mouse-like hops. The cat watched, fascinated.

"Come on, puss. Want to play?"

Tentatively the Siamese reached out with one paw. Gray jerked the cord just out of its reach. The cat regarded it with a quizzical expression, then tried again. Gray drew the rope toward him in fits and starts, while the cat, its fear forgotten in the excitement of the hunt, scrambled in reckless pursuit, squirming out from under the table.

Smoothly Gray seized it by the scruff of the neck. He rose to his feet, lifting the cat in one hand, while with the other he pocketed the rope.

He studied the animal as it fidgeted in his grasp, mewling and hissing. He caught a glint of silver at its throat. An I.D. tag.

He snapped the tag free of the cat's blue nylon collar, then held it up to the window. A fork of lightning dazzled the sky, briefly illuminating the square of metal.

Angel, it said.

"So," Gray breathed, tightening his grip on the Siamese. "You're a girl cat, then? My little Angel? How sweet. How very, very sweet."

He dropped the nametag on the floor.

Gray was almost sorry for what he had to do next. He liked animals, he truly did; they always seemed so innocently trusting.

But the cat had seen the crime.

And in his line of work, there must be no witnesses.

He wrapped both hands around the cat's delicate neck and squeezed. The Siamese writhed furiously, her tiny legs bicycling, her paws slashing empty space. Gray felt the pulsing energy in her body, the frantic palpitations of her heart, the beat of blood in the veins of her neck. Life. That was what he felt. He squeezed harder.

The cat struggled a moment longer, then gave up, going

limp, a furry rag doll in his hands. Her eyelids fluttered weakly. Still squeezing, Gray drew the animal close to his face, staring fascinated at her eyes, hoping to see them glaze over, to catch the exact instant of transition from life to death. He was a connoisseur of such things.

Abruptly the cat was jolted with a last spasm of energy. She lashed out at Gray, her claws raking his cheeks, drawing blood.

He screamed in surprise and pain. His fingers splayed. The cat fell free, dropping to the floor where she landed with feline adroitness, and then she was a blurred streak, arrowing out of the living room, down the hall, gone.

Gray mopped his face with one hand; the glove came away tacky with blood. Dammit. That little bitch had hurt him.

He marched into the kitchen, found the cutlery drawer, and removed a knife with a sharp serrated blade. Its small clever teeth caught the lamplight and smiled at him.

"I'm coming, kitty," Gray said low under his breath. "Coming for you."

He strode down the hall and stopped at the first open doorway, looking in on a dark room smelling faintly of sweat. He found the wall switch and flipped it up.

A bedroom. His circling gaze took in a bed sloppy with tangled sheets, a nightstand displaying a telephone in the shape of a football, and, against the far wall, a towering bookcase, its tiers of shelves crammed with paperback books in dusty disarray.

On top of the bookcase, between a globe of the earth and a silver-plated amateur sports trophy of some kind, was the cat. She was hunched there, regarding him coolly with her green gaze, flicking her tongue like a large furry lizard sunning itself on a rock.

Gray returned the cat's stare while he ran his thumb over the knife blade. A familiar tension in his facial muscles told him that he was smiling.

He approached the bookcase, his eyes locked on the cat, then stood on tiptoe and stabbed at her. The cat drew back, flattening herself bonelessly against the wall, staying inches out of his range.

Gray swore. He stared up at the Siamese.

"I find you most annoying," he said quietly.

Angel returned his stare in silence.

He considered using his Luger. One squeeze of the trigger, and a metal-jacketed .22-caliber hollow-point round would be embedded in Angel's heart. Nice and easy.

But the sound of a gunshot might attract some neighbor's attention, and Gray hadn't hidden Allen's remains yet.

With a sigh, he gave up on the idea of shooting the cat. He would have to find another way to take care of her.

He left the bedroom and returned to the kitchen. Clamping the knife between his teeth, he took hold of one of the four tubular kitchen chairs and carried it down the hall. When he got back inside the bedroom, he was pleased to see that the cat had not moved from its perch.

"Should have run and hid when you had the chance," he said around a mouthful of stainless steel.

He planted the chair directly before the bookcase, then stood on it. His new elevation brought him face to face with the cat. She was easily within his reach now, trapped between the globe and the trophy, with nowhere to run. Slowly he guided the knife toward her glossy belly. Her jade eyes flicked from Gray's face to the blade to his face again.

"Going to skewer you, puddy tat. Going to make puss-kabob out of you."

His arm tensed as he prepared to drive the knife home, and in that instant the Siamese sprang straight up in the air and sailed over his head.

Gray spun on the chair, slashing wildly at the cat and missing. The effort cost him his balance. The chair tipped. He teetered, windmilling his arms, then crashed down on his side. The knife punched a ragged gash in his left forearm. He cried out like a child spread-eagled on the asphalt of a playground.

When he turned his head, he saw Angel looking at him from across the floor. He lobbed a curse at her. She turned and vanished out the bedroom door, racing in the direction of the kitchen.

Gray was really mad now. He was the Pinellas County Killer, for Christ's sake. He had murdered ten people. The entire St. Petersburg area was afraid of him. All of Florida knew his name and feared it. And here he was, being shown up, humiliated, outwitted and outmaneuvered, bloodied and beaten by a lousy stinking little house cat. It just wasn't right.

He got to his feet, tore off a strip of the cotton bed sheet, and wound it around his bleeding arm to form a makeshift tourniquet. Then he ran out of the bedroom in pursuit of the cat.

"Come on out and fight, you coward," he gasped, wincing at the bright steely pain of the knife wound. "Come on!"

In the kitchen he stopped, his attention caught by a soft rapping sound. Thump. Thump. Thump. He tracked the source of the sound to the back door and looked down. At his feet, a small pet door was swinging on its hinges, banging softly.

Gray unlocked the back door, opened it, and squinted into a mist of rain sizzling with intermittent lightning strokes. A violet sky hung over a cement patio scattered with a few sticks of lawn furniture: a recliner and a couple of web-backed chairs. Past the patio lay the back yard itself, small and green and fenced in.

The cat was nowhere in sight. But she was out there somewhere.

"I'll get you," Gray murmured. "I swear I will."

He no longer remembered exactly why he had to get the cat. He knew only that he wanted, *needed*, to kill her. He yearned for it, he craved it, the desperate imperative of it burned in him with monomaniacal intensity. That cat was a monster, demon, hellspawn—Angel, indeed!—and he would be doing the world a favor when he expunged her from existence, as he soon would.

Gray stepped outside into the punishing rain. He staggered around the yard, searching for the cat, whispering her name over and over in an ugly, chortling monotone.

At the side of the house stood an oak tree. He gazed up at it, and a thrill shuddered through him as he saw the black Siamese perched in its branches.

He threw aside the knife and drew his gun. He no longer cared if the neighbors heard the shot or if a whole platoon of cops arrived in response to somebody's 911 call. He was going to get rid of that goddamn cat, and he was going to do it right now.

But before he could fire, Angel hopped nimbly from the tree to the roof of the bungalow, then scampered up to the ridgeline where the two sloping sides of the roof met. She hunkered down there, a small black shape in semisilhouette against the stormy sky.

Gray tried taking aim. The spiky TV aerial blocked his view. He maneuvered to the left and squinted through the gun sight again, then shook his head. His target was too far away, and he wasn't much of a marksman. He knew he would miss at this range.

He had to get closer.

He stripped off his gloves and pocketed them along with the Luger, then grabbed hold of the oak tree's lowest branch and hoisted himself up. Muscles popped in his shoulders and arms. Grunting with strain, sneezing as rainwater swirled over his face, he rose from branch to branch, till finally he was level with the roof's overhang.

He jumped. He landed on the roof with a good solid thud that jarred his teeth. For a moment he lay motionless, gripping the ragged shingles and gathering his strength. Then he began crawling up the thirty-degree incline on all fours, not unlike a cat himself. Lightning crackled and hissed. Rain beat at his face. Wet strands of his wind-whipped hair flew around him in a fishing-line snarl.

A yard from the peak of the roof, he stopped. Angel stood above him, hunched and frozen, a gargoyle glowering down at him as balefully as the blue-black thunderheads boiling in the sky.

"You're history, kitty cat," Gray breathed. "All your nine lives are up."

He rose to a crouch, bracing himself against the TV antenna, then fumbled the Luger out of his coat pocket and aimed directly at the cat. No way he could miss at this range. He smiled, imagining the small furry body dropping like a bag of blood to the ground.

Gray was still smiling as his index finger drew down on the trigger, and then thunder boomed directly overhead, and he was burning—oh, God, oh, Jesus—he was on fire, his jaws locked, eyes dazzled, brain hissing with static.

Lightning. The TV antenna—he'd been leaning against it—*Christ*.

Convulsions took him. He tumbled down the roof, turning cartwheels and somersaults like a giddy child, his trigger finger twitching spastically, firing the gun again and again, blowing bloody holes in his gut. He flopped onto the gurgling drainpipe, which cracked under his weight and sent him spinning toward the white square of the patio, and he heard himself screaming, a high-pitched womanish shriek, in the instant before he smacked into the cement with a wet snap of bone. It was the sound of his neck breaking.

Then he just lay there on his back, paralyzed, numb all over, leaking blood, gargling rainwater, and trying desperately to breathe.

Can't die, he told himself. Can't. Not me. It's the other ones who always die. Isn't it?

At the edge of his vision he caught a flicker of motion near the base of the oak tree. Angel.

The Siamese crept toward him, impelled by the proverbial curiosity of felines. She circled his body, mewing softly, then climbed onto his chest and gazed down at him from inches away. Her small quizzical face filled his world. Gray wished he could move. Wished he had the use of his hands. His wringing, squeezing, strangling hands.

I hate you, he told the cat voicelessly. Hate you so much. You bitch. You goddamn furry little bitch.

Angel studied him a moment longer in respectful silence, then lowered her head and licked Leonard Gray's face, bestowing on him a last loving kiss of her own.

Little Cat Feet

·

Les Roberts

The first thing I noticed was the smell. You'd have noticed it too, unless you're one of those people who's cut off your nose to spite your face.

It was an acrid, ammonia odor that made my eyes water; I could feel it sinking into my clothes and hair, the kind of stink that makes door-to-door political canvassers and magazine salesmen and Jehovah's Witnesses do a direct about-face and go away before they ever ring the doorbell. I sneezed. It was the smell of a cat litter box that hadn't received enough attention—magnified to the tenth power.

The house was a Moorish wet dream, all inlaid mosaic tile and squinches and horseshoe arches, with jacaranda and fever trees and hummingbird-enticing bottle brush growing in profusion up to the carved wooden door set into the wall around the house. It was set high in the sere hills above Cahuenga Boulevard and the Hollywood Bowl, in a neighborhood where all the eccentric has-beens from moviedom's Golden Age are holed up waiting for the bean counters who run the industry now to once again start doing films like Mr. DeMille used to make. Only an eccentric would choose to live in a house accessible only to mountain goats or four-wheel-drive vehicles, solely for the privilege of having a high-angle view of a city so socked in by brown air pollution that it makes you cough just to look at it. They all like to go out on their balconies at night, shake their fists at the lights behind the smog, and vow, "Big town, I'll lick you yet."

I pushed the button inset into the stucco arch, and immediately got an answering buzz. As I'd been instructed, I opened the wooden door and went through into a walled garden where several varieties of palm and exotic shrubbery imported to Southern California from someplace else grew in overprofusion. The place was badly in need of pruning shears—or a machete. The door to the house was open and Louise Manaster stood framed in the archway. She was dressed in billowy crepe lounging pajamas in a rich shade of gray, and her hair was pulled back into a matching turban. Unlike many Hollywood women of her generation, she didn't resort to makeup by the trowelful, and if she'd had any cosmetic surgery it was the good kind that didn't show. I knew from my movie history that she had to be around seventy years old. She looked fifty-five, and though she was not beautiful, she was handsome instead, conveying the illusion of beauty. And in this town, the illusion is all that matters.

"Mr. Saxon?" she said. "Please come in."

The litter box smell was stronger inside the house, almost overwhelming. In the air everywhere were fine little cat hairs, and a ray of sun coming in through one of the arched windows turned them silver, dancing on a current of air. From where I stood in the atrium entry I could see eight cats in various stages of recline and repose—three Siamese, two Persian, and three shorthairs whose ancestry could probably be traced back four generations in the past year alone. One of the Siamese, a bluepoint, came over to me and muttered, her tail a vertical question mark over her back. I sneezed violently. I have a slight allergy to cat hair.

If you've ever seen a movie produced in Hollywood before 1962 you've seen Louise Manaster's costumes on the bodies of every leading actress in the business. Back when people knew the stars as well as their own families and the only director they knew about was Hitchcock, most Americans could have told you her name and what she did for a living. On the mantle in her living room were a row of her Academy

Award statuettes, more than anyone else in film history, displayed as casually as a stone mason from Jersey might show off his bowling league trophies.

She led me into the living room and indicated that I should sit on an ornate Chinese-red sofa that curved around in an L-shape for about fourteen feet. It was covered with cat hair. Louise Manaster arranged herself on a low-slung silk pouffe as big as a poker table, hands clasped around one silk-clad knee. One of the cats, a gray, jumped up on my lap and began kneading my thigh with her needle claws. I gently pushed her onto the floor with the back of my hand, and sneezed three times.

"Don't you like cats, Mr. Saxon?"

"Yes, but not when I'm wearing a dark suit. And their hair gets into my nose. I guess I prefer dogs."

"Pity," she said. "Dogs are subservient, fickle, fawning, and co-dependent, and will lick the hand of whoever feeds them. But a relationship with a cat cannot be taken for granted. It must be carefully negotiated on both sides." She drew herself up proudly. "I am a cat person," she said, which told me I was in for a negotiation.

"What did you want to see me about, Miss Manaster?"

The frail shoulders rose and fell. "Do you investigate theft?"

I shrugged, not wanting to commit myself. I've been in Hollywood long enough to know that. "What's been stolen?"

She uncoiled herself from where she'd been sitting, and went over to the fireplace. She was a tall woman, slim and elegant, and only her hands, liver-spotted with enlarged knuckles, tattled on her age. She took something from the mantle where it had been half-hidden between two of her Oscars and brought it to me, holding it in the palm of a hand that trembled slightly. It was a jeweled pin, black onyx in the shape of a sleek cat in motion. The eyes were two emeralds, the collar was made up of tiny rubies, and there were enough diamonds embedded in the backing to purchase a small yacht.

"This," she said. Two more cats wandered in from another part of the house. That made ten, and still counting.

"I don't understand. You have it in your hand."

Her lip curled into an unpleasant sneer. "It's obviously a copy, Mr. Saxon." It wasn't all that obvious to me. "The original was given to me by the head of a major studio many years ago, as a sort of thank-you gift. I discovered it missing the same night Derek left me."

"Derek?" She was going to tell it in her own way, I could see that, and in her own sweet time. I leaned back on the hairy sofa, ready to dig in for the duration.

Derek Hawke had come to town eight months earlier from someplace in the Midwest where they grow corn and mine gypsum, determined to hit it big in films or television. You've heard the story before; we all have. He was a big hunky guy with blue eyes and golden hair, and had gotten a job as a stock boy at the May Company on Wilshire Boulevard and Fairfax Avenue, where after only two days he was "discovered" by Louise Manaster. She'd installed him in her Moorish palace in the hills and footed the bill for a new wardrobe, acting lessons, and a leased Cadillac convertible, and had made a few calls to old friends who were still alive and hanging on at the studios. She didn't have as much influence in town as the bus boy at Spago's—she hadn't costumed a film since the early seventies and half the hairy-nosed children who now run the business never even heard of her. But poor Derek, the movie-struck kid, had heard of her, counted the Oscars over the hearth, and perceived in her a ticket to fame.

And then two nights ago, the love-birds had quarreled—loud enough for all the neighbors to hear them—and after making a phone call Derek had stomped out, taking with him only a small overnight bag.

"What was the argument about?" I said.

She waved a vague hand. "He felt his career wasn't progressing as it should have. I tried to explain that some things take time, but . . ." She sat down again, playing with the pin, rubbing it between thumb and forefinger like a lucky penny.

It's amazing how many innocents of both genders come

from the provinces and drop their drawers in this town for a chance at stardom, and how few of them actually sleep with the right people.

"Why didn't he take his convertible?" I interrupted.

She looked sad, ruined. "He threw the keys at me. He said he didn't want anything of mine. That's why he left all his clothes here."

I was impressed. A gigolo with scruples. Every day brings something new, I suppose.

"He called me—oh, he said some terrible things to me, Mr. Saxon. I don't think I can ever forgive him for that." She covered her face with her hands.

I put my knuckle up under my nose to stifle another cat-induced sneeze. "And you think he stole the real pin?"

"Certainly not!" she said.

I held my hands out, palms up. "Then . . . ?"

"It was a mistake, a—an impulsive misjudgment, that's all. Derek is no thief. The pin was out on the coffee table—I'd just reclaimed it from the jeweler, who'd replaced a loose clasp. I think he just—took it by accident."

Sure. And Santa Claus, the Tooth Fairy, and the Easter Bunny were all paid-up members of the Screen Actors Guild.

The story stunk. It had a lousy beat, you couldn't dance to it, and I gave it about a fifty-five. "What is it you want me to do?" I said.

"Get my pin back," Louise Manaster said.

Cute. She was figuring if I found the pin I'd find her precious Derek. Maybe I would.

I could have just said no. That would have been the smart thing. But I'm an old movie buff, too. How could I refuse the woman who had dressed Lana Turner, Ava Gardner, Katharine Hepburn, Lauren Bacall, and Rita Hayworth? Besides, this way I could bill her for having the cat hair cleaned out of my suit.

Otherwise I'd be sneezing for a month.

The first thing I did was to check the sleazy hock shops down on South Main Street, and on Sherman Way in the

San Fernando Valley, but I did so with small faith. The pin was probably in the pocket of some junkie trying to unload it in a parking lot along with ten or twelve watches he'd wear all up and down both arms. There must be at least ten thousand down and outers to fit that description in L.A.

Louise Manaster had given me a list of names she'd called on Derek's behalf, people she knew in the industry. They obviously hadn't gotten him a contract, but other than the guys in the stockroom at the May Company, all of whom were themselves stars of tomorrow, I couldn't think of anyone else in town who knew him.

Albert Sussman wasn't one of the original founders of Monarch Pictures, but he'd been there since the beginning and produced several films which you've probably seen on a cable station specializing in oldies. Now in his eighties, he maintained an office on the lot, the oldtimers from the prop department or studio security tipped their hats to him and called him Mr. Sussman, and everyone else pretty much ignored him. There were high-level executives at Monarch, guys in their late thirties or early forties who oversaw every phase of the filmmaking operation, who hadn't the foggiest idea who Sussman was, and were just waiting for him to die so they could utilize his office.

He was wearing a light-colored suit, white shirt, and black string tie the morning I visited him at the studio, and was smoking an expensive cigar, the tip of which he'd managed to gum into a disgusting soggy mess. He looked like the owner of a Brazilian rubber plantation.

"Ah, one of Louise's protegés," he said, nodding. "They come and go so quickly, it's hard to keep track. It's a god damn shame, a woman like that, at her age, running around with some young putz the age of her grandchildren . . ."

"Don't you go out with women young enough to be your grandchildren, Mr. Sussman?"

He switched his cigar from the left corner of his mouth to the right. "I don't 'go out' with them. They're hookers. It's an entirely different proposition."

"Could you take a look at this for me?" I said, showing him a head shot I'd found in Derek Hawke's personal effects. In fact I'd found about five hundred of them, a not-yet-arrived actor's calling card. He looked handsome, vulnerable, and nearly indistinguishable from all the other kids his age who were waiting on tables or working in stockrooms or had latched on to some rich and ultimately powerless patron like Louise Manaster.

Sussman studied it. "This one, yes. He was in here about a month ago, wanting to be a star. I didn't see much magic in him, Mr. Saxon. There's a million pretty faces and bodies out there—youth is a commodity that's a drug on the market—but there has to be magic or else it's no good. James Dean. The young Brando. Cagney, Gary Cooper, Jimmy Stewart—that kind of magic. This kid?" He smacked his lips around the cigar and gave a deprecating little wave. "I made a few calls for him, but nobody much listens to me anymore around here, so it came to nothing." He shook his head sadly. "He seemed to know he was on a treadmill. There was a sadness about him." He raised his eyebrows. "Not that good, bankable Montgomery Clift kind of sensitivity, mind you. Just a sad kid."

"Sad about what?"

"What did he have to be glad about?" Sussman said. "No talent, no career, not a pot of his own to piss in, and screwing a woman fifty years his senior just to survive. Of course he was a sad kid." He pushed the picture back across the desk at me as though it were grossly pornographic. "I give him one more month in this town before it chews him up and spits him out."

"Sad, Mr. Sussman—do you mean desperate, too?"

"You go beyond that here," he said. "You realize that your whole life you've been chasing the wind, you don't get desperate. You get down—lower down than a worm's ass—once you realize you aren't worth two cents in a town that loves a buck the way a nun loves her beads."

"Is that where Derek Hawke was when you saw him?"

He carefully, deliberately blew smoke at me. Most of the

time I gag on cigar smoke, but this cigar was so fine and so expensive that I didn't mind it. I rather liked it, in fact.

"Close," he said.

The Bolt-Sharman Agency was located south of Wilshire on Beverly Drive, in one of those two-story low-rent office buildings that survive only because there's not enough room to build a high-ticket glass monolith in its place. The building had been there for forty years, and so had Frank Sharman, whose heyday had coincided with those low-budget *Attack of the Giant Puppet People* features of the middle fifties. Then Irving Bolt died, and the agency, now on hard times, handled day players—pretty young people who could stand around looking good and not have to act, who might pick up a few days' work a month but would never see their name above the title. If they had anything on the ball they left Frank Sharman early in their careers; in fact it was well known in casting circles that if Bolt-Sharman represented you, you were pretty much a loser.

"Derek Hawke? Yeah, I sent him out on a couple of calls," Frank Sharman said. He was seventy-two years old, and affected the rich hippie look of the late, lamented Love Generation—long sideburns, a vivid silk shirt, faded blue jeans, and a scarf. His glasses were steel-rimmed, perfectly round, and the lenses were tinted gray. All that was missing was a Liverpudlian accent and Yoko Ono hanging on his arm.

"I only bothered with him as a favor to Louise. It's not enough to look nice—the kid just doesn't have any pizzazz. I knew it when he walked in the door. I'm surprised Louise didn't know it, either." He smiled and gave me one of those just-between-us-guys leers. "Of course, her judgment was—ah—clouded." He made a circle of his left thumb and forefinger and made an in-and-out motion through it with his right middle finger. Just in case I hadn't gotten his drift. Just in case I was terminally stupid.

"You have an address for him?"

He pursed his mouth. "Louise's house."

"Do you know his friends, then? Who he hung out with?"

"Hung out?" Sharman sat forward in his chair. "He hung out here. In my waiting room. Every goddamn day, whining for a job, for an audition, for some crumb." He shook his head. "All actors are crybabies, but they ought to frame him."

All of a sudden he remembered who he was talking to, but he was discomfited only a little bit. "Sorry, I forgot you're in the business, too. But I've been an agent forty years and I can spot a winner coming down the street—or a loser. You know what I mean?"

"Yeah, I know what you mean," I said. I hate movie people—they're all very impressed with themselves. In my hunt for Louise Manaster's cat pin I was running into a lot of them. "Do you remember what calls you sent him on?"

"That was six weeks ago!" he said. "I don't even remember if my bowels moved this morning. Ask Paige."

"Paige?"

He waved his hand toward the door. "The girl."

Frank Sharman's "girl" was a fresh-faced kid of about twenty-three, with honey-colored hair and a complexion right out of Iowa. Periwinkle-blue eyes. The body of a cheerleader. The nameplate on her desk said she was Paige Smith. Smith, for God's sake. She'd probably been a straight-B student, was voted Best Personality by her senior class, and made Toll House cookies that'd knock your socks off. You know the type. I wanted to ask what a nice girl like her was doing in a place like Hollywood. But I knew. The same thing they're all doing here—chasing after empty dreams and trying to convince themselves they're living. The entire city of Los Angeles is in denial.

She was going through her casting sheets, her tongue sticking out between her teeth as she concentrated, running down the list of names with a pink-tipped fingernail that was too long for a secretary but just right for an aspiring movie queen. I noticed the finger trembled a bit, and that there were purplish smudges beneath those blue eyes. Hollywood was giving her a rough time, I supposed. What a surprise. I wondered if it was drugs, booze, or a shattered love affair. Or maybe just that she'd come out here to be a star too, like Derek Hawke, and had suddenly opened her eyes to find herself someone's "girl" at a fly-by-night agency that couldn't have gotten Olivier a job if they were doing *Hamlet* down on the corner.

"We sent Derek Hawke over to ABC for extra work on a soap on the seventeenth of June," she said. "And to Disney—well, Touchstone, really—about a picture on the twenty-fifth." Her voice sounded soft and muffled, like she'd just drunk a glass of milk.

"Did he get either one of them?"

She shook her head sadly. "Not even a callback. Look, he isn't in any trouble, is he?"

"I don't know," I said. "Why?"

Her shrug was elaborately offhanded. "He just seemed like a nice guy, that's all. He was over here a lot, and I sort of got to know him."

"I don't suppose you'd know where he might be."

She stared at something absolutely fascinating about four inches above my head. "I didn't know him *that* well."

"Oh."

"Sometimes when people come in here a lot, you get involved with their problems whether you want to or not. You know, they sit around waiting for something to come in so they can go out on a call, and you get to talking . . ."

"Uh-huh."

"It's no big deal."

"No," I said. I pointed at the casting ledger. "Anything else?"

She resumed her search, and when she spoke again her voice was lower, less shrill. "Here—he went to read for Andrew Nicholson on the third."

"June third?"

"Uh-huh."

I jotted Nicholson's name down on my little spiral pad. "Do you remember the last time you saw Derek?"

"Last Monday," she said promptly. The day he disappeared from Louise Manaster's bed and board. With the cat pin.

I gave her my business card. "It's kind of important that I find him. Will you call me if you see him again?"

"I probably won't see him again."

"I thought he hung out here a lot."

"Oh, well, yes, but if he's in some sort of trouble . . ."

She didn't finish her sentence. She didn't have to.

At about eight o'clock the next morning a Korean gardener discovered Derek Hawke's body. He was down at the foot of Louise Manaster's hill, just off the edge of her property line, staring at the smog-stained sky with sightless eyes. There were stab and slash wounds in his neck, stomach, and finally in his chest. A subsequent coroner's report said that he had been dead since Monday evening, and that the cause of death seemed to be from a pointed, dull-edged instrument like a nail file. Wherever he'd been heading when he slammed out of Louise Manaster's house, he hadn't gotten very far. I heard the news on the radio, and immediately checked with Lt. Joe DiMattia of LAPD Homicide, who told me the only belongings they'd found on or near the body were an overnight bag with underwear and socks, a shaving kit, a wallet with a driver's license from the state of Missouri, and forty-six dollars and change in his pocket. No cat pin. Maybe the Korean gardener had swiped it before he called the cops—but I didn't think so.

It was DiMattia's personal opinion that the Manaster woman had killed Derek Hawke because he was trying to leave her, and all my protestations that she would hardly have dumped him down the hill and left him there for two days fell on deaf ears. Maybe it was because she was my client and he wanted to believe the worst of her. Maybe he really thought his scenario made sense. Joe DiMattia could be the poster boy for that slogan about a mind being a terrible thing to waste.

When I got to the house, a grave-looking older man in a vest, tie, and shirtsleeves opened the door, announced that he was Miss Manaster's doctor, and said she couldn't see anyone right now because she was "prostrate" and under sedation.

If I had Joe DiMattia suspecting me of murder I'd be prostrate, too. She had the motive and the opportunity, but somehow she didn't strike me as the type of person who'd kill a young man and leave him down at the bottom of her hill for the mice. Or care that someone else had. Louise Manaster had been in Hollywood long enough to know that everything is temporary; careers, lovers, TV series, they all had their time and then they were no more. That's why almost ninety percent of the buildings in town have been built since 1956.

Several cats, including one I hadn't seen before, swirled lazily around the doctor's feet like water rising in a bathtub. I said, "Please tell Miss Manaster I came by."

He looked at me with distaste. "You're a trifle older than her usual companions. You won't last, you know."

I sat in the car and smoked a cigarette before driving back down the hill. I repressed a shudder; being mistaken for Louise Manaster's fancy man wasn't my idea of a joke. How many other young men and women, coming to Hollywood to chase a dream, had fallen into the same kind of dead-end trap? I was glad I had my investigations agency to support me during the lean times. At least I could face myself in the bathroom mirror every morning.

Louise Manaster had given me a healthy retainer, which made me feel better about the whole thing. I'm not dumb—I knew that the object of the whole exercise was not to recover her gem-encrusted cat but to recover her young lover. With him dead, it seemed rather pointless. Items like that are usually insured, and can be replaced.

But I did have her money, and a contract to find the jeweled cat pin, so I doggedly kept at it. Maybe Andrew Nicholson knew something about it.

He was one of those Hollywood characters that seems to show up at every party, every charity function, every major premiere. He had produced a few low-budget pictures that no one remembered, but ask anyone in town about Andrew

Nicholson and they'll either tell you about his open predilection for good-looking young boys, or the fact that he had inherited more money than he knew what to do with from his mother, who had not only been a mid-level star in the thirties, but had made several marriages to movie moguls and investment bankers that had been, to say the least, financially if not emotionally rewarding.

Nicholson's house was up above Sunset Plaza Drive in West Hollywood, with an even better view of the smog than from the Manaster place. Alabaster statues of well-endowed Greek males standing before Doric columns flanked the doorway. I don't know who it was that let me in, but he was about nineteen, with beefy shoulders and biceps and the kind of tan that you have to work at, and was wearing a lavender tank top and white rayon shorts. He had violet eyes and a full, sensual mouth, and tufts of black hair stuck out from under his arms like the wings of a raven.

"Andrew is out by the pool," he said. He wasn't very happy to see me; maybe he was worried that I'd cut in on his action. Andrew Nicholson's relationships with his young men tended not to last much more than a few months, and perhaps this one was sensing that his time on the hill was running out. In any case, he gracelessly left me standing in the atrium while he went off to do whatever it was he did to fill his waking hours. Probably there was an exercise room somewhere in the house that had been built just for him, or his predecessor, or twenty predecessors past.

Andrew was indeed out by the pool, which I managed to find without much trouble on the other side of a thirty-foot wall of glass. That's why they pay me the big bucks.

"Mr. Saxon, how delightful to see you again," he said, not getting up. I couldn't remember where I'd met him, and I'm sure he couldn't either, but the way he said *delightful* left no doubt in my mind that it wasn't.

He was stretched out on a chaise longue, wearing a skimpy black bikini and basted from head to foot with tanning oil. An expensive tape deck was playing Tchaikovsky next to his ear. He was in pretty good shape for a man of fifty, but he didn't look as though he used the exercise room the way his live-in friend did. He invited me to sit down by patting the pad next to him, but I chose a deck chair several feet away. No fool I.

"Shall I have Sean bring you something to drink?"

I politely declined and told him why I was there.

"Of course I remember Derek Hawke," he said. "A lovely young man. He read for me some weeks ago."

"For what?" I said.

"I'm preparing to do a picture. The script is nearly finished."

I knew what that meant. Nothing. It was either the standard brand of Hollywood bullspeak to cover the fact that he had nothing going at the moment, or else Frank Sharman was sending him handsome young actors to interview just for the hell of it. There is little difference between a Hollywood agent and a pimp anyway, but most aren't quite as blatant about it. At least pimps get to wear more interesting clothes.

"When's the last time you saw him?"

He lay back on the cushion, eyes closed, baking in the afternoon sun. "I don't really recall. Perhaps two weeks ago."

"But he read for you on June third. This is July eighteenth."

"Mmm-hmmm," he said, his tone insinuating.

"So you saw him after the reading?"

"Of course I did. Don't be tiresome, Mr. Saxon."

I leaned over and snapped off the music. "If you'd listen to the radio instead of your tapes, Andrew, you'd know that Derek Hawke has been murdered."

His eyes flew open and beneath his tan he lost a lot of color. He sat up. "My God," he said.

"If I could trace him back here, the police can, too. So I suggest you talk to me."

"Are you insinuating . . . ?"

"No," I said. "I just want to talk."

He mopped his face with a fluffy red towel. In the bright

204

sunlight I could tell he'd had extensions done in his hair. "What can I tell you about?"

"The relationship, for starters."

He smiled without mirth. "There was none."

"Hard to believe, knowing you."

He put a hand over his heart. "Scout's honor. Our friend Derek suddenly got religion. The seeds of corruption were in that young man's soul—but he finally said no more. It seems the little slut was in love with someone else and just wouldn't feel right about—making any arrangements with me."

"And you accepted that?"

The smile turned nasty. "Never let it be said that I stood in the way of the course of true love." He leaned over toward me. "I hope my name can be left out of any official inquiry. If I'm going to be dragged through the tabloids at least I should get something out of it."

"If you're telling the truth, you shouldn't have any problem," I said. "Derek didn't happen to mention who he was in love with, did he?"

He shook his head. "Some *woman*." The way he said it made it a dirty word. Then all at once he looked at me as if he'd never seen me before. "Hmmm. I don't suppose *you'd* be interested in—auditioning for me?"

I looked off toward the house, where the young man who'd let me in was lurking near a french door, watching us sullenly. "I don't think Sean would like it."

"The Seans of the world come and go, you know that. The Derek Hawkes, too. But someone more mature, someone that I could actually talk to . . ."

I stood up, heading for the exit. "Dare to dream," I said.

I waited outside the office until about six o'clock, unnoticed in the general Beverly Hills evening rush. Finally I saw her come out the front door of the building, looking ashen and drawn. She headed for the public parking garage down the block as though picking up each foot was an effort. I followed her up to the second level, to a white 1982 Toyota

Corolla with a crumpled fender and a sagging headliner. She fumbled with her keys to open the car door.

"Hello, Paige," I said.

She jumped and screamed, her voice echoing in the parking structure. Then she saw who it was and put her hand to her chest in the valley between her breasts. "Mr. Saxon!" she giggled breathlessly. "You scared me to death."

"Sorry. I just wanted to talk to you some more. Away from Frank, away from the office."

"What about?" she said. It might have been skepticism I saw on her face—a fresh, wholesome-looking kid like that walking around Beverly Hills, I'm sure a lot of guys "just wanted to talk" to her. Or it might have been something else.

"About Derek Hawke," I said.

She dropped her eyes. "Oh." She fumbled at the door lock, finally swung it open. "I heard what happened to him. That's just awful."

"Do you want to grab a cup of coffee somewhere?"

She looked at her watch and shook her head. "I don't think so. I have to get home."

"Can we just sit in the car a few minutes, then?" That seemed to frighten her, so I added, "I'm relatively harmless."

She pressed her lips together, her brows knitting prettily, and she got into the car and reached over to unlock the passenger door for me. I slid in next to her over brand-new sheepskin seat covers.

"Paige, how long had you and Derek been seeing each other?"

"How did you . . . ? We weren't—he was just an actor who came into the office . . ."

"He told Andrew Nicholson he was in love. It couldn't have been Louise Manaster. From the way you acted when I talked to you yesterday, I took a shot that it might be you. Both you and Derek were the same type—you could have posed for an all-American-couple-goes-to-Burger-King ad. I thought perhaps you might have—found each other out here."

She just stared, eyes wide and level.

"Am I right, Paige?"

She turned sulky, Molly Ringwald rebelling against her parents. "All right, we were seeing each other. What of it?"

"He walked out of Louise Manaster's on Monday night without the car she'd leased for him. The house is way up in the hills—I think he called you to come and pick him up." My nose began itching and I rubbed it almost violently, feeling the cartilage pop.

She didn't answer.

"He made a phone call before he left the Manaster house, and I'd be willing to bet he called you to come and get him. You hadn't known about Louise Manaster until that moment, had you? You thought you had Derek all to yourself. You didn't know you were sharing him with a seventy-year-old woman. You were in love with him, and when you found out he was a kept plaything, you got angry and stabbed him with your nail file. Right here in the front seat. That's probably why you have brand-new seat covers on a car that's ready for the junk heap."

Her face had turned several shades grayer, and the dark smudges I'd seen beneath her eyes when I first met her were back. I found myself feeling sorry for her.

"You didn't mean to kill him," I said as gently as I could. "You found out the man you thought you loved was just a notch above a male hooker, and you lost it—struck out. You had to get rid of the body, so you dumped him right where you were—down the hill from the Manaster place. You figured the police would suspect Louise, and there was no way they could connect Derek to you. Except the cat pin. Did you keep it as a memento? Expensive souvenir—about two-hundred-grand worth."

She fell back against her door, stricken. Her hand was at her throat and she looked to be in deep shock. Anything in the six figures does that to people.

"That was a mistake, Paige. I wasn't after Derek—I just wanted the pin. If you'd left it in his pocket I would have dropped the whole thing."

"You can't prove anything," she said, voice quivering like a little kid's when you tell her she has to go to sleep.

"Sure I can. Just tell the police to search your apartment for the pin. But I don't even have to do that," I pointed down to the floor of the car at my feet. "Cat hair," I said. "From Derek's clothes? Gets me every time."

I sneezed twice and took the car keys away from her.

Finicky

·

John Lutz

Mandy placed her foot on the spade and leaned hard, driving the pointed scoop no more than a few inches into the hard earth of the back yard. At her feet the cat Hector lay motionless on his side. She straightened up and exhaled loudly, looking down at three-year-old Robert Jr., who was clutching his stomach and whimpering.

"I know it's sad, but sooner or later comes a time for everything to die," she said, wishing as she hadn't for months that Robert Sr. were still here. But the boy's father was gone, the police had no idea where, and she was a woman alone. Well, not alone, exactly, but the single head of household the government talked so much about but about which it knew so little.

Life had been hell *with* Robert Sr., and at first she'd been glad to be alone and independent. Just Mandy and Robert Jr., cozy family unit. But a boy so young was hardly company for a middle-aged woman, and the loneliness had crept in around her and then into her, sinking her heart and mind like water inundating a doomed ship. It wasn't fair to Robert Jr., she knew, but even little things became major irritations and she'd snap at him, or lock herself in her bedroom and sob in despair. A life like hers was enough to drive a weaker woman mad.

In the moonlight, she peered down again at the scant progress she'd made with the spade. She nudged the motionless cat aside with her toe, then bent to her task once more. *Ouch!* She'd pulled something in her side, but she kept digging.

This was a job for a man, burying something even this small. Since Robert Sr. had gone the pressure had built and built in her, growing like a cancer fed on loneliness. Money was a problem almost immediately. The only job an un-skilled, uneducated woman in her late thirties could get was hamburger flipper at a fast-food restaurant. It paid little more than minimum wage, and she soon found herself skimping on groceries, making excuses to creditors, dressing Robert Jr. in clothes he'd already outgrown. And though she loved the boy, he sometimes made her solitary anguish even worse. He was supposed to be through the ''terrible twos,'' but with Robert Jr. the terror continued. He was constantly in motion, unreasonable as only a three-year-old can be, breaking things, causing her to lose sleep. Lately, with his father gone, he'd been crying at the slightest provocation. The worst part was, when he screwed up his face and began to bawl his discon-tent, he so closely resembled his father it caused her heart to go cold. She hated that feeling.

Tonight had been particularly bad. First he'd bumped his head in the bathtub, his screams echoing in the old tile bath-room and exploding her peace of mind. She'd been at the kitchen table with the pocket calculator, trying to work math-ematical miracles with the bills, but that had stopped and she'd run to his aid, to quiet him. Later he'd screeched and complained at supper, refusing to eat. Capped the meal by knocking his bowl of vanilla frozen dessert onto the floor, then her bowl when she stooped to clean up after him. Screamed until she'd given him a second dessert. While Mandy was doing the dishes, Robert Jr., in the living room, had done something to Hector, who himself screeched deaf-eningly and shot into the kitchen with Mandy.

At first she could find nothing wrong with the trembling gray cat, and put him down when Robert Jr. yelled for her to come into the living room. Leaving the still disconsolate Hector, she'd hurried from the kitchen, and in the doorway to the living room she'd stopped and stared.

Finicky

The picture on the screen of the console TV, the only expensive piece of furniture remaining, was rolling soundlessly. The long ladder of Robert Jr.'s metal fire engine had penetrated the speaker, ripping the material and obviously wreaking havoc inside. The toy fire engine had been the last thing Robert Sr. had given his son.

Trying to quiet Robert Jr., Mandy bent over the TV and manipulated the dials. The picture stopped rolling but she couldn't coax sound from the set. Damn!

Damn again!

The shovel had struck a root, probably from the willow tree Robert had planted the week after they'd moved here five years ago. He loved willow trees. Mandy hated them. Melancholy things.

Unable to see the partly exposed root in the darkness, she chopped at it with the spade by feel, careful not to hit Hector. She had to get the shallow grave dug, had to be done with it and end this nightmare evening and finally climb into her empty bed. She bent over to see if she was making any progress, resting her hand on her son's narrow shoulder. The ground was still too shadowed to afford her a glimpse.

"We all gotta accept the fact of death sooner or later," she said, glancing over at Robert Jr. as she worked. "Maybe this is the best way, hard as it is."

There! The spade had severed the root.

She attacked the hard ground with renewed effort, feeling dejected and alone, spending her rage on her task. It gave her satisfaction to see the dark shallow grave opening up beneath the plunging, scooping spade.

Finally she decided it was deep enough. She bent low, feeling an ache in her back, and slid the small still body into the grave. It made a horrible sound as it hit the bottom. She swallowed the lump of sorrow that swelled in her throat.

Immediately she began scooping loose earth into the grave, ignoring the strain in her arms and shoulders, working, working to finally draw the curtain on this suburban backyard tragic scene.

When the loose dirt lay in a mound over the tiny grave,

she slammed the flat of the spade into it over and over until the bulge was almost at ground level. Rain would eventually take care of the rest, soaking the ground and causing the dirt to settle. By Robert Jr.'s birthday next month, grass would have spread over the bare spot, and it would be as if the yard had never been disturbed. Life would continue almost as if nothing had happened, leaving only a sore spot best not touched in the memory.

Breathing raggedly, Mandy leaned on the shovel and wondered if she should say a few words over the grave.

No, she decided, that would be ridiculous. This night had been enough of a travesty; she didn't want to continue it. She threw back her head, almost like a wolf about to howl, and stared up at the dark sky and tilted half-moon. Clouds were scudding along up there like black stains on the universe. She must have gotten dizzy for a few seconds, because it seemed the pinpoints of stars began to whirl.

She sucked in her breath and dropped her gaze.

The dizziness passed.

"Okay, that's that," she said. "Let's get back inside now and try to put all this behind us." As tired as she'd ever been, dragging the shovel behind her, she plodded toward the sliding glass door leading inside from the patio.

She tossed the shovel aside on the ground; she'd put it back in the garage tomorrow morning before work, didn't want to do a single thing more tonight.

Inside, she washed her hands at the kitchen sink, using dishwasher detergent and scrubbing each individual finger beneath the trickle of water from the faucet that dripped constantly now that Robert Sr. was gone. She picked up a soap-impregnated steel wool pad and began to use that. Scrubbing, scrubbing. Through the window over the sink she could see out into the moonlit back yard. There was the barbecue pit, the forsythia bush near the fence, the willow tree under which Robert Sr. was buried, the smaller fresh grave that held Robert Jr.

When fifteen minutes had passed she finished washing her hands, dried them on a dish towel, then put the box of roach powder back beneath the sink. She bent down and patted Hector on the head. He arched his back and slid sensuously through the tunnel of her cupped hand, purring softly.

With a final glance out the window, she trudged from the kitchen to the bedroom. She was smiling.

It was quiet in the house.

The Duel

.

J. A. Jance

Howard was nothing if not dependable. Living up to his reputation for constant vigilance, he was at his assigned post and standing guard, carefully studying the parade of home-bound cars that tooled down the rainy, winter-darkened street. He examined each pair of fuzzy, rain-softened head-lights, waiting for the one, all-important pair which would slice away from the others and turn onto the graveled drive-way.

The atmosphere in the room was charged with floating particles of waiting while the graceful old Seth Thomas clock on the mantel ticked hollowly away. Every fifteen minutes it gave sonorous voice to each quarter-hour interval. The only other sounds in the chilly and ominously expectant house came from a single person playing cards. The cards slapped down angrily on the faded finish of the rosewood table where Anna played her ever-present game of solitaire.

The hands of the clock marched slowly, inevitably past the delicate Roman numerals on the mother-of-pearl clock face. It was late and getting later and still Edgar wasn't home. With each passing moment, Anna's playing grew more impas-sioned and frenetic. The cards hit the table with increasing force and urgency. The periodic shuffles were like threaten-ing claps of thunder preceding an approaching storm.

"Any sign of him?" Anna asked without looking up.

Howard didn't move, and he didn't answer, either. That

214

was to be expected. Howard never had been the talkative kind, nor was he particularly sociable. He seldom remained in the same room with them once Edgar arrived home. As soon as the Lord and Master stepped inside the front door— Lord and Master was the nickname Anna and Howard called Edgar behind his back—as soon as L&M came home, Howard would stalk off upstairs, leaving Anna to fend for herself, to deal with her husband on her own. Howard's position was that Edgar was Anna's problem.

Up to a point, that was true. But now, thank God and Federal Express, the two of them were evenly matched. Edgar no longer had her outgunned, as it were.

Her use of the word *outgunned* made her smile in spite of herself. Pausing briefly from her game of cards, Anna slipped one hand into the deep pocket of her heavy, terrycloth robe and let her fingers close tentatively around the rough grip of the still-almost-new Lady Smith and Wesson she kept concealed there. She touched the gun because it was there for the touching. She touched it for reassurance, and perhaps even for luck. Stroking the cool metal of the short barrel, she wondered if the confrontation would come tonight. If so, it would finally be over and done with, once and for all.

Anna Whalen no longer cared so much what the ultimate outcome would be. She just wanted out of limbo. Whatever the cost, she wanted the awful waiting to end.

And how long had she been waiting? Forever, it seemed, although it was probably only a matter of months since the situation had become really intolerable. Howard, ever observant, was the one who had first pointed Edgar's dalliance out to her. He was also the one who had realized and warned her that Edgar might try poison.

Initially, the idea of Edgar's poisoning her had seemed like a wildly farfetched idea, a preposterous, nightmarish joke. Anna had laughed it off, but later, the more she thought about it and the more she observed Edgar's increasingly suspicious behavior, the more it had made sense. After all, he was the only one in the house who did any cooking, such as it was. Eventually she realized that it would be a simple thing for him to slip some kind of death-inducing substance into her food.

Faced with this possibility, Anna and Howard had wisely hit upon a countermeasure. True friend that he was, Howard had generously agreed to taste whatever food appeared on Anna's plate. Howard tried everything first—everything that is, except green beans and snow peas. Howard despised green vegetables. Unfortunately, the frozen-dinner people were very big on snow peas this year. Friend or not, when servings of suspicious green things turned up on Anna's tray, Howard wouldn't touch them.

If she hadn't been cagey about it, green vegetables might well have been Anna's undoing, her Achilles heel. Instead, she carefully slipped the offending green things off her plate and surreptitiously stuffed them behind the cushion of her recliner whenever Edgar wasn't watching. Every morning, as soon as the Lord and Master was safely out of the house, she'd return to the chair and dispose of the previous evening's incriminating evidence. So far, so good.

Outside a passing car slowed, but it turned left into the Mossbecks' driveway across the street. Anna still called it Mossbecks' although the Mossbecks hadn't lived there in fifteen years. She had no idea who lived there now—some nameless, childless young couple who both had important, well-paying jobs in the city. Why someone like that needed a house as big as the Mossbecks' Anna couldn't imagine.

But then, to be fair, she and Edgar didn't need such a big house, either. They lived in only four of the downstairs rooms in Grandmother Adams's gnarled old house. Edgar was too tight to heat the rest of it. He claimed they couldn't afford it. He slept on a day bed in what had once been Cook's room off the kitchen. Anna's ornate bedroom suite had been moved downstairs into what had once been her grandmother's parlor. For years, no one but Howard had ventured upstairs, but he had assured Anna that he didn't mind the cold. In fact, he preferred it.

Actually, the escalating warfare between Edgar and Howard was what had finally alerted Anna to her own danger and to the possibility that another woman might be the root cause of all the trouble. Most of it anyhow. For at least six months now, Edgar had been coming home late on Tuesday nights, and only on Tuesdays. Howard, whose nose was particularly sensitive to such things, had detected a hint of very feminine perfume, the same scent every time, lingering on Edgar's clothing on each of those selfsame Tuesday nights. Anna had racked her brain to figure out who this perfume-drenched homewrecker might be.

Anna's forty-year marriage to Edgar had never been an especially happy one, but then neither one of them had been brought up to believe in happy marriages. Marriages lasted, of course, because that was expected. How one functioned inside those lasting marriages was left to the good grace and wit of the individuals involved.

Part of the problem was due to the fact that there had been certain misunderstandings from the very beginning which were traceable to parental meddling and mismanagement on both sides. Edgar had been touted to Anna's family as having "good breeding and good prospects" although the chief touter, mainly his widowed mother, should have been somewhat suspect as a source of reliable information. But then Anna's family wasn't entirely blameless when it came to stretching the truth either.

Edgar had presumably married for money without realizing that Anna's father, Bertram Quincy Adams III, had done an excellent job of concealing his own foolhardy squandering of the family fortunes. By the time Edgar discovered his wife was practically penniless, except for her grandmother's house and a small trust fund, he himself was far too committed to the gentlemanly lifestyle.

Anna Quincy Adams Whalen wasn't rich, but her pedigree opened doors that otherwise would have been closed to her husband on his own. Constitutionally unfit for regular work, Edgar shamelessly used Adams family connections to procure himself a couple of corporate directorships and a private school trusteeship. The small income from those combined with minimal Social Security checks kept the wolf from the door and paid the property taxes, but that was about it. They lived on the right side of town with a fashionable address but behind a closed door which carefully concealed their genteel poverty. To Anna's way of thinking there was nothing genteel about it.

She looked around the chilly room. What had once been a large, elegant dining room had been forced into the mold of dining and living room both. The extra leaves had long since disappeared from the rosewood table. Grandmother Adams's remaining furniture, quality once but now faded and dingy, had been pushed up against the walls to make room for a monster television set and two La-Z-Boy recliners which Anna found ungainly and uncomfortable both, but that was where she and her husband sat, night after night, matching bookends in their matching chairs, eating frozen dinners on TV trays while CNN droned on and on.

It would have been nice, every once in a while, to watch a sitcom or even one of those dreadful made-for-television police-dramas, but Edgar was the keeper of the remote control, and he liked to watch the news. When he was there they watched what he wanted. When he was gone, the television stayed off completely because Anna found the push-button controls far too complicated to understand.

Naturally, Edgar had bought the set without consulting her which may have been one reason why Anna hated it. The first she had known anything about it was when the delivery man rang the doorbell and asked her where she wanted him to set it up. Oh well, she had gotten even. Anna had made an unauthorized purchase of her own. The mail-order Smith and Wesson had come to the house less than five days after she phoned in her order. She had intercepted the VISA card bill for three months in a row, paying it herself out of her own paltry Social Security check until she had gotten the balance down low enough that Edgar hadn't questioned it.

Just then headlights flashed across the rain-splashed window. Tires crunched in the driveway. Edgar was home.

Howard got up at once. "Please don't leave me alone with him tonight," Anna begged, but Howard only shook his head and wouldn't stay. She resented it that he could so callously abandon her and leave her to face Edgar alone, but that was just the way Howard was. Over the years, it seemed as though she would have gotten used to it.

Edgar came into the room, set down his briefcase and grocery bag, and immediately closed the drapes. "How many times do I have to tell you to close the drapes in the winter? You're letting all the heat out."

"I forgot," Anna said, and continued to play her game of solitaire with diligent concentration.

Edgar went over to the television set and picked up the remote control. For a moment he stood staring down at the small electronic device on top of the set.

"Have you let the damn cat sit up on the cable box again? You let it wreck the last one. That's what the guy said, you know, that the insides were all plugged full of cat hair."

"Maybe it keeps his feet warm," Anna offered.

"Don't start with that 'the house is too cold' stuff again," Edgar said irritably. "If the house is too cold, close the damn drapes. Are you hungry?"

She wasn't, but Edgar liked to eat as soon as he got home so he could watch the news for the rest of the night without any unnecessary interruptions. "Yes," Anna said. "I could eat a horse."

"It's chicken," he said, picking up the groceries and carrying them into the kitchen. "Fried chicken, mashed potatoes, and corn."

Good, Anna thought. Howard liked corn. She listened to the familiar sounds from the kitchen—the tiny bleatings of the control on the microwave, ice tinkling into a glass, something, gin probably, being poured over the ice. Suddenly Anna found herself feeling sorry that it was corn instead of snow peas. She had wanted it to be tonight. She had wanted to end the uncertainty and get it over with.

The swinging door to the kitchen banged open. She knew without looking that Edgar was standing behind her, staring down over her shoulder at the cards scattered across the smooth surface of the table.

"Did you win today?" he asked.

"No."

Anna played a complicated, two-deck kind of solitaire which she won only once every year or so. If she had cheated, she probably would have won more often, but she was always scrupulously honest. She didn't like it when Edgar looked over her shoulder, though. Having him watch made her nervous, and she missed plays she could have made.

"Why don't you try a different game?" Edgar asked.

"I like this one," she replied.

The beeper on the microwave went off. Edgar returned to the kitchen. As soon as he left, Anna could see that she had missed putting the six of spades on the descending spades pile for at least three turns. Damn him. She threw down her cards in disgust and went to set the table.

That's what they called it, setting the table, although it was really nothing more than setting up the two TV trays. Edgar always brought the silverware and napkins in with him from the kitchen, but he liked to have the trays set up by the time he got there so he didn't have to stand there with his hands full and wait for her to do her part of the job.

The microwave was going again, and the door to the kitchen was shut. Edgar couldn't hear her.

"Howard," Anna called softly. "Howard. You come back down here. I need you." But for some strange reason, Howard didn't appear.

"Where's Howard?" Anna asked when Edgar brought the food in from the kitchen.

Edgar shrugged. "Beats me," he said. "I haven't seen him since I got home."

Anna waited, but still there was no sign of Howard. She didn't dare make a fuss or call to him again. Edgar was soon eating away, his eyes glued to the television set. Only when there was a station break did he turn to look at her.

"You're not eating your dinner," he said accusingly. "I thought you said you were hungry."

She was hungry, now. The smell of the food, the look of it, had made her hungry, but without Howard there to try it for her, she didn't dare eat any of it, and she was afraid to stuff the chicken, bones and all, down behind the cushion.

This must be it, she was thinking. He must have locked Howard away somewhere, so he can't help me. She slipped her hand into her pocket and screwed up her courage.

"Why are you doing this?"

He looked over at her, surprised. "Doing what? Watching television? I always watch television. You know that."

Her fingers closed around the grip of the pistol, but she didn't take it out of her pocket. Not yet. She didn't want to give everything away at once.

"Why are you trying to poison me?" she asked.

Edgar choked quite convincingly on a piece of chicken. "Me? Trying to poison you? Anna, you've got to be kidding! You've been reading too many books."

"There's another woman, isn't there, Edgar," she continued. Anna kept her voice low and even. She didn't want him to think she was just being hysterical. "You've been seeing another woman on the side for some time now, and the two of you are trying to get rid of me."

"My God, Anna, that's the wildest thing I've ever heard. Wherever did you come up with such a crazy, cockamamie idea?"

"Tuesdays," she answered. "It's because of Tuesdays. You're late coming home every single Tuesday without fail."

He looked relieved. "Oh, that," he said. "I've been seeing a counselor, trying to sort some things out in my own mind. And it's been helping more than you know. Maybe you should try it, see if it wouldn't help you as well. I could come home early enough to pick you up, and we could go see the counselor together. What would you think of that?"

The story about the counselor sounded vaguely possible, but she wasn't about to fall for it. "I don't believe you," she said, and pulled the gun.

Edgar's eyes filled with shocked disbelief. "My God, Anna! Where did you get that thing? Is it loaded?"

Of course it was loaded. What would be the point of carrying a gun that wasn't? Edgar started to get up, but she shot him square in the chest before he ever made it to his feet. The force of the blow flung him back into the chair which shifted automatically into the reclining position, leaving him with his feet jutting into the air like a helpless, overturned turtle. He lay there for some time, groaning and clutching his chest.

Anna watched him curiously. If he had tried to get up, she would have shot him again, but he didn't. Eventually he stopped groaning. His hands fell limply to his sides. Meanwhile, the news droned on and on, talking about something that was going on in the Middle East again . . . still. Anna didn't pay much attention. She wasn't particularly interested in world affairs.

After a while, though, when they started talking about a nationally known murder case, a trial that had been in process for several months and was just now going to the jury, she got interested in the program. Forgetting her customary caution, she began to eat her dinner. Anna was so interested in what the lady news commentator was saying, she barely noticed the funny almond taste of the corn.

Howard did, though. Much later, thinking Anna and Edgar must have fallen asleep in front of the droning television set, he finally crept back down from upstairs. The big yellow cat sniffed disdainfully at what was left of the corn on Anna's plate, but he had sense enough not to eat it. Howard's nose was far too sensitive for that.

Archimedes and the Doughnuts

·

Gene DeWeese and Barbara Paul

I'm not sure when it started, but I know when it ended. It was shortly after noon on Sunday, the ninth of June, just six months ago. That's when Clara Murphy came pounding on my door, surprising me in more ways than one.

At the time I was sitting at the kitchen table staring morosely at an assemblage of grease, cholesterol, calories, and triglycerides that would keep me up all night if it didn't kill me first. I'd been conned into buying it by two small monsters from outer space that my son Warren keeps insisting are my grandchildren. Monster Number 1 had started chanting "Pizza! Pizza! Pizza!" and of course Monster Number 2 had quickly joined in, as he always does. So we'd stopped by a pizza parlor with the fine old Italian name of Willoughby's, and then back home I was faced with the disagreeable prospect of actually eating the stuff.

Clara's pounding on the door stopped me just in time; need I say I was glad to see her? Truth to tell, I was always glad to see Clara Murphy. We'd known each other all our adult lives. Her Harry had been dead for ten years, my Emma for twelve; but there'd been a time when the four of us were inseparable. We had a lot of good years behind us, Clara and I. But we were older now, less active; I hadn't seen her for, oh, three months at least, since last March when she'd brought her cat Archimedes into my clinic for his annual shots.

This time, though, the sight of her shocked me. She'd

looked fine when she'd brought Archimedes in, but now she looked as if twenty years had gone by, not three months. I'd never seen her so pale, not even when she'd had the heart attack a few weeks after Harry died. And she looked tired, tired right down to the bone, as if she barely had the strength to stand up.

But I didn't get to say anything; I didn't even have a chance to say hello before she was grabbing at my sleeve and using what breath she had to urge me to come with her. "It's Archimedes," she gasped, as if it was all she could do to get the words out. "I have him in the car, I came home from church and found him, he's never been like this before, never, and I don't know—"

"Easy, Clara, I'll take a look at him—try to relax." From past experience I knew Clara's idea of a feline emergency could be nothing more than a temporary loss of appetite; the only true emergency she'd come to me with had been a BB lodged in the back leg of a cat named Desdemona. I told the monsters to finish their pizza and went to get my bag; Clara trailed after me, trembling and unsteady. "You didn't drive over here in that condition, did you?" I asked her.

"Jerry drove me." The words were faint.

I nodded and said nothing; Jerry was the one serious point of contention that had ever arisen between us. I held out a hand to steady her as we went down the steps toward her car; I was more worried about her than I was about Archimedes. Despite a sweet tooth that almost matched Clara's—Archimedes was one of the few cats I'd ever seen who would actually eat plain sugar—he'd never been more than a pound overweight and was usually in excellent health. But I knew there was no way I was going to get Clara to answer questions about her own health until I looked after the cat. Clara loved that animal, just the way she'd loved the half-dozen other cats she'd had since she first came into my clinic with Darius (he was a Persian) over thirty years ago.

A lanky young man unfolded himself from behind the wheel of Clara's Mercedes. "Hello, Milton. Sorry to bother you on a Sunday, but . . ." He gave me a look that meant *You know Aunt Clara*.

I didn't answer the look. "Jerry."

"He's in the back." Jerry opened the car door.

The moment the door was open I could see this was something more serious than a BB in the leg. Archimedes, a fifteen-pound tiger stripe, was moving restlessly over the back seat, whining painfully. His breathing was almost as rapid as a human's pulse. And he had thrown up, partly on the seat, partly on the floor.

"He just now lost his breakfast," Jerry said. "Aunt Clara, I told you it was nothing to worry about. Archimedes isn't as young as he used to be and he simply can't digest everything he eats anymore. Isn't that right, Milton?"

I took the stethoscope from my bag and checked the cat's heart. Like his breathing, it was rapid and weak. "We'd better get him to the clinic," I told Clara. "I'll need more than I have in this bag."

"What is it, Milton?" she asked, even more alarmed.

"Has he been outside?"

"No, of course not. Ever since Desdemona—"

"Could he have slipped out? That's happened before."

"Not this time, Milton—I'm sure of it. He was asleep on the dining-room window sill when Jerry picked me up to go to church. You remember, Jerry."

Jerry cleared his throat. "I don't think I saw him, Aunt Clara."

"Well, *I* saw him," Clara insisted. "And he was asleep when we left. He didn't slip out." The effort of talking left her exhausted.

I asked, "Is there anything in the house, then, that he could've gotten into? What about ant pellets? You still put them out in summer, don't you?"

"Yes, but not where Archimedes could get them. I put them under the stove and the refrigerator—he couldn't possibly reach them."

"Well, we'll figure this out later," I said. "We'd better

tend to Archimedes first. You two go on ahead to the clinic—I'll follow in my car in just a minute.''

I could barely hear the sound of the Mercedes starting up as I hurried back up the steps and into the house. I picked up the phone and tapped out my son's home number. ''Warren?''

''Hey, Dad, what's up?''

''You're going to have to come take the monsters home. I have to get over to the clinic—something's wrong with Clara Murphy's cat.''

''Aw, too bad. Is it serious?''

''Yes, I'm afraid it is.''

''Then you might want to let Jerry know. Clara—''

''Jerry drove her here. Look, Warren, you can pick the monsters up at Mrs. Tanner's next door. I can't wait around 'til you get here.''

''Monica will come get them. I have to go to work.''

''On Sunday?''

''Bert's sick and Jack's off to Willow Bend today, and I don't have anyone else to send in. But don't you worry about the kids, Pop—you go take care of the sick kitty.''

''Don't call me Pop.'' I hung up the phone, shooed the monsters next door to Mrs. Tanner's, and backed the car out of the garage.

Archimedes' symptoms had me worried. I'd seen this sort of thing before, in farm cats that had ingested something that had had rat poison mixed into it. On the whole cats have too much sense to eat something that will kill them, but they can be fooled; pesticides are getting more sophisticated all the time. That's why I'd asked Clara about the ant pellets, even though it was implausible that Archimedes would have eaten one. Why would he ignore them for four or five years and then suddenly decide to sample one?

Clara had stopped letting her cats out of the house ever since the day poor Desdemona came dragging herself home, her right rear leg virtually useless. That damned BB in her leg had been a gift from a particularly loathsome ten-year-old who was—and unfortunately still is—Clara's nephew.

Yep, it was Jerry who'd shot Desdemona, the same Jerry who was now so solicitously driving the ailing Archimedes to my clinic. I had to wonder if Jerry had slipped the cat something; he was just mean-spirited enough to do a thing like that. But Clara said Archimedes had been all right when Jerry picked her up for church.

All those years ago, Jerry had never admitted to shooting Desdemona. When I told Clara that not only had Jerry done it, but he'd shot her deliberately—she flatly refused to believe me. Said I was just guessing. But I'd seen too many other cats with the same kind of wound that summer. There'd been at least half a dozen during the two months that ten-year-old Jerry and his BB gun had stayed with Clara and Harry—that's half a dozen that I *saw*. How many other cats were wounded or even dead that I knew nothing about? Once Jerry returned to his own home, the incidence of cat-shootings dropped to zero. When I'd tried to point this out to Clara, she'd called me spiteful and unreasonable, saying I'd never liked the boy and always thought the worst.

Well, that last part was true; I didn't like him. And I was pretty much alone in that opinion. Even Warren thought Jerry was an okay guy, and he's usually pretty good at seeing through people's façades. But the first time I'd ever seen Jerry, he'd been holding a wounded bird in his hand—broken wing, I think. The boy was in Clara's front yard and didn't see me walking up the driveway. I was about to offer to take a good look at the bird when he put it on the ground and crushed it with his foot. Ground its head right in. Jerry liked hurting things—small things, that is, things that couldn't hurt back. Of course he'd shot the cats. And probably had a lot of fun doing it.

But Clara steadfastly refused to see that side of her nephew. I could understand why; Emma and I had had Warren, but Clara and Harry had remained childless. Jerry's parents died the year before Harry did, and it was logical that the two surviving members of the family should draw together. I'd taken to checking in on Clara now and then after Harry died; but now that Jerry was grown, she was turning to him more and more. That's why I hadn't seen her for three months; in a way, I'd been abrogating responsibility to Jerry. The thought of that didn't make me any too pleased with myself.

They were waiting at my clinic when I got there, Clara in the Mercedes with Archimedes and Jerry pacing nervously outside. I lifted the cat carefully out of the back seat. His breathing was more shallow than ever.

"Are you going to give him something to settle him down?" Jerry asked.

Inside, the first thing I did was to flush out the cat's stomach, although Archimedes had done a pretty good job of that himself in the car before I got to him. Then I gave a shot of dimarcaprol, to help neutralize any poison still in his system. Then all we could do was wait.

Slumped in a chair under the bright lights I need for my job, Clara looked worse than ever. Her face was gray and pinched; her shoulders drooped forward. She looked old, old. Haggard, even. Clara, pretty Clara, looked *haggard*. I offered her a chocolate bar I found in my desk, but for once Clara had left her sweet tooth at home. She just shook her head, *no*. Jerry kept up his pacing until I was ready to yell at him.

After about an hour Archimedes weakly lifted his head and started sniffing in the direction of the candy bar I'd left out. The cat had almost died of poisoning, and now he was ready to celebrate with a little Hershey's chocolate! Tell me about resiliency. I checked him over; his heartbeat was stronger and his breathing was slow and easy.

"He's going to be all right," I said.

Clara gave a little cry of relief, and even Jerry looked as if a load had been lifted from his shoulders. I told Clara I wanted to keep Archimedes at the clinic for a few days, just to keep an eye on him.

Jerry looked at his watch. "Aunt Clara, now that the emergency is over, well, I have a date, and . . ."

"Of course, dear, you run along," Clara said. "Take the car. Oh—you don't mind driving me home, Milton, do you?"

"Be glad to. Just let me get Archimedes settled in." I was

putting fresh water in his cage and this time didn't even hear the Mercedes start up and drive away. I wondered if Jerry would clean up the mess in the back seat.

On the drive to Clara's house I again brought up the subject of where Archimedes had gotten the poison. "It had to come from *somewhere*," I pointed out. "And if we can't find the source, Archimedes could get into it again."

"I know," she said tiredly. "I've been trying to think, but there's nothing in the house that could have made him sick. I'm sure of that."

"All right. Then you have to consider the possibility that the poison was given to him deliberately."

"What?" She sounded shocked.

"It's the only other explanation. Archimedes would never have eaten that much poison unless it was mixed in with something else, something he liked. A few licks out of curiosity, maybe, or to clean the stuff off himself if he'd gotten it on his fur—but not as much as I found in him, Clara. I suppose you've already washed his food dish from this morning?"

"Yes." She turned her head away. "You know what you're saying, don't you?" she asked in a small voice. "You're accusing Jerry of poisoning Archimedes." I said nothing, letting the thought fester. Finally Clara burst out, "This time you go too far! I know you've never liked Jerry, but to accuse him of putting poison in Archimedes' food . . . you're getting obsessive about him, Milton!"

That was a nice cold bucket of water in the face. Obsessive? Me? I tried to think about it objectively . . . but that was impossible, of course. So I said, "Okay, if it's not Jerry, then the source of the poison has to be somewhere in your house. I'd better come in and look for it. We have to find out."

"We'll both look," Clara said.

I glanced over at her tired face. "I'll look. You're going to lie down before you fall down."

Clara's house was on a small rise at the peak of a long curving driveway. It was a magnificent old house, built by her grandfather around the turn of the century and full of the little niceties so sadly lacking in much of modern housing. It was far too big for one person but Clara wouldn't dream of leaving, even though it was costing her a fortune in up-keep. But Clara's family had always had money; if she wanted to spend her inheritance maintaining an Edwardian-style mansion, that was her business. Personally, I thought it was money well spent; it really was a magnificent old house.

We went in the front door, which Clara had neglected to lock when she'd rushed out with Archimedes. "Go lie down," I said to her. "There's no need for both of us to look."

She shook her head. "I want to see this through. Where do we start?"

"The kitchen. Then the bathrooms, then the basement."

Clara led the way into the gargantuan kitchen, but stopped short just inside the door—and laughed. "Oh, that *naughty* cat."

It took a second, but then I saw what she was looking at. On the floor by the kitchen counter was a cardboard box, one of the flimsy white ones you get from the bakery. It was upside down, and the cardboard had been clawed apart until you could see what remained of the chocolate-covered doughnuts inside; Archimedes had had himself quite a feast.

"It's my own fault," Clara said ruefully. "Normally when Jerry drops off the doughnuts I put them in the refrigerator where Archimedes can't get them—you know how he loves sugary things. But this morning I just couldn't seem to get moving. I've been so tired lately, I simply put them down without thinking—"

"Jerry brings you doughnuts every day?"

"Not *every* day, Milton," she said with a faint smile. "A couple of times a week, though. Isn't that thoughtful? I do so love doughnuts, especially the chocolate ones." She bent over to pick up the box.

"*Don't touch that,*" I said sharply, and felt like kicking myself for being such a damned fool. I should have guessed. I went over to the phone on the wall by the refrigerator and tapped out a number. To the woman who answered I said, "Give me the Sheriff. It's urgent."

"Milton?" Clara said. "What are you doing?"

When the familiar voice came on the line I said, "Warren, listen up. There's a box of doughnuts on the floor of Clara Murphy's kitchen that you've got to get tested for poison." I looked at Clara's shocked face. "Tell them to test for arsenic first."

Warren was quick. "The cat. That's what was wrong with him?"

"That's what was wrong with him. He got into a box of doughnuts meant for Clara, and it was Jerry who brought them here. He's been bringing Clara doughnuts a couple of times a week for . . . how long, Clara?" She was too stunned to answer. "For a long time, I'd guess," I said to Warren. "I've got to get her to the hospital."

"I'll pick up Jerry," he said. "You take care of Clara, Dad—leave the rest to me."

So I bullied that poor sick woman into the car and off to the hospital, where she got the care and attention she needed. And that's when it all ended, six months ago. The lab tests found arsenic in the chocolate frosting of the doughnuts, as I'd suspected. I'd gone with Warren to Jerry's apartment, where Warren found the package the arsenic had come from. I hadn't seen one like it for nearly thirty years, since they found safer ways of getting rid of rats. But there were probably other packages like it still around, out in abandoned farm buildings around the county. Still available, and still lethal. In Jerry's kitchen were several containers of the ready-to-use kind of chocolate frosting you can buy at the supermarket.

We found something else as well. Jerry wasn't much of a reader; he had only one two-shelf bookcase in the place, crammed with paperbacks—adventure stories, spy novels, porn of varying degrees of softness. An adolescent boys' book collection. The one exception was the single hardback book he'd bought, a biography of Napoleon.

Warren and I stood staring at the book shelf. "Did you ever hear Jerry talk about Napoleon?" Warren asked me.

"Never," I said emphatically.

"Me neither." He pulled the book off the shelf and riffled through the pages. A newspaper clipping fluttered to the floor; Warren picked it up. "It's a review of this book," he said, reading quickly. "Well, well, what do you know. The author says that Napoleon died of arsenic poisoning and that no one knew at the time because it'd all been done so gradually."

"Huh. So that's where he got the idea." He'd probably enjoyed watching his aunt deteriorate, the sadistic little wretch.

Warren shook his head sadly. "You were right about Jerry, Pop. He's twisted, all right."

"Don't call me Pop," I said.

Jerry never did confess, of course, any more than he'd confessed to the BBs. But this time even Clara knew the truth; she had to accept the evidence of the lab reports, as did the jury when Jerry was tried for attempted murder. Clara is still anemic and I check on her almost every day. Other than that, she's pretty well recovered from her ordeal—only it took her six months instead of the six days it had taken Archimedes.

But I knew Clara was getting better when she announced one day that she was worried about me, living alone as I do, and that she was going to start checking in on me now and then to make sure everything was all right. I didn't say no to that. We'll watch out for each other—and for Archimedes, of course, who gets a doughnut for breakfast now and then; he's earned it. We still have a few good years ahead of us, Clara and I, thanks to his sugar-thieving ways.

The Lower Wacker Hilton

·

Barbara D'Amato

"**S**o, eight-fifteen A.M. we go screamin' in there," Officer Susannah Maria Figueroa said, "like it's a burglary in progress, and here's this guy—"

"Five foot zero," Norm Bennis said, "with four hairs on his head, all four of 'em combed across the top."

"Know the type," said Stanley Mileski, leaning back against his locker.

Figueroa pulled her walkie-talkie off the Velcro patch on her jacket and stuck it back on in a more comfortable position. "So it's eight-thirty give or take and he'd just got to the office, looked in the back room where the safe was, now he's hoppin' up and down on these *little* feet and yelping, like, saying 'It's gone! It's gone!' Pointin' through the door. Well, we go in and take a look and sure enough, the safe's gone. No doubt about it."

Norm Bennis said, "Big pale patch on the wall, clean patch on the floor."

"So he's jiggling and yelping and stuff, and he says, 'This safe's supposed to be burglar-proof, can't be jimmied, can't be opened, can't be blasted, made right here in Chicago, they promised me it can't be opened, and *now look*!' and he puts these little tiny hands up to his face and he starts to cry."

Stanley "Lead Balls" Mileski said, "Jeez, I hate it when citizens do that."

Kim Duk O'Hara, their rookie, said, "Me too."

"So Norm here," Figueroa cocked her head toward her partner Bennis, who was a black man of medium height and *very* wide shoulders, now lounging back against the water fountain, "Norm says where in Chicago'd you buy it and the guy tells us. Norm says to the foot officer wait here and we go tearin' over to the safe company. Go in. There's the manager just unlockin' his office. Guy looks like Dwight Eisenhower, manages the Presidential Safe and Security Company."

Mileski said, "I ask you."

O'Hara said, "Who's Dwight Eisenhower?"

Bennis said, "He confirms. Safe can't be blasted, can't be opened without the combination, door's flush so you can't pry it. Set o' numbers on a horizontal dial, you have to slide 'em to the right combination. Can't hear any tumblers fall. Nothin'."

"So Norm says, here it's nine A.M., you just gettin' in? Manager says yeah. Bennis says 'Your company name on the safe?' Manager says yeah. Bennis says, 'Can't be opened? I got an idea.' "

"Years of experience," Norm said, who was thirty-six to Figueroa's twenty-five.

"Phone rings. Bennis says 'May I?' and picks it up before Eisenhower even had a chance.

" 'Why, yes, sir,' Bennis is saying, nice as a cemetery plot salesman. 'We can help you with that. We'll come right on over.' Hangs up, says 'C'mon.'

"We slide on over to North Sedgwick, up the stairs, apartment three-F, ring the bell, door opens, Bennis yells 'Surprise!' We leap in, Bennis to the left, me to the right, I mean procedure was seriously followed here. And there's the safe and there's the perps."

"You coulda tied a ribbon on 'em," Bennis said.

"And there's the most humongous collection of crowbars and files and hammers and broken screwdrivers and crap you ever saw in your life."

Mileski was all bent over, laughing.

"Turned out," Figueroa said, "brother in law o' one o' the perps just won the lottery. Little lotto or some such. Won twelve thou. Here it is just before Christmas. Our perp was jealous. Wanted to do just as good for his family."

Norm Bennis stood upright, drew down his cheeks and eyelids and intoned, "Ah, yes. Jealousy is a dismal thing."

"Six fifty-nine and forty-seven seconds," Mileski said, looking at his watch. They all piled through the door into the rollcall room and sat down. As the digital clock on the wall changed to 7:00::00 he said, "Ding!"

Sergeant Touhy's face showed expression number four: Extreme Patience with the Behavior of Children.

"Settle down, troops, let's read some crimes."

The rollcall room at Chicago's First District station had its Christmas decorations up. Two loops of tinsel garlands over the door and a plastic wreath near the blackboard. The tinsel had shed as if it had mange and the bow on the wreath was sagging like a weeping willow.

"Figueroa," Bennis whispered, "this needs a woman's touch."

"Screw it, Bennis."

"Somebody to iron that bow, like."

Sergeant Touhy had a raft of pictures of shoplifters. "The stores are crowded. But some of these jerks are after big-ticket items. They're your diamond, expensive-watch gentlemen. You get a call and find the store detective got one o' these babies, hold him."

"There's gotta be a million shoplifters in Chicago, Sarge," Mileski said.

"Hey, these got a history. *Career* shoplifters."

"But—"

"They're easy to prosecute, Mileski."

"But—"

"Mileski, you see somebody picking up a Honda under his arm and taking it home, be my guest."

"But—"

"Mileski, these are the ones if we don't get 'em, we get criticized, get my drift?" Touhy's voice was taking on a dangerous edge. "You want to bail out Lake Michigan with a spoon, do it on your own time, okay?"

Mileski shut up.

"About yesterday, Bennis and Figueroa?"

"Yes, boss," they said in chorus.

"You were outta your district."

"Two blocks, Sarge," Bennis said.

"Districts is districts, Bennis. Plus you're supposed to leave that crap to the detectives. What's the area commander gonna think when he hears about this stunt of yours with the safe?"

"That they saved some work?"

"Bennis! You're on the edge of a—"

"Gee, Sarge," Figueroa said. "Tell the commander we were in hot pursuit."

"Shit!" Touhy slammed down the notebook. "Okay, you clowns. Hit the bricks and clear."

Figueroa and Bennis were almost to the door when Touhy yelled, "And don't do it again!"

Susannah Maria Figueroa was not in the best frame of mind today. She didn't really like working second watch. Third watch, three to eleven P.M. was better. Today she was missing her daughter Elena's first-grade holiday play. Elena was going to be half of a reindeer.

Suze Figueroa said, "I'll drive," and climbed into the car with Bennis. After a minute or two the seriously macho mars lights and all the seriously macho dash stuff had her feeling better. Like they always did.

The radio kicked in.

The dispatcher said, "One thirty-one."

"Thirty-one." It was Mileski's voice.

"See the woman at Chestnut and Michigan regarding found property."

"Michigan and Chestnut. Ten-four, squad."

"Thanks."

"Or was that Chestnut and Michigan?" Mileski said.

"Try Chestnut and Michigan and if she's not there try Michigan and Chestnut," the dispatcher said, laughing.

" 'Four."

"Someday he's going to go too far at the wrong moment," Bennis said. "With the wrong person."

The radio said, "One twenty-seven."

"Twenty-seven."

"Check the alley behind Clark Street in the four-hundred block. Supposed to be a nine-year-old kid driving a blue Oldsmobile. Citizen called it in."

"Ten-four."

The radio went on with its usual chatter. Bennis and Figueroa cruised their beat, admiring the Christmas lights.

"Cars going to the strongarm robbery at Eight-six-oh North Lake Shore take a disregard."

Silence for a few seconds.

"One twenty-two?"

"Twenty-two."

"Take an ag batt at Seven-one-seven North Rush. One twenty-three?"

"Twenty-three."

"Your VIN is coming back clear."

"Thanks, squad."

The radio said, "One thirty-three."

Bennis picked up and said, "Thirty-three."

"Complaint from a citizen, approximately Two-oh-oh South Wacker. Citizen says somebody's moanin' down in the sewer there."

"Name o' the citizen, squad?"

"Concerned's the name. Concerned Citizen. Not likely to be around when you get there."

"Ten-four, squad."

With the mike key closed, Bennis said, "Shit. Sewers."

Bennis and Figueroa rolled down Wacker, but they didn't see anything. There wasn't any citizen standing around wringing his hands in the two-hundred block. Since Figueroa was behind the wheel, Bennis got out on the sidewalk and stood listening. Figueroa saw him shiver a little.

"Jeez, that was eerie," he said, getting back in the car.

"What?"

"There's a kind of howlin' comin' outta that grate in the sidewalk."

"See anything?"

"Figueroa, my man, wouldn't I let you know if I did? Hang a left and let's get into Lower Wacker."

Two hundred years ago, the place where the center of Chicago now stands was a swamp. Some people think not much has changed.

When Chicago was a young frontier town, the swampy areas were mostly left as they were, filled with water and mud and garbage, and as the town grew, filled with the poor, living in tents and shacks. After the Great Chicago Fire, things were different.

There was big money in Chicago—lumber money, meat-packing money, money from making harvesters and combines, money from the burgeoning railhead. Big money went into improving the city. The downtown streets were raised above the swamp or flood level. Whole areas of the Loop were built on iron stilts, the pavements were raised, and gradually the sidewalks were filled in and the vacant land stuffed with buildings until you could walk from one end of downtown to another and not realize it was underlain by swamp.

The only remnant of all this raising of the city was a series of secondary streets below the level where the sun shone. Some, like Lower Wacker, which runs under Wacker Drive along the Chicago River, are regularly used and are favorites of taxi drivers and city cognoscenti for getting places in a hurry.

Others are used primarily by loading trucks and delivery vans, picking up and delivering to the sub-basement levels of glitzy hotels and posh restaurants. Still others carry heat conduits, sewer mains, or parts of the underground transportation system.

Occasionally, one of the daylight-level streets will collapse without warning, leaving a hole at street level, a few cars in the muck at the bottom, pedestrians standing around on top gaping, and the rats underneath scurrying away. The last time this happened a passerby took one look at the hole, which was fifteen feet deep and forty across, and threw himself into it, hoping to collect big damages from the city. Several bystanders saw him do it, however, and the ploy failed.

But many of the tunnels and leftovers under the city are unexplored and forgotten. There are homeless living there, and the Mud People. Down in these tunnels it is always dark. They are perfect places for people or deals that don't want to see the light of day.

Figueroa and Bennis slid into the downgrade and pulled up at a stop sign. "That way," Bennis said.

Dimly lit, Lower Wacker stretched away in both directions. They couldn't see any great distance because of the forest of support beams. Vertical iron beams ran down the pavement between the traffic lanes; cement pylons with iron cores held up the fifty-floor hotels that loomed unseen above them. Produce trucks roared out of the gloom from side alleys.

"Go about thirty yards," Bennis said.

Thirty yards in was a side alley. "Let's try this," he said.

"Yeah, it looks like real swell fun," Figueroa said.

The side alley was actually a tunnel, lit by very dim bulbs at hundred-yard distances. Most of it was sunk in gloom. Ahead the pavement was too narrow for the squad car.

Bennis started walking. Figueroa stayed ten seconds more to lock up the car. Leave one unlocked, come back and it's gone. Plus, God forbid you should leave the door open. Get rats in the car.

Figueroa caught up with Bennis and together they picked their way slowly along the tunnel, listening. The tunnel walls were concrete, striped vertically with a hundred years of ooze from the streets above. In some places stalactites of dried road salts and minerals and dirt depended from the pitted ceiling. Puddles of dank ooze lay in the low spots.

They turned down the sound on their radios. They had

gone about forty or fifty feet when they heard a howl. For an instant it sounded animal. Then it broke apart into sobs.

Figueroa and Bennis grimaced at each other, aware that they both had just resisted an urge to hold hands.

There was a still smaller side tunnel nearby. Inexplicably, two el tracks ran into this side tunnel on crossties and then ended, dead, having run twenty feet from nowhere to no-where.

"Kelite?" Figueroa said, very softly.

But Bennis, thinking that a flashlight beam would only give warning that they were coming, shook his head.

The moaning increased.

In the cavern ahead was a dim glow, flickering yellowish on one side and bluish on the other. It outlined a group of figures so mingled in the dimness that Figueroa couldn't guess whether there were two or six. Over the figures loomed what looked like an ancient oak tree. The scene, Figueroa thought, was Druidic. She shivered.

As she and Bennis drew closer, the light seemed brighter. It came from two sources, a squat candle in an aluminum pie tin on the cement floor and indirect light on a part of the wall farther along that looked like it slanted in from an air shaft. The ancient tree became a heat duct that split into three arms near the top of the tunnel.

There was silence now ahead. The people had seen them.

Bennis and Figueroa moved closed.

"Jeez," Figueroa whispered, "The Corrugated Card-board school of interior decoration."

Between the heat duct, which was nearest them, and the air shaft, which was farthest away, were four areas against the wall. Figueroa thought of them as areas, because *rooms* was too strong a word and *beds* wasn't quite right, either. They were personal spaces, most separated by corrugated cardboard. The one nearest the heat duct was made from the top of a refrigerator or stove carton, laid on its side. Into this its owner had pushed a cracked piece of foam rubber pad, long enough to make a bed. The carton would enclose the upper half of a sleeper, for privacy. The space next to this was made of a big carton cut lengthwise. This formed a coffinlike bed and inside it were several layers of corrugated board, raising the bottom ten inches or so off the floor, away from the cold and damp. The other two, which were farther away, were also made of portions of corrugated board padded with many layers of newspaper.

In and around all of them were ripped scarves, dirty jackets, magazines, pieces of blankets, shoes, a pink bedsheet, Band-aid cans, soup cans, toilet paper, potato chip bags, duct tape, plastic bags, a saucepan, three or four lopsided pillows, a small pile of maybe half a dozen potatoes, several wine bottles, and a plastic-wrapped package of carrots.

On the pavement against the far wall was a tea kettle, a piece of bread, a small metal trash can, a circle of bricks with a lot of ashes and black coals in the middle, a can of charcoal lighter fluid, a can of Sterno, and a badly dented skillet.

Figueroa took all this in at a glance, at the same time keeping an eye on the human component of the scene.

Two men stood holding a third, who had been crying.

Figueroa said, "What seems to be the trouble here?"

They all stared at the two cops. Figueroa had the impression that a silent message of caution had gone out between them.

The smallest man, whose head jiggled on his neck said, "He's dead."

"Who's dead?" Bennis said.

"Chas. Chas. He's dead. He's dead." He was pointing, his finger trembling, toward the bed nearest the air shaft. It was so tumbled with clothing that they had not seen the body. "Dead, dead," he said, nodding over and over. The other men shifted their feet and waited.

"Stay here," Bennis said to the three men.

The job of the first uniforms on a scene is to check it out, see if a crime has been committed or if somebody is hurt. If somebody's hurt, call the EMTs. If there's a dead body, close down the scene and call the techs and the detectives.

Bennis went to the body and knelt down. Figueroa kept a watch on the other men.

"Dead?" she asked Bennis.

"Dead."

"Paramedics?"

"He's cooling off already. Dead a coupla hours, maybe."

When Bennis came back Figueroa went and looked at the body. There was no obvious sign of violence. No blood. No knife sticking out. Just a gaping mouth, unshaven chin, and staring, clouded eyes.

Figueroa said to the three men, "Can I see your driver's licenses?"

The man who had been crying giggled briefly. "Don't have any."

"Why not?"

"Got rolled. Inna shelter."

"I have one," the oldest of the three said. Bennis turned to the others and said, "Names?"

Willie Sims was a smallish black man of indeterminate age with white whisker stubble and a coating of dust that made him look gray. Samo Marks was a smaller white man with dark whisker stubble and a layer of dirt that made him look gray. His head twitched, and when Bennis made a note of his name in his notebook he also made the comment "Addled."

The third man was slightly cleaner. Louis Papadopolous, who had a driver's license, had washed sometime in the last few days.

Samo hadn't washed recently, but the tears had flowed so freely down his cheeks that most of the lower part of his face was clean, if streaky. Even around his eyebrows, across which he had apparently swiped his sleeve, there was a clean patch.

"Occupation?" Bennis asked, in a tone of voice that suggested he was required to ask it, but thought it was stupid in this case.

Willie Sims shrugged, "I owned a restaurant. Had a fire. No insurance."

Samo Marks said, "Nothin,' nothin' a-tall." He waved

his head back and forth. "Useta set pins," he said. "Bowling alley."

Papadopolous nodded at Samo as if he were doing very well. "They automated," Papadopolous said.

"And what about you, sir?" Figueroa asked, using her be-nice-to-the-public voice.

Papadopolous said, "Ad exec. We had a few—mm—deep cutbacks."

"Oh."

"I got into the sauce. Not any more." Figueroa gestured at the wine bottles. Papadopolous said, "Samo drinks, some. Chas too."

"Chas was zonked last night," Willie said.

"Zonked! Wasted!" Samo said.

"He 'as real nice, Chas, he 'as real nice," Samo said over and over. "Never hurt anybody." He started moaning again. *Emotionally labile,* Figueroa said to herself, having just spent four Thursday evenings in Supplemental Sensitivity Training.

"Useta lie there, look up the air shaft and tell us what went by," Willie said. "Mornings, people on their way to work. Like, just before we'd go to sleep."

"Yeah?"

Samo said, "Tell us all about the legsa the girls on the sidewalk up there. You know."

"Um, legs."

"Yeah, and some of 'em wouldn't be wearing any underwear. Sheet, you shoulda heard some a what he saw—" He stopped, abruptly realizing he was talking to a female-type officer. "Um, yeah, like shoes," he ended up.

"Well, sure."

"Kept us entertained," Papadopolous said.

"No TV here, ya see," Willie said.

"Who sleeps where?" she asked.

"Thas me," Willie said, with some pride, pointing at the piece of foam rubber near the heat duct.

"You got the choice place," Bennis said to Willie.

"Yeah. Nice and warm."

243

"That's me," Papadopolous gestured at the spot next to Willie, the layers of cardboard.

Samo said, "Over there," pointing to the pile of newspaper and tattered blankets that lay next to the dead Chas. All the while, Samo was moving his head back and forth, as if listening to music.

Chas's bed was a hodgepodge heap of old clothes, including a couple of stocking caps and a shoe. There was a torn plaid scarf over his lower body, though, and while it was a mess, neither that nor any of the bedding looked like it had been kicked around.

"He been sick?" Bennis asked.

"No, just the sauce."

"Well, we'll get the experts on it." Bennis grabbed his radio.

To Figueroa, watching, it looked for an instant like Papadopolous was either going to hit Bennis or run. Her hand moved an inch toward her sidearm.

"One thirty-three," Bennis said. "We've got a downer."

The radio said, "Bagzzt-*skeek*-urty-three."

"One thirty-three."

"Pzzzzmmmmm."

To Figueroa, Bennis said, "Shit. Reception's cruddy down here." Again he said, "One thirty-three."

Clear as day the radio said, "Thirty-three. You're not makin' it with your radio, sir. Borquat-muzzzzz. Pip."

"Oh, excellent, swell, really sweet. I'd better go up the street and put out the word." He gave Figueroa a glance they'd exchanged maybe five hundred times, him to her or her to him. It meant, "You okay with this?"

She nodded.

"Back in two seconds."

Figueroa believed that Papadopolous's fear had less to do with Chas's actual death and more to do with the possibility that the police would arrest them or move them along to some less desirable place.

"Pretty sheltered here," she said, hoping he'd talk about it.

"We fixed Thanksgiving dinner in that," Papadopolous said, pointing to the small garbage can.

"Store give us a lil' turkey," Samo said.

"You roasted a turkey! In that?"

Papadopolous said, "We made a bed of charcoal briquets and put the can on top." He grinned at her, knowing she was finding it hard to believe they weren't all incompetent morons. "Shucks," he said, laying it on, "anybody'd been a Boy Scout could do it."

"Stores throw out stuff, it doesn't look fresh anymore," Willie said. "Vegetables, like. Pastry."

"How long you been living here?"

"How long?" Willie echoed. "Maybe since November?"

He looked at Papadopolous, who said, "November tenth we came here. The police drove us out of O'Hare."

"O'Hare, yeah," Samo said. "Druve us out."

Willie cackled. "They're bundling us into these buses. So they say, all horrified: 'Do you want O'Hare to look like *New York*?' "

"Took us a while to find this place," Papadopolous said, obviously uneasy, still thinking they were going to be moved along.

"This is a good place," Samo said, head nodding.

"Yeah, sweet," Willie said, chuckling again. "We call it the Lower Wacker Hilton."

"What do you do all day?"

They were all averting their eyes from the corpse.

"Well, day, see, we don't do anything, days," Willie said. Samo said, "We sleep."

"Stores and all those fancy restaurants, they don't want us millin' around, see?" Willie said. "In daylight."

"They don't mind so much at night," Papadopolous said. "So we get back here just before dawn, go to bed. Get our healthful eight hours. This time of year it's not light until seven, seven-thirty anyhow. Sleep to four-thirty. It's dark at four-thirty, so we get up and go to work. Works out real neat."

Willie chuckled. "Yeah, out there movin' and shakin'."

245

"Dumpsters!" Samo said brightly. "Garbage cans!"

Papadopolous said, "They don't mind too much as long as you don't throw stuff all over the street."

Samo suddenly broke out, "You oughtasee some guys they just dump over a can, throw everything, throw shit all over the sidewalk. We allus been real careful." He grabbed a quick glance at the corpse of Chas and started to snuffle.

Willie said, "Some folks make a bad name for honest street people."

"Basically you're scavengers, then," Figueroa said to Willie.

"Scavengers? No, I don't think we're scavengers."

"What are you?"

"Beachcombers," Willie Sims said.

Bennis came back. Figueroa raised her eyebrows at him. He said, "They will be with us, my man, as soon as is consistent with the pursuit of their other duties."

"Gawd!" Figueroa said.

Figueroa caught sight of two eyes glowing in the darkness behind the heat duct. She jumped but covered it by pretending to turn to get a better view.

"Aw, gee," Samo said, seeing what it was.

Papadopolous made a clucking sound.

An animal stepped out of the shadows.

"Jeez, a cat!" Figueroa said.

Papadopolous said, "We feed him. Bring something back for him every night. When we can. Keep him around as much as possible."

"Why?"

"For the mice. And the rats."

"Rats!" Samo shrieked. "Get yer toes."

"Not yours!" Willie said scornfully. Samo's feet were extremely dirty.

Figueroa said, "We got rats down here the size of Toyotas. No cat can deal with Chicago tunnel rats. These rats scare cats outta seven lives."

"Not this one."

It stalked farther forward.

The cat was a marmalade tom with a huge ruff. He had a round face that looked more like bobcat than tomcat and his body was a barrel.

"Weighs thirty-five pounds," Papadopolous said.

"Yeah, okay," Figueroa said. "I guess rats wouldn't scare him."

"Name's Adolf."

There was the sound of heavy feet in the distance, getting closer.

Suddenly Samo started crying. "He kilt'm."

"Killed who?"

"Chas. Smothered'm. Adolf smothered'm. Slept on his face and smothered'm."

"Okay," said Figueroa, "that's enough."

She turned and took Samo's arm.

"Look," she said, "the court's probably gonna say you're not really responsible." Willie and Papadopolous were staring at her as if she was nuts. "You've been drinking crap. You got a can of Sterno over there and a piece of bread to strain it through. You were depressed. You didn't have anything in this world. You wanted something. Any one thing of your own. And you went out of your head. You smothered Chas with your pillow."

"Nooooo—"

"Figured Papadopolous'd help move him, lose the body, rather than have your space here get discovered."

"Nooooo—"

"Come and look up here."

Figueroa dragged Samo over the airshaft. They looked up. There was a vertical cement shaft with light at the top, light coming through opaque glass disks set in an iron grid. There was nothing else to see. Absolutely nothing.

Samo shrieked.

"How'd you know, Figueroa?" Bennis said.

"Brilliance."

"C'mon, my man. This is me you're talkin' to."

"Cats don't smother people, Bennis. Useta say they smothered babies, but they don't."

"So the guy was wrong. Chas could of died of natural causes."

"Then why'd he think up an explanation for Chas being smothered? Huh?"

"Beats me."

"Who benefited from Chas's death? What did they have of value, any of 'em? Two things. The heat pipe and the view from the air shaft. Willie and Chas. They had the prizes."

"Yeah."

"See, they always lie low in the daylight. None of 'em ever had a chance to look up the airshaft. That was Chas's spot. They got back before daylight and everybody had his own space. None of 'em had ever looked up the airshaft, so they didn't know there was nothing to see. They didn't know that Chas was just entertainin' 'em."

"And when Samo realized—"

"I think he was already feeling remorse. When he realized, that was when he really broke."

"Well, I'll tell you what *I* think, Figueroa. I think you go on workin' at this, my man, you gonna get real good at your job."

A Proper Burial

.

Barbara Collins

Officer John Steele didn't want to do it.

He didn't want to tell Ernie and Marie Finley that the police had found their Sarah—who'd been missing for several days—dead.

As Steele stood on the doorstep of the Finleys' modest white stucco house, he hesitated to ring the doorbell. It wasn't as if he'd never been the bearer of bad news; like the time he told the Johnsons their son had been found—just so many body parts—in the woods of Wildcat Den State Park. And then there was the Penmark girl who was raped, doused with gasoline, and set on fire . . .

But somehow this one was harder for Steele. His fellow officers on the force would be surprised if they knew just how much John was upset by the death of little Sarah. Because what they didn't know about John—whose cold, harsh manner made children quiver and criminals cower—was that behind those piercing Clint Eastwood eyes, and inside that six-foot-three body-by-Hulk, lived a pussycat.

Suddenly the front door opened. Mr. Finley, who had either seen or sensed Officer Steele out on the porch, stood in the doorway. He was a small man, about five foot five, with a mustache, thinning brown hair, and a kind face etched with worry.

"You have news about Sarah?" he asked anxiously.

Officer Steele didn't answer immediately. He stepped inside, removing his hat, turning it slowly in his hands. For a brief second or two he took in the surroundings, which surprised him.

Everything in the very formal living room was purple.

And now, something made sense: earlier he had trouble finding the Finleys, who'd just moved into the neighborhood. When he stopped some kids down the block to inquire about the family, one older boy had said, "You mean the purple people?"

Mrs. Finley joined them, having come out of the kitchen, wiping her hands on a lavender dishcloth. She was a few inches taller than her husband, and a few pounds heavier. Her jet black hair, piled on top of her head in huge, looping curls as if wrapped around soup cans, appeared to have a deep purple sheen under the light on the ceiling.

Officer Steele opened his mouth, but before he could speak, Mrs. Finley burst into tears, burying her face in the towel as if she knew what he was about to say.

"I'm sorry," Steele said, his voice cracking as he fought to get himself under control. "Your Sarah's been killed."

Mr. Finley threw his arms around his wife, and they stood sobbing so close together, the two became one.

"She was hit by a truck," Steele continued, "in front of a convenience store about half a mile from here."

The Finleys sobbed harder.

Officer Steele, feeling awkward, touched the arm of the husband, whose face was burrowed into his wife's shoulder. Steele said quietly, "It was dark outside when she crossed the street, probably attracted by the lights . . . a woman—an off-duty nurse—saw what happened and ran to Sarah, but it was too late. The nurse eased her over to the curb and called us. The driver of the vehicle never stopped."

Mrs. Finley pulled away from her husband. The tears streaming down her face left tracks of purple mascara. "It's all my fault!" she wailed. "I left her in the kitchen to go upstairs . . . and she must have gone out on her own, and gotten lost . . ." She looked toward the heavens—in this case, the ceiling—and screamed, "Oh, my baby! My baby!"

Mr. Finley grabbed his wife by her arms, almost shaking her, pleading. "It's *not* your fault! You *mustn't* blame yourself."

Officer Steele shifted his weight uneasily and cleared his throat. "Mr. and Mrs. Finley. I need you to come with me. To identify her."

Mrs. Finley's hand flew to her face as she gasped in horror at the thought of it, but Mr. Finley looked directly at the officer. "We're ready," he said firmly. "Where do we go?"

"Downtown. The forensic lab," said Officer Steele softly.

"The forensic lab?" Mr. Finley asked, raising his eyebrows.

"Yes," said Officer Steele, putting on his hat, "we're gathering evidence so we can nail the killer who ran your little Sarah down."

Walter Graves was the best forensic expert in the state—hell, the whole *country*—but he'd be damned if he could figure a way to get the evidence the D.A. wanted for *this* case.

He unzipped the small body bag that lay on the shiny chrome table, then stroked his close-cut gray beard as he stared at the bag's contents. Coming in the wake of his brilliance in the Fernando trial, which brought him nationwide—hell, *worldwide*—publicity, this one could only make him look like a fool!

He picked up the bag with both arms and carried it to a locker nearby, within which he carefully placed it before shutting the drawer. Yes, this one was important. Not because a life was lost—but because the eyes of the forensic field were upon him. Watching. Waiting . . . for him to step on his dick.

The door to the lab opened and a police officer Graves recognized—but did not know by name—entered, along with a middle-aged man and woman; he looked like Mr. Whipple from the old toilet-paper commercials, and she had weird hair.

"Mr. Graves," said the cop, gesturing to the couple, "this is Mr. and Mrs. Finley."

"Yes?" Graves said, keeping the irritation of this interruption out of his voice.

"They're here to identify . . . Sarah."

"Sarah?"

"Didn't someone from the desk call?"

"Oh, *Sarah*," Graves said, nodding. "Yes. But I don't know *what* they expect to be able to identify."

The missus began to cry and the husband tried to comfort her. Graves thought the cop shot him a dirty look.

"She's over here in cold storage," Graves said, moving to the wall of lockers.

The husband started forward, but the wife, shaking, held back. The cop put a massive arm around her shoulders, and with the help of the husband, they all moved forward.

Graves pulled open the drawer.

The trio advanced and stared.

"If it makes you feel any better," Graves said, trying to be helpful to the obviously distressed couple, "she didn't suffer—well, suffer *much*. I mean, she *did* get hit by a two-ton truck."

The little woman wailed, and the cop glared.

Graves, unable to make his voice sound pleasant any longer, said, "Well, is that her?"

"Yes," answered the husband, softly.

The wife nodded, unable to speak, wiping her eyes with a hankie.

"Reminds me of old Cornwall, back on the farm," sniffed the cop. "Got caught in a combine."

"Can we take her now?" said the missus, reaching for the body.

Graves lunged forward, covering the plastic bag protectively, with both hands. "No!"

The wife's face turned angry. "No? *Why not*? She's *ours*!"

"She's state's evidence now," Graves said flatly, withdrawing his arms from over the flattened form.

"For what?" asked the husband.

"For a murder investigation."

The cop intervened. "Mr. and Mrs. Finley, just moments before Sarah was run down, the manager of the convenience store was robbed and killed. A woman—the nurse who went to Sarah's aid—saw a man leave in a truck. While the nurse was able to give a good description of the man, the prosecutor needs corroborating evidence to make his case."

"But I don't understand what that has to do with Sarah and why we can't take her!" said the wife.

"Because *Sarah* is the prosecutor's key piece of evidence!" Graves almost shouted at the woman. "I'll make this as simple as I can," Graves continued. "Do you see those tire tracks?" He pointed to places on the remains. "They can identify the vehicle and, in turn, the killer. Consequently, I can't release her until the suspect goes to trial."

"So you're talking . . ." said Mr. Finley, clearly ahead of his wife.

"A year. Maybe more."

The missus turned to her husband, her eyes pleading. He shook his head. She then faced the cop. "Officer Steele, please, make him give us Sarah! I can't bear to think of her lying in a *freezer* . . ."

The cop looked down at her. "You want the murderer convicted, don't you?"

"I suppose so," she said, halfheartedly. "But it's just not fair! First our Sarah is killed, and now we can't even give her a proper burial."

Graves had had it.

"Jesus, lady!" he said, "It's just a goddamn *cat*!"

The cop gave Graves one last look that could kill, before walking the grieving couple gingerly out.

Marie Finley couldn't eat, could only sleep fitfully since the death of Sarah. Under different circumstances she would have been thrilled to lose the ten pounds that melted away like butter; but she barely noticed, staying in her bathrobe most of the time. Her hair, normally so carefully done up in the same style as when she and Ernie first met, hung straight, limp, matted to her head. She sat in their bedroom, in a chair in the corner, caught in the grasp of depression, which was squeezing and squeezing.

"Honey, please," said Ernie softly, entering the room with a tray of food. "You have to eat."

She didn't look at him.

"Sarah would want you to."

"How do you know what Sarah would want?" Marie snapped viciously. "Sarah is *dead*!"

Ernie's face looked as if it had been slapped, and she was sorry she said it, but didn't take it back.

Ernie set the tray down on the bed, and turned to leave. "She had a good life," he said in a lame attempt to cheer her.

She didn't respond.

"I'm going to run an errand," he sighed. "I'll be back soon."

Marie watched him leave. Poor Ernie, she thought, poor, sweet Ernie. She knew he was hurting. But she couldn't help him. Not now. How could she, when she couldn't help herself. No, he would have to be the strong one. He always was.

They'd met at a concert almost nine years ago. It was during the summer of '83. "The Golden Boys of Bandstand," featuring Bobby Rydell, Frankie Avalon and Fabian, had played to a soldout crowd of middle-aged bobby-soxers trying to relive *their* golden years. Afterwards, backstage, Marie managed to get Fabian to autograph her "Like a Tiger" 45 picture sleeve she'd brought along, and when he did, he looked at her and grinned, "Darlin', I *love* your hair." She thought she would *die*! She turned to the man next to her—another autograph seeker—and said, "He's still *so* cute!" When the crowd began to leave, the man—Ernie—and she walked back to the parking lot, talking excitedly about the performers—Ernie had every record Bobby Rydell ever made—and ended up going out for a malt. It was just like high school, but better!

She and Ernie were married a year later, a first time for both. But living together was hard after being alone for so long. And when the children they wanted didn't arrive, Marie became depressed and the marriage faltered. Ernie had read somewhere that the color purple was supposed to spark passion, and set about redecorating their house. When that didn't work, he went away.

It was a cold, overcast day in November, several months later, when Ernie came back to Marie, begging her to give the marriage one last try. He was holding a package—a brightly wrapped box—and when she opened it, she saw a cute, cuddly, furry yellow cat with the most adorable blue eyes!

And they called her Sarah.

Marie got up from her chair in the bedroom. Like a phantom she floated down the hall, as if drawn by some invisible force, until she stood in front of a closed bedroom door. She knew if she opened it and went in, she'd break down. But she couldn't stop the hand that reached out and turned the knob, no more than she could stop the ache in her heart.

The late summer sun shone through a window and across a small bed—Sarah's bed. Marie felt the tears beginning to flow.

It was Christmastime, and she and Ernie were out shopping when they saw the doll bed—along with a little dresser and nightstand—in the window of Ingram's department store. They bought the whole set for Sarah, laughing and giggling all the way home . . .

Marie could bear to look no longer, and turned to leave, shutting the door behind her; the room would remain untouched until Sarah was brought home to rest under the magnolia tree, in the back yard.

Ernie came in the kitchen door as Marie shuffled in, returning the untouched tray. He walked over to her, cupping her face in his hands.

"Marie," he said, "I went to see Officer Steele."

Marie looked right through him.

"The man that killed Sarah is out on bail."

She continued to stare.

"I found out where he lives."

Now his face came into focus.

"I know how we can get Sarah back," Ernie said, then smiled.

And for the first time in weeks, Marie felt blood in her veins.

And saw life in Ernie's eyes.

Virgil Wykert sat on his davenport and belched—loudly, rudely. He loved to do that, and was sorry no one was around to hear it. No one, that is, except for Dave, his pit bull. Dave lifted his huge head off the floor, where he'd been sleeping, stuck out his tongue, panted and drooled. Virgil's friends said the dog stunk, but *he* never noticed. Virgil leaned back and took another swig of beer, then reached down and scratched at his crotch. He'd better do something about those fleas, though, or the mutt would have to find his *own* bed to sleep in.

It was well after midnight but Virgil was up, playing with his new toy, a Turbo Graphx 16, one of the perks from the convenience-store robbery. He'd gone out and bought it the very next day. The system was so much *better* than Nintendo. And the graphics of the games were sharper—like in the one he was playing—"Splatterhouse"; when the guts began to splatter, it looked so real! But the ghouls were getting the better of Virgil, partly because he was tired but mostly because he was drunk. He used the control pad to decapitate one of the monsters, and watched the blood ooze . . .

He hadn't planned on killing that store manager. But when the guy started whining about how he had a wife and a baby and all, something snapped inside Virgil. He just wanted him to *shut up*! Hell, *everybody* had it tough these days!

Virgil paused the video game, freezing its gory image on the television screen. He'd have to ice that eyewitness, too— that nurse who fingered him . . .

There was a knock at the front door.

Virgil jumped as if the control with its wires had shocked him; he reached for the .38 hidden under the cushion, in case it was the cops, or some vengeance-seeking relative of that store manager.

"Yeah?" he hollered from the couch.

The knocking persisted.

Virgil got up and went to the door, holding the .38 hidden with his right hand while cracking the door with his left.

"Whadaya want," he growled to the small, wimpy-looking man on his stoop.

"Mr. Wykert?" said the man, politely.

"I don't need any of what you're sellin'," Virgil snarled.

"Oh," the man said, "I'm not *selling* anything."

"Then *what*?" Virgin opened the door wider, flashed the gun and smiled smugly as the little man's eyes popped. Dave, now next to his master, growled viciously.

"I . . . I just wanted to talk to you about my cat . . ." the guy stammered, looking down nervously at the dog.

"Cat?" Virgil's eyes narrowed.

"Yes. The one you ran over in front of the convenience store you robbed."

Virgil reached out and grabbed the man by his coat collar, pulling him roughly to him, sticking the .38 under his chin. "I don't know what you're talkin' about. And if you don't want to be my dog's next meal, you'd better *leave*!"

Virgil gave him a shove, then reached out and grabbed him again. "No, *wait*!" he said, having a thought, "time is money. An' you just *wasted* my time—so give me some *money*!"

Still held in Virgil's grasp, the man got out his wallet, hands shaking. "Fifty's all I got."

Virgil grabbed the wallet and took out the money, then tossed it back and started to shut the door. "Oh, and by the way, *pop*," he smirked, "I coulda *missed* that kitty, but I *didn't*. Because, know what? I *hate cats*!"

Virgil slammed the door in the guy's startled face, and threw the lock.

He returned to the couch, laughing, thumbing the money in his fingers. Now he could get the *other* Turbo Graphx game he wanted: "Legendary Axe."

But his laughing stopped abruptly at a noise he heard outside: the unmistakable sound of the engine of his Chevy truck.

Virgil dropped the cash, picked up the .38 and ran out the door with Dave right on his heels.

It was dark outside, but a three-quarter moon hung high in the sky, throwing a small spotlight on his most prized possession, which sat on the crest of his driveway about five hundred feet from the house. The truck faced him, its headlights cutting through the air like laser swords in a video game. The teeth of the custom-made chrome grill glinting in the moonlight made an awesome mouth. The engine went *Ba-room! Ba-room!*

Virgil, face red with rage, started up the incline, gun in hand, snarling dog at his feet.

"Get outta my *truck*, you *son of a bitch*!" he hollered above the noise of the engine.

But as he approached, the truck slowly moved backwards, keeping its distance. He broke into a run now, pointing the gun, wanting to blast the bastard away, but he *couldn't* because he didn't want to hit his truck.

Suddenly big wheels squealed, and the Chevy jumped forward.

Dave took off for the hills, but Virgil froze in his tracks as the truck lunged toward him. He turned and started to run, but the teeth snatched him. And the mouth chewed him. And the truck devoured him, before coming to a stop, belching up smoke and blood . . .

The first purple-pink rays of the sun appeared on the horizon as Ernie opened the back door to the kitchen for his wife. They had driven around aimlessly, silently, for a long time, caught in those late hours between darkest despair and the dawning of hope.

"Ernie," Marie asked, breaking their self-imposed silence, "where on earth did you learn to hot-wire a car?"

Ernie removed his jacket, hanging it on a coat rack by the door. He turned to look at her, smiling shyly. "I used to work on jalopies when I was in high school. Trying to get the girls to like me.''

She went to him, and looked at him the way a man always wants a woman to. ''*I* like you,'' she whispered, putting her hands on his shoulders. She kissed him; and the kiss that began soft and sweet turned hot with love—and passion.

''Are you hungry?'' she asked when their lips parted.

''Starving,'' he said.

''Me, too! I'll make us some breakfast.''

Ernie sat down at the round oak table, and Marie busied herself at the stove, and before too long she placed a big plate of scrambled eggs, bacon and hash browns in front of him.

''Oh Ernie,'' she said, excitedly, joining him at the table, ''that was such a *great* plan. Without a suspect there'll be no trial, and they'll give us Sarah back.'' Her eyes were large and bright; then suddenly they clouded. ''But I was so worried about you, when you went to his door.''

Ernie stopped eating, fork in mid-air. ''I had to make sure it was him.''

''I know, but when he grabbed you and I saw a *gun*, I didn't know . . .''

Ernie sat up straight in his chair, looking toward the kitchen door.

Marie's eyes followed his. ''What?'' she asked quietly.

''Did you hear something? Outside?'' Ernie said, putting his fork down on his plate. ''There. That.''

Marie looked frightened. ''Ernie,'' she whispered, ''what if we were followed?''

''Couldn't have been,'' he said, then patted her hand, which was resting on the table. ''It's nothing. We're just . . . jumpy.''

He pushed his chair back, motioning Marie to stay put, went over to the door, and cautiously opened it.

Ernie looked out and didn't see anyone, but Marie let out a blood-curdling scream.

Ernie spun around, his heart pounding. He thought she

had screamed in terror, until he saw the joy on her face and the yellow fur in her arms.

"Sarah!" Marie cried from down on the floor where she now sat with the cat held tightly to her chest. "It's *Sarah*!"

Ernie stared in disbelief, then ran to them, and fell on his knees, "Oh, my God . . . oh, my God . . . it *is* her!"

"You bad, bad cat!" Marie scolded between sobs. "*Where* have you *been*? Don't you know how *upset* we were?"

The cat, struggling to get free, jumped out of Marie's hands and ran to its dish that lay empty by the door.

"Ernie!" Marie shouted, "she's hungry! Quick, get the food!"

Ernie dashed to the cupboard and got out a can and emptied it in the dish. And they watched the cat eat, tears of happiness running down their cheeks.

Then Marie picked up the cat. "Mama's baby must be *so* tired," she said, kissing its diffident face. "We're *all* tired. Let's go to bed."

"Good idea," Ernie yawned, turning out the kitchen light, following his wife out of the kitchen. "What a night!"

But at the bottom of the stairs, Marie, cat cradled in her arms, stopped in her tracks. "Oh, Ernie," she said, horrified, "what about that *man* . . . ?"

Ernie's face turned to stone. "He got what he deserved."

Marie nodded slowly, scratching the top of the cat's head. "That's right. After all, he was a *murderer*." She turned and climbed the stairs, nuzzling the cat, cooing quietly to it.

"I should say," Ernie said, following her up. "He killed a cat."